THE WATCHER

LISA SELL

Published by Continue Books, 2024.

Copyright © Lisa Sell, 2024.

The right of Lisa Sell to be identified as the Author of the Work has been asserted by her in accordance with the Copyright, Designs and Patents Act 1988.

Apart from any use permitted under UK copyright law, this publication may only be reproduced, stored, or transmitted, in any form, or by any means, with prior permission in writing from the publisher or, in the case of reprographic production, in accordance with the terms of licences issued by the Copyright Licensing Agency.

This book is a work of fiction. Names, characters, businesses, organisations, places, and events other than those clearly in the public domain, are a product of the author's imagination or used fictitiously. Any resemblance to actual persons - living or dead -, events, or locales is completely coincidental.

Print ISBN: 9798329424065

For Dad, who was a huge supporter of my writing.
I wish you were here to keep reading my books.

CHAPTER 1

The Watcher

I am the Watcher.

I am everywhere.

There is no escape from my scrutinising eyes.

Many watch.

No one makes it their reason for being like I do. Watching is seductive, necessary, and a compulsion. Those who claim to attend only to their own business are liars. Apathy kills. We must look around us to survive.

It's a basic human need to observe people and our surroundings. Compared to me, though, you're amateurs. Only the most observant and intelligent prosper. I always win.

Look behind you.

I'm right there.

Eye spy with my little eye someone is going to die.

CHAPTER 2

Sophie

What a fool I've been. I should have known he'd see. Wrapping up my secret seemed to be a solution. Now it's revealed, lying on the coffee table.

'When did our relationship get to a place where you hide things from me?' Ben asks.

Like a dubious game show host showing the loser what they could've won, my husband flourishes a hand towards the fertility predictors and pregnancy tests.

Victory became my obsession. Every time I peed on a stick, I hoped for the winning shot. I was always off target. Ever since we lost our child, my sole ambition is to fill my empty womb again. I want to be a mother.

From the moment I knew I was pregnant, I connected with my baby. I spoke to the dot inside me, sharing what I was doing throughout the day and confiding my hopes for their future. As soon as *Yes* appeared on the digital test, I became a mother. My mind couldn't process the change when I miscarried. Once, I was a parent. What am I now?

Ben's legs buckle as he sits. Now the fight has left him, I don't know what to do. I'd rather we fought this out and called it a temporary blip. Rendering my husband exhausted signifies the severity of my mistakes.

THE WATCHER

Ben places a splayed hand next to him on the sofa. Like a chastised child, I retreat to an armchair in which I don't belong. Despite the frayed, hideous, orange and brown paisley pattern, Ben insists on keeping it. This was the chair his mum used to commandeer. Whenever he sits in it, Ben's face softens as he connects with childhood memories of her. Since his mum's death, it's the only way.

If I'm allowed to sit on his mum's throne, maybe he doesn't despise me. My ever-present companion, Shame, creeps in. When I'm alone, I've created a ritual of reclining in this chair, hoping a place where a mother sat would work its magic. You hear of women working in supermarkets who claim to have fallen pregnant after sitting at the same checkout. Heat flushes my cheeks as I consider the lengths I've trawled. I'm not even superstitious. Whenever Ben salutes a solitary magpie, I tease him. This desperate version of Sophie Walters is a stranger to me as well as to my husband.

Test sticks fall off the table as Ben slaps the table. 'Why did you keep this to yourself? We agreed not to intervene with fertility stuff, and see what happens.'

'It felt like you decided for us. Sometimes I didn't get a say in if, when, or how I'd get pregnant again.'

'All I did was look after you. You were in such a bad way after the... the...'

'Miscarriage. We need to stop avoiding it like it's a dirty word.'

Ben slumps. 'I didn't think you could cope with saying it. Everything I've done after the miscarriage has been for you. My feelings didn't matter. I always put you first. The doctor advised taking it slow and focusing on your mental health. I've been nothing but supportive of you and tried to help with the anxiety. I understand how it got worse for you after the baby died.'

For someone who has trouble with saying *miscarriage*, Ben doesn't struggle with the "d" word. I try not to use it. The finality is unbearable. *Miscarriage* and *loss* hurt, too. They imply my lack of ability to carry a baby. When your treasured child is gone, words often wound.

Ben reaches over to touch me. I grab his hand and kiss it. He's hurting as much as me. How can we move beyond this pain? Our marriage hangs on a flimsy thread, frayed by my deception. I am not this woman.

'I wish I'd known how desperate you were to get pregnant,' Ben says. 'At first, you appeared relaxed about it. Hiding fertility predictors and pregnancy testing kits is worrying. You promised never to lie to me again.'

'I lied before because your mum begged me to. She didn't want you to know how ill she was. I hated knowing the truth when you didn't. I wish I'd never seen that oncologist's letter.'

'I'm sorry. That's not fair of me. It must've been a difficult secret to keep. But you don't need to hide things from me. From the number of kits here, I expect you've been doing this since we lost the baby.'

The evidence seems to increase as we inspect it in the suffocating silence. Not only do I wish I'd never done this, I also regret the subterfuge of disposal. After using the sticks, I put them into a carrier bag, hidden in my underwear drawer. When they stacked up, I had to remove them from the house. Every day they were in our bedroom was a day closer to my lies being discovered.

'Those foxes are tenacious buggers.' My usual humour as a default mechanism falls flat. Ben's hard stare confirms the joke about the fox that raided our bin is in poor taste. He's right. I'm so ashamed I can barely look at him.

'If you wanted a baby so much, we could have discussed it,' Ben says.

'I tried.'

'When?'

The air in the room thins. 'When we planted the memorial tree in the garden, I said we should try again.'

I don't want to think about placing bootees in the ground. On reflection, burying something signifying death alongside roots that will flourish was wrong.

Ben strokes my hand. 'I didn't realise you meant so soon.'

'I should've been more open about what I wanted.'

THE WATCHER

'We were both broken when I planted the tree. I wondered if I'd ever stop crying. For your sake, I kept going.'

The tightness of my grip on his arm surprises us both. I cave into his chest.

'I want a baby, Ben. Our baby.'

'Before the miscarriage, you never said that. Your desperation is worrying.'

A weird laugh escapes from my mouth. 'You don't know the half of it.'

Revealing the hours I've spent trawling the internet for fertility tips won't help. A snake of shame coils in the pit of my stomach at the forums I joined for those desperate to conceive and the old wives' tricks I tried.

'I want us to have a child.' With the statement finally made, the vipers inside me are silenced.

'Even before the miscarriage, we agreed to let nature takes its course. Neither of us felt paternal.'

'After getting pregnant, my perspective changed. When you've had life inside you, it's hard to give it up.'

'What's happened to my quirky, easy-going wife? Where did the person who called kids a pain in the arse go? I feel like I'm losing you.'

My grief is reflected in Ben's eyes. Why didn't I see it before? Remorse makes me look away. I lost sight of our love. Please don't let my marriage be over.

CHAPTER 3

Sophie

My best friend gives me an appraising look.

'I said this wouldn't end well. You were obsessed with all the fertility stuff. I can't recall a recent conversation where you haven't mentioned getting pregnant. It's not healthy.'

'Please don't lecture me. I'm so ashamed of myself.'

Normally, I value Emma's honesty. She's an expert in talking me down from stupid situations I used to hurtle in to. This was when we were young, waitressing, and life wasn't meant to be taken seriously. Now I'm in my forties, I should know better.

The joviality of a group watching football in the corner of the pub mocks my misery. How did I lose myself in the empty pursuit of a futile goal? Usually, I'd be joining in with the merriment and getting a round in.

Emma shuts her laptop as the landlady comes over with a bottle of wine and two glasses.

'Just the one glass, please,' I say. 'I'm not drinking.'

'Sorry, I keep forgetting,' Holly replies. 'I'm so used to you two sharing a Malbec. It's second nature to bring it over.'

'I'll have some,' Emma says. 'My throat's drier than the bottom of a budgie's cage. Soph won't get pregnant if she's full of vino, though.'

THE WATCHER

I let it pass. Emma's bluntness is usually appreciated. At least we don't mess around trying to figure out how the other is feeling. I'm wondering now if leaving the house and sending an SOS to Emma was a good idea. Today I've done nothing but disappoint Ben. While he wanted to keep talking things through, I needed to escape. At the merest sniff of confrontation, I'm gone; the product of judgemental parents and a brother who strives to outdo me.

I take a glass. 'Stuff it. I might as well have a drink.'

Holly pours the wine. 'I'd love to join you for a catch-up but...' She holds out a hand towards the football crowd. Catching her eye, a man at the bar bellows for service.

'I'm coming!' she shouts back.

The man clicks his fingers as a summons.

'I'll snap his flaming fingers off,' Holly says.

'No one messes with Holly Reynolds.' Emma giggles.

As Holly stamps towards the bar, her hoop earrings sway. I almost pity the dickhead who thinks he's in charge of the situation. She's normally a pussycat, but when provoked, she transforms into a lioness.

Despite my sadness, I have to laugh. 'Bloody love that woman.'

'Surely you'll work things out with Ben.' Emma brings me back to crushing reality.

'At the moment, I'm worried we can't. There's too much tension from wanting different things. Ben doesn't want kids right now. I do.' Taking a large gulp, I savour the novelty of alcohol tickling my tongue and warming my throat.

School teacher style, Emma peers over the top of her glasses. 'Stop exaggerating. Ben said it wasn't the right time and you both need to recover.'

'What if there isn't enough time? We're both forty-two and were lucky to become pregnant.'

Emma takes my face in her hands as I struggle for air. 'Focus and breathe. Don't let that bastard anxiety win.'

People I recognise, mixed with strangers, express judgement and interest. On my behalf, Emma scowls back. The patrons soon return to their conversations.

'I don't like myself anymore,' I say. 'I used to think I was a nice person. What have I become?'

'Someone who's grieving. A woman who doesn't have the family she expected. A person who invested hope in what was inside her, only for it to be snatched away. You are the loveliest human I know, Soph. Kindness flows from you. It's standard behaviour to harden your heart after going through a trauma. You're protecting yourself from further emotional onslaughts. Be real. You don't have to put up a front with me.'

Speaking through the sobs is difficult. Emma waits while squeezing my hand. I take a breath. 'Thanks. You've always had a way with words.'

'Considering it's my job, I should hope so.'

'How's the book coming along?' I ask, while stripping the top layer off a beer mat for distraction.

'Tricky. I'm struggling with the characters' timelines. It's difficult concentrating at the moment. It's proving harder than *Mastermind*. I think I might be coming down with something.'

'You'll get there.' I wipe my wet cheeks on my sleeve. After months of crying, I believed there were no more tears to shed. Somehow, there's always more. 'By the way, I'll send some designs over to your publisher to consider soon.'

'Fab.' Emma claps like an excited toddler. 'Book covers are my favourite part. My publisher loves your stuff. You're one talented lady. Don't say you heard from me, but they're considering using you for other authors. If you get the call, act surprised.'

'I expect you've talked me up to them. Thanks so much. I wouldn't have started this without your help.'

'We're far away from waitressing at Luigi's on Cowley Road.' Emma looks up at the ceiling, as if summoning the past from above us. 'Sometimes I miss it. Things seemed a lot simpler back then.'

'Those heady days of finding our ways in the world, often smelling of garlic and parmesan. Who can forget the dreadful accordion player who rocked up on Saturday nights? No one booked him, but we didn't have the heart to make him leave.'

THE WATCHER

Emma chuckles. 'He kept coming back because you gave him a pity tenner every time. You're such a pushover for helpless cases, waifs, and strays. Do you remember the plastic tablecloths in the restaurants and how they stuck to everything?'

'Oh, and the night I took away a bloke's pasta because he complained it wasn't warm enough, and I peeled the bowl off the table?'

'His expression when the linguine flew...'

'Indeed, considering it smacked him in the face.' We join in a fit of laughter. Working at Luigi's was a great era. Despite earning paltry wages, we were happy. Future possibilities glowed within us. I tried to sell my paintings hanging from the restaurant walls, and Emma scrawled plot ideas on napkins.

Emma's a fantasy fiction author, currently working on book seven. I'm a freelance artist and, after her "encouragement", she ensured her publisher only uses my designs for her books.

Having half my best friend's bravado would help. I wouldn't be hiding from my husband for a start.

Emma tilts her head to one side. 'Has your mood dropped into your shoes?' It helps having a friend who understands me. Emma's prone to depression. Anxiety is my particular flavour of mental illness. We've learned to notice the signs in each other, often before we're aware of them ourselves.

'I don't think I can stay in Oxford anymore.' I can barely get the words out. This has always been my home.

'Don't be silly.'

'I've got to leave.'

CHAPTER 4

The Watcher

Harmony House is my kingdom. It's an observational project masquerading as a building.

My many eyes, installed within others' homes, scrutinise everything. When people shed tears, I revel in them. Their laughter raises a rare smile from me in knowing it's often a front to conceal troubles.

Along with their clothing, people put on a mask. You can't see it, but I know it's there. The insecure check in the mirror, putting a best face in place. The world is watching. Many fear being unmasked and revealing their genuine selves. Who will love you then?

The Watcher peels away the veneer. I reveal secrets, warped minds, confessions, routines, and lies. I am more than Big Brother. My strength isn't derived from setting dictatorial rules. I seldom intervene. When I have to, it's always deserved.

Hints dropped, notes through letterboxes, and anonymous reports to the police have exposed adulterers, deceivers, and criminals. Never call me a vigilante. The only justice I care about is my own.

It's as simple and damning as this; I enjoy watching people suffer. Suffering shows a person's true nature. When a person is broken, you discover what they're made of. How I love to make them break.

CHAPTER 5

Sophie

Emma takes a gulp of wine. After moving the glass away, her mouth drops open.

'Don't look at me like that,' I say.

'Seriously, you're not giving up on such a good marriage?'

'I'm not leaving Ben, you dopey mare. He's my everything. I was just thinking random things. Don't listen to me. I'm a mess.'

'Running away won't help. Your problems will go with you. I know you don't want to hear this, but you have a tendency to flee from issues rather than face them.'

'I do not!'

'Dropping out of university,' Emma begins, getting her fingers ready to list my acts of cowardice.

'I went to art college instead.'

'True, and it worked out, but you didn't have a plan. It was a stressful time for you. What about when we were pissed and we set off the security lights in Sainsbury's car park? You scarpered!'

Despite my friend's harsh tone, I can't help erupting into giggles.

'I wouldn't've minded so much,' Emma says, her voice shaking with laughter, 'but my knickers were caught around my ankles.'

THE WATCHER

'That's what you get for not having a pee before we left the pub. Security still happens at 1am in car parks.'

'Okay, I'll let you have that one.' Emma gives me a nudge. 'You must acknowledge your tendency to avoid things if they're getting too complicated. How is leaving Oxford and Ben behind going to resolve this?'

'I was only thinking of a short break, a breather to destress. Although I love him, because I love him, I can't work stuff out with Ben nearby. Time away will help me sort my head out. My marriage is the most important thing. I can't and won't imagine life without Ben in it.'

'Fair point. I know you won't settle until everything's been considered thoroughly. You've got to be honest with Ben, though. He'll only panic and think you're divorcing him. Maybe consider it as a mini retreat.'

'Don't think it's going to be easy. Ben and I haven't been apart since we were sixteen. Every moment away from him will be a wrench. The one good thing is I can work anywhere. Have pencils and paints, will travel.'

Emma slaps her forehead. 'I've got an idea! I can't believe I forgot to tell you. This is what happens when I'm working on a book. I forget everything. There's an author, Bekstar Paroz - great name - who's renting a flat in Southbourne. It's a suburb in Bournemouth. Bekstar only recently took on the place but has to go on her travels to write a guidebook. She's asked me to look after the place for a month. I was still deciding, but now we can go together. There are some pictures and details of it here.' Emma opens her laptop, scrolls through emails, clicks, and then offers a breakdown of the property. 'There are only eight flats, so it won't be full of people. Harmony House is in the perfect place from what I can make out on the map.' She turns the screen towards me. 'Gull Lane. Seaside cliché, but we'll let it pass.'

'The property appears to be on a quiet road,' I reply. 'Being right next to the beach would be a pain in the arse. It's nestled between the beach and a grove. What's that?'

Emma taps words into the search engine. 'A grove is usually a wooded area. This certainly isn't. Southbourne Grove sounds right up my street. Pardon the pun. It's a long street of mostly independent shops, cafes, and restaurants.'

I move closer to the screen. 'The beach and shopping areas won't take long to get to on foot. I could do with walking more.'

'Let's go on a guided tour.' Emma clicks through a series of photos.

Harmony House's upper glass balconies jut from a pristine white brick foundation. The boxy shape has a contemporary edge I'm not usually drawn to. Jutting lines separate the flats. The clinical feel is pervasive, right down to the white fencing along the entrance. A small patch of grass, flanked by a line of vibrant flowers, offers the only natural touch.

My terraced house in Marston is a quaint cottage, indicative of my liking for character in buildings, people, and paintings. Why I'm drawn to this feat of cool modern architecture is beyond comprehension. Light hitting the glass emits flashes like a camera, drawing me into the scene. This isn't my world, and yet this building is seducing me.

'Have you noticed how Harmony House is one of a kind?' Emma points at a photo showing where the building is situated on the road. 'The few other properties on the lane appear to be houses, bloody enormous ones, too.'

The distinctiveness calls to my quirky nature. Despite being an occasional ball of anxiousness, I let my weirdness shine. I shouldn't be drawn to this overtly wealthy road, and still the words are ready to tumble from my mouth.

'Let's ask Bekstar about us going there together.'

I can't believe I've said it. Huge changes normally make me nervous. This seems right. The fiery sun kissing the edge of the rooftop over the Harmony House building feels like a welcome.

'This is temporary, isn't it?' Emma asks. 'Ben will kill me if you're doing this as a way to leave him.'

'Don't be silly. I promise you, it's only for a month to get my head together. You know I can't stay away from Ben for long.'

Emma composes a message on her phone. We await a reply.

I check the property details again. 'Calling it *Harmony House* is a bit hippyish.'

'Soon, we might be saying we're living in Harmony.'

'If only.'

Emma's phone pings. She reads the message. 'We're on! Bekstar says all we have to cover are the bills. She thinks the warden will be okay with us being there as long as we behave and slip him a few extra quid.'

'A warden? What is this place, a prison where the screws take bribes?'

'Nah. It's a swanky block of flats where a warden oversees things. We should feel protected, being watched over.'

CHAPTER 6
The Watcher

The Harmony House building is a watcher's paradise. Eight flats are enough for me to observe without feeling overwhelmed. It's a sensory cornucopia. Sea air spritzes saltiness on my tongue, just by opening a window.

Past projects taught me to value quality over quantity. The things I've witnessed within these walls are the stuff of dreams and nightmares. My observational methods have led to death. No regrets. Humans make their own choices. Their particular watching preferences can turn even my cast iron stomach.

As a man dragged a razor down his wrists, I celebrated the blood flowing. You probably think me an unfeeling creature. You'd be right, although he deserved to die on the bathroom floor of his squalid flat. Getting your kicks from making and watching child porn sullies the excellence of intelligent observation. My tapes sent to the police of this individual's deeds led to him ending his life. Don't confuse my actions for caring about abused children. After a miserable childhood of trying to evoke any latent sympathy, I discovered I have none. It's not a lack. Being unhindered by emotions makes my viewing clinical. Exposing a paedophile was merely sport. His death was the perfect result. I will not have watching brought to the level of gratuitous seediness.

THE WATCHER

Previous suburban apartments overloaded my mind. The expanse of a city may seem like a watcher's dream. Boxed up flats, packed into concrete towers, make their residents weep for something with soul and heart. Giddy with looking in all directions, the sensory overload made my head spin. One moment I'd focus on a couple's argument, the next a drug deal took place in the hallway, and then a teenager shooting characters on a screen planned how to do it for real.

London tenants in high rises infected my screens with their filthy lives. Contamination seeped into my retinas and rippled under my skin. I needed to get clean. Seaside air was the tonic.

Harmony House is my promised land. When I arrived here, earlier observation had drained me. The intention when I came to Southbourne was to rest. It didn't last long. The thunderous crashing of the sea carried over a breeze, summoning me to action. The ebb and flow resurrected my stagnant sense of purpose.

Watching nourishes me. An appetite for seeing gnaws inside, demanding fulfilment. The journey from the screen and into my mind is lightning fast, but unlike those who passively stare at their phones, I absorb what I see. Images nestle within me and flood my veins. Viewing is my lifeblood. Without it, I wither.

Watching is my weakness and strength. Observing others is my raison d'être. I tried to be human. This probably sounds ridiculous. Of course, I'm a human being, right? Except, I don't possess your humanity. I don't care or emote.

Despite a hatred of people, I acknowledge their usefulness. People teach me how to be more human. As a child, I riled against the norm until I learned to emulate it. Years of observance have made me human, or at least passable as a person.

Although they can offer teachings, people are often dull. They always revert to type. No one has surprised me yet. Not a single being has proved themselves worthy of my complete attention. Still, I never give up on seeking the perfect specimen. It's time to prepare for new arrivals; something new to feast my eyes upon. I'm hungry and one of the women coming here has particularly whetted my appetite.

Welcome to Harmony House, Sophie Walters.

CHAPTER 7

Sophie

'Okay, I understand. Just make sure you get plenty of rest.' I end the call and wonder if it's fate telling me not to go to Harmony House.

'What's happened?' Ben asks, standing by my suitcases.

'Emma has glandular fever. She was feeling a bit off-colour when I saw her in the pub last week. The doctor's just left her house. She can't come with me.'

I try not to notice the glimmer of hope spreading across my husband's face. It would be so easy to stay. Should I?

'I can't believe I'm saying this,' Ben begins, 'but I think you should still go.'

I swallow against the pain rising up inside me. 'Do you want me to leave? I know it's been hard, and I haven't been easy to live with.'

He kisses me on the forehead. 'No. I wish I never had to let you go, but maybe that's our problem. We spend so much time together we don't always get time to think. It's only a month. You've already told the publisher you'll do seaside sketches for them.'

'You're right. I could make it up from my imagination, but it's never quite the same. You know how I love a good research trip.'

THE WATCHER

'Exactly. Think of it as a month of work and then hopefully it won't be so hard to be away.'

My resolve to leave wavers. As always, he's looking after me, but I've relied on him for too long. Since we met at a youth club in our teens, Ben's been my constant. I confess I've allowed him to do things I could've done myself. It's not his fault. My husband is the most caring person I know. Now, I must stand alone. If I don't work problems out for myself, we'll never get through this. Maybe fate intervened, so that I had to go alone. If Emma had been with me, I'm not sure much head sorting would have happened. Going to Southbourne on my own will make me stronger and ready for an altered future, probably without children.

Outside, I take in a last view, etching every piece of my house upon my mind. When we moved in, I beheld the home we would create. The walls hold many memories, joyful and tragic. Failed dreams and confirmed hopes seep out of the foundations. Ben and I are this building. How will a flat in Southbourne compete? The two properties couldn't be more different.

Our terraced cottage, nuzzled into a secluded road on the outskirts of Oxford, epitomises warmth. Golden stone, clematis crawling up the front wall to reach for the sky, and a sun trap garden, bathes us in positivity.

Harmony House's stark white bricks, sharp glass features, and jutting edges shouldn't feel like a prize in comparison. What it offers, though, is a place to heal.

I must leave behind this haunted house, with its spirits of dead opportunities. Hopefully, Harmony House will teach me how to find peace with an altered future and make this a home again.

'I'm so nervous,' I say. 'Leaving you behind is the hardest thing I've ever done. This is huge.'

'I understand. I see you're wearing the silver boots usually reserved for special occasions. Is this a celebration?'

As I tighten my hold, he breathes against my neck. Heaving shoulders betray his attempt at holding tears at bay.

'I could never celebrate being away from you,' I say. 'You and I could never end. From the moment I first saw you, I knew that was it forever. I need to get things in order. That's all. This baby business will never be resolved while I'm flailing around, losing direction. I'm doing this for us, Gentle Ben.'

He stands back and treats me with a generous smile. Ben is stocky and ridiculously tall. His parents adopted the moniker from the TV bear of yesteryear, and it's stuck.

Ben composes his face into a front of stoicism. 'I'll miss you every day.'

I slump against the car. 'I don't think I can do this. Maybe I'm not strong enough.'

'You're the bravest person I've ever met. Face your fears.'

'I'm also an anxious mess,' I add.

'Aren't we all sometimes? It's what makes you so strong. Even though you have anxiety, you conquer it.'

Unable to speak against the lump in my throat, I focus on getting into the car. Vera, my dilapidated Mini, groans as I take a seat. The chair springs threaten to burst out of the fabric. Rust feasts on the paintwork. I daren't fix anything. The car would probably fall apart. We're in this together. Until the day she gives up, Vera is mine. I send a silent prayer to make it to Southbourne. Vera's packed to the rafters with my stuff and she's not a fan of chilly weather.

Ben taps the hood. 'Go well, Vera, and get my Sophie there in one piece.'

'If the outlaws call,' I begin, 'unlikely as it is, please don't tell them where I am.'

'Definitely not.' He's well aware of the complicated relationship with my parents. Thankfully, since they moved to Australia, we've not had many interactions. Their constant switches from apathy to judgement are exhausting. If they find out Ben and I will be apart for a while, cries of "I told you so" will resound across continents. They're not my husband's biggest fans, based on snobbery about him coming from a dodgier part of Oxford.

With the turn of the key in the ignition, Vera starts on the first attempt. Is this a positive sign of what's coming?

'Wait!' I cry. 'I forgot to say goodbye to Doris!'

THE WATCHER

Ben darts into the house and then reappears with our guinea pig. Doris's nose twitches as I nuzzle in.

'Look after my baby.' I regret the words as soon as I say them.

'I love you.' Ben kisses my forehead. 'Doris and I will be waiting.'

'I love you too, more than I can ever express.'

As I drive away, Ben decreases in the rear-view mirror. I diminish with him.

CHAPTER 8

The Watcher

Observation isn't a passive act. You think a glance at the person walking towards you is subconscious. One look sets your brain alight. Opinions, conditioning, your upbringing, and attitudes ignite in your brain. The person's appearance and movements flood your mind bank with facts and opinions. Knowledge is power.

My viewing is always conscious. Authority lies in The Watcher's eye. I see, assimilate, and destroy.

Look behind you. Cast a glimpse around the room. Heed the hairs prickling on the back of your neck. Trust your instincts. Take a moment in the busyness.

Someone is always watching.

I am always watching.

CHAPTER 9
Sophie

Good old Vera served me well. My usually thirsty Mini only needed one slug of water throughout the journey. She wasn't the only one who lost water on the way here. Gut-wrenching sobs held inside me for far too long, unleashed. Every mile further away from Ben jabbed at my heart.

I assess the car now parked on Gull Lane. Everything's still in place; no mean feat for a vehicle that's lost wing mirrors on motorways. Maybe it's a sign this is meant to be. I'll take anything as a positive related to this mad idea to leave Ben behind and live in an unknown area.

Looking up, I note the muted scarlet sun gripping onto remnants of the day, blanching the dusky blue sky. Night forges a battle. I recall the photograph of a more vibrant sunset in the photos Emma shared of the building. Light merging with the rooftop, softening the harsh lines, attracted my artist's eye. Perhaps this similar setting sun in front of me is another sign things will work out. Maybe I'm like the sun, trying to hold on despite the dark odds against me. Where is this airy-fairy nonsense coming from? Bereavement must have pickled my brain.

Unpacking the car signifies the beginning of a new phase. There's nothing like moving house to discover how much stuff you've accumulated. Ben joked how he wouldn't miss things falling out of cupboards. I can't be a hoarder here. The flat is too small. A month isn't enough time here to accumulate too much crap.

'Ow, bloody thing.' The easel jabs me in the ear as I wrench it from the boot of the car. It slips from my grip and stubs my toe.

Photos of light spilling into the flat inspired me to bring most of my art equipment. A lot of my recent work is digital. This is the perfect opportunity to return to my first loves of sketching and painting. I'm craving the chalkiness of charcoal beneath my fingernails and glistening acrylics on a palette. The beach offers many artistic opportunities. Images of frothy waves and gritty sand form a backdrop in my mind. My reverie is broken by a committee of seagulls circling overhead, laying claim to the lane named after them.

Battling against the birds' cawing, a man sitting on the steps of the Harmony House building clears his throat. He gives a wry smile while watching me struggle with the easel. I note his patchy russet hair dye, double denim, and cowboy boots. Deciding to unpack after I've got the key, I lay the easel down.

'Giving up already?' dodgy cowboy man asks. With clearly practised ease, he blows smoke rings.

I slam the car door and wince, remembering Vera's held together by duct tape and hope.

Dodgy cowboy man removes the cigarette dangling from the corner of his mouth.

'I hate to disempower women,' he says as he stands. 'You get your knickers in a knot when men try to help, unless you want me to overpower you?'

I concentrate on hair dye stained below his hairline, rather than the smut. I edge past him towards the main entrance. This creep is ruining my moment to start something new. I can't even take a proper look at the building. Driving here, the anticipation of seeing Harmony House for the first time kept me going.

A plump ginger cat appears and rubs its body against the man's shin. I fuss the moggy who offers loud purrs in return. The man kicks out at it.

THE WATCHER

'Don't!' I try to shield the cat with my hands. 'That's cruel.'

'I'm allergic to cats. Can't stand the mangy things.'

Before taking cover in the shrubbery, the cat hisses. Dodgy cowboy man takes no notice as he punches in a code at the main door.

The man grins. 'Sorry, sweetness, you can't get in without my help.' He holds the door open. A stale odour of cigarettes emanates from him as I dart past.

'I'm Rory, by the way.'

He sticks out his hand to shake. The clammy palm makes me shiver.

'Pleased to meet you,' I reply. My mother may be a snob, but she taught me manners.

'And you are?' Rory leans in far too close as I try to find a space in the hallway.

Getting away from you, I think. His intense stare feels violating.

A door opens to a flat.

'Sophie, I presume?' another man asks, leaning in a doorway. 'I'm Adam, the warden. Come in out of the cold. Thanks for letting her in, Rory, although I keep telling you to leave visitors to me.'

'You know me. I never could resist a pretty lady. It's a pleasure to meet you, Sophie. Welcome to Harmony House. Good to see a new face around here.'

CHAPTER 10

The Watcher

Testing, testing. The clarity of my voice is superb on this new audio equipment. Only the best for me. The Watcher likes to talk, too. How else will you know my interpretations? I'm not a silent player. My opinions matter. *I* matter.

Should I name myself right now? If you're listening to the complete recordings, my identity has been revealed. The project will have ended, and I claimed my fame. You will recognise the genius of my scheme and how I avoided capture.

Dear listener, you and I engaged in a power struggle the moment you heard the first word I recorded. You are only privy to what I want you to hear. All knowledge is derived from me. I will treat you to occasional truths hiding in between the lies. I may even offer the odd recording before this project ends. Prove your worthiness first.

For now, I'll narrate as if I could be anyone. It keeps it interesting. My chosen listener, when you have all the recordings, you'll know who I am. So, why do I record my observations as if I could be any of Harmony House's residents? Toying with perceptions helps alleviate my occasional boredom.

I may describe an individual's actions when the person is actually me. Why not have fun with the narrative structure by

THE WATCHER

hinting I could've been anyone? Everyone looks. Don't dare tell me you don't.

You might think I'm a frustrated writer wanting to control the story. I'm far more accomplished. Instead of characters, I manipulate people's lives. No one knows who's controlling the observation tower. You're not even aware I'm watching. Don't believe we're on the same level because I chose you.

Perhaps you wonder why I want a listener. Let's be clear, I don't need you. You are part of my project: an appendix in a dissertation of watching.

I refuse to make this venture easy for either of us. Where's the challenge in handing these recordings over to a do-gooder who goes to the police after hearing the first recording? You, The Listener, will listen to all my narratives. I'll know you well enough to be certain of this.

Each new day, my recordings will call to you, demanding to be heard. You'll despise yourself for craving more. Occasionally, you'll wonder if you're as bad as me in your curiosity to know what others don't. You'll tussle with a sense of justice and be angry with me for forcing a decision upon you. Goodness states you must hand these recordings to the police. Rage doesn't want you to give me notoriety. Eventually, decency will win.

Since I found out about Sophie's arrival, a burgeoning excitement has increased. Maybe she will hear my audio diaries. This feels like the last opportunity to find my listener. Other possibilities proved disappointing. The gnawing in my gut, an intensity of an unbidden knowing The Listener is in Harmony House, keeps me here.

Sophie's shuffles competing against squared shoulders disclosed trepidation, undermined by a fighting spirit. There are others to observe in the flats, but it's becoming tedious. Familiarity breeds my contempt. There are only so many times you can witness breakfasting, washing, and getting dressed before boredom threatens to paralyse your mind. The residents try to engage when we pass by in the building. I go through the mill of small talk while suppressing the desire to spill their secrets.

Upon my arrival at Harmony House, I mistakenly believed the tenants would be sophisticated. Properties within a suitable walking distance of the beach command top rental rates. Landlords allow residences to crumble and still people will snap them up, desperate for a coveted postcode. Harmony House's landlord is far away from the building, but his penchant for turfing out residents and making demands keeps his authority close. Wardens and guardians preside over his buildings across the world. Sometimes we need to use others to accomplish our aims.

My Harmony House observation began as a two-person operation. We were never accomplices. That would make us equal. Eventually, the other person will learn of their place. This time I'm going solo in my watching. The Listener will do my bidding. It might be Sophie, although she's given me some cause for concern.

Anxiety shone from her like a neon light. Shaky hands dropped the easel. A cautionary check over a dilapidated car showed her ability to assess. Searching eyes drifted up to the rooftop, detecting something to spring a smile. I hope she isn't one of those addicts, desperate for a seaside fix. I've been stagnating in a building of predictability. New blood is required.

It's pleasing to see Sophie's an observer, too. Perhaps she's more than an anxious being. Banal mental illness won't disrupt my plans. Sophie must prove she can work with anxiety, not make it her ruin. I've defied the restrictive labelling of mental illness conditions. She might, too. Her friend, Emma, isn't here. I hope this means Sophie is alone.

Yes, indeed.

Sophie Walters is one to watch.

CHAPTER 11
Sophie

Adam's scowl deepens by the minute. Are all the men who live here weird? If Rory and Adam are any indication, the answer is a firm yes. Note to self: keep the front door locked.

'Is Rory always such a charmer?' I ask, trying to lighten the warden's intensity.

'Don't mind him,' Adam replies. 'Rory's been here for years and doesn't present too many problems.' He offers me a mug so huge it requires both hands to hold it. 'Rory's bark is worse than his bite. Thinks he's a ladies' man and can't come to terms with getting older.'

'Bit of a player?' I take a sip of tea, letting out a gasp as it burns my tongue.

'More milk? Sorry, I have it piping hot. Not to everyone's taste.'

'Please.'

While Adam's in the kitchen, I look around the flat to get an idea of the layout. The lounge is smaller than mine at home; cosy and cramped. I expect he's downsized from a house and couldn't part with his possessions. Feminine touches are everywhere, from a floral-patterned three-piece suite to shepherdess ornaments in a display cabinet. The girls' various poses signify the life of a shepherdess must be a busy one. There was me thinking it's just holding a crook and whistling.

'Do you collect ornaments?' Adam returns, noticing me looking at the figurines. 'These were my wife's.'

'I'm a bit of a hoarder.' I chuckle. 'Ornaments aren't in my stash yet, but give me time.'

'This was my wife's only collection. She liked tidiness.' He teases a hint of a smile. Moroseness soon returns. 'I miss her nagging me to get rid of piles of magazines. Even though she passed away ten years ago, it still feels like yesterday.'

If Ben died, I'd never recover. Being apart from my husband is incomprehensible. But I am. Trust me to make this complicated.

'You shouldn't really be here,' Adam says.

'Why?'

Adam glugs the rest of his tea and whacks the mug onto the table. 'Sub-letting isn't allowed. The landlord likes to vet potential tenants.'

'I thought Emma sorted it out with you.'

To be gracious, I neglect to mention the money Emma paid as a bribe. No doubt, it's currently in the warden's bank account.

'Right enough. It's only because I don't want the place lying empty that I've let you live here. I believed Bekstar was going to stick around. Unreliable tenants won't be tolerated.'

As Adam's chest puffs out, he probably thinks it displays authority. He's more like a scrawny pigeon with illusions of being a peacock.

'I thought there was another woman coming with you, this Emma person?'

'She has glandular fever and is suffering with it. I didn't want to leave Emma behind, but she insisted. I'll only be here for a month at most. Bekstar will be back by then. I'm most grateful for you allowing me to live in this lovely place for a while.' I give a sweet, forced smile.

Adam spreads his legs across the sofa.

Okay, mate, I understand. You're in charge.

THE WATCHER

'Here's the code for the main entrance.' Adam gives me a slip of paper. 'I change it occasionally. Residents kept giving out the codes because they can't be bothered to buzz guests in. When I change the code, I'll let you know in advance.'

I put the note in my pocket, reminding myself to check my jeans before they go into the wash. Ben had to fix the washing machine after a build-up of paper I forgot to take out bunged it up.

Adam assesses paperwork he insisted Emma and I filled out. He places it into a folder labelled with our names.

'No parties, no drugs, no smoking, keep the noise down, and pets only by my consent.'

'I'll be a very good girl and not make a sound.' Despite my best effort, sarcasm trickles out.

Adam's knuckles whiten as he grips the folder. 'That's what the woman who lived here before Bekstar said. Louise was a right one for being noisy, although she soon became quiet.'

Overwhelmed by the heat in the room, I unzip my jacket.

'Did you have a word with her about the noise?' I ask.

'I didn't need to. Hasn't anyone told you? Louise died in your flat.'

I scan the room, wondering if I'm on *Candid Camera*, being *Punk'd* or whatever people watch nowadays.

'Someone died where I'm going to live?'

'I'd have thought your friends would've told you.'

'How did she die?'

'Accident.' Adam's face is devoid of emotion. Earlier shows of superiority hint he's enjoying making me work for information.

'What happened?' I try not to show my fear, but my wobbling voice betrays me.

'Louise fell and hit her head on the edge of a cabinet in the lounge. The coroner said she likely tripped over a rug. There were fancy oriental ones in most rooms. Louise had more money than sense. Apparently, catching a foot on a rug is a common household accident.'

'Who found her?' A sudden desperation consumes me. Louise and I are connected by the flat. Do I believe in bad omens?

'Unfortunately, it was me.' He shuts his eyes, as if conjuring up the scene. 'One of her colleagues from the optician's came here. Louise hadn't turned up at work for days. They tried calling but got no reply. I unlocked the door and found the body.' Adam's voice breaks. Maybe he has a heart in there somewhere.

He continues. 'It was Halloween night last year. I usually stay indoors. There are too many kids about playing nasty tricks. At least they can't get into the building. I detest Halloween. Why do people celebrate monsters and being dead? Kids nowadays have far too much leeway, messing about and upsetting people, even more so when they're dressed as devils. Little beggars wouldn't have wanted to witness what I saw, though. The amount of blood seemed fitting, I suppose, considering the time of year. Don't let it put you off. It's an unfortunate incident. Terrible business, but it didn't deter Bekstar from moving in.'

Maybe she doesn't know. If Bekstar does, she certainly didn't tell Emma. Emma would have been all over it as something to use in the crime novel she's considering writing.

Adam stands, pats his back pocket, and pulls out a set of keys. 'Shall we?'

Within the bewilderment, I try to gather my senses. 'Shall we what?'

'Go to the flat, of course.' Adam opens his front door.

I take slow steps behind.

Dare I enter a place of death?

CHAPTER 12

The Watcher

Louise Penrose was difficult to ignore. She was a stunning woman, but reticent with it. What she lacked in self-confidence, Louise more than made up for with a penchant for booming pop music. Banal tunes blasted from her flat until the day she was silenced.

The commonality between Louise and Sophie is fortuitous but also a concern. Louise was in her forties when she left her husband; the same as Sophie. Both had and have a quiet demeanour shielding a more sassy edge. Will Sophie disappoint me, too?

Initially, Louise was a complex study. At night, she'd tuck the covers in around her legs; a security routine. It brought to mind the shrouding of a corpse. She recorded her hopes, dreams, and memories in a diary. Continual references to her husband's multiple affairs were tedious. Thankfully, the mistake Louise kept making in Harmony House made for more enlightening viewing. Zooming in on the pages, I entered a private world of words. Each punch and insult her husband had inflicted created images in my head. Louise and I connected in wanting to end the life of an abuser.

For too long, I allowed someone to exert control over me. They thought they could mould me into their vision of perfection.

I played along. Sometimes you must fight dangerous instincts and allow your superior mind to fix the problem. By seeming compliant, I'm the stronger of the two. Those who usurp others' power are reprehensible. Everyone should know their place. I'm teaching my pseudo controller this. The fallout will be worth the struggle. I won't be a victim.

Louise prided herself on leaving behind a cheating spouse and starting anew. Despite a liking for uncouth music, her home was tastefully furnished. Antiques and flea market finds filled the flat. Most Saturdays she'd return from bargain hunting with something to add to the decor.

Bookcases boasted literary classics and medical journals. Louise was an accomplished optometrist who soon secured a job upon arriving in Southbourne. She thought she'd done well by securing a flat in a coveted area. When I heard her telling people of the new beginning, my knowledge of her impending doom was thrilling. Imagine, if you will, a woman's excitement, declaring Southbourne as a place for renewal. Louise was an unstamped old-fashioned library card until a last date was printed and made permanent upon her body.

A craving for company was destructive. The wrong kind of men buzzed around her. Enjoying being the honey, she never looked at or listened to the clues surrounding her. I gave many hints of an imminent demise and still she chose the fatalistic path. Vanity kills.

Louise drowned out regrets by developing a drinking problem. Although they're called *functioning alcoholics*, Louise wasn't operating effectively the night she died. The booze in the cabinet might have killed her, eventually. Instead, the cabinet itself did the job.

I recall the delivery men trying to get it into the flat. The flagrant machismo as they sparred over how to perform the operation was insulting to my ears. When clumsy hands made the cabinet strike walls and doors, the men's words changed to profanities.

THE WATCHER

The cabinet's arrival heralded Louise's demise. The foolish woman beheld the bargain find with wonder. Once in place, it became a medicine chest, full of tipples to ease the pain.

Rather than being her salvation, the cabinet was destructive. Solid mahogany shatters skulls. Whenever I play the video, the thud and crack are astounding. I saw it happen in real time, too.

No regrets. No guilt. Louise was the perfect study in seeing and hearing death. Her demise was one thing that took me by surprise. I believed I was solely an observer. It turns out I enjoy death, too.

CHAPTER 13

Sophie

Adam's "hospitality" ended as soon as he let me into the flat. Going in alone was terrifying. Before entering, I questioned the reality of ghosts. Would Louise be waiting? I'd cast a look at Adam's flat opposite mine, wondering if I should ask him to come inside with me. Then I decided the fear must stop, to pull up my big girl pants, and enter. I've left my husband behind for this. Returning to Ben because I'm afraid of spooks isn't an option. I have to allow Southbourne its best chance to heal my marriage and me.

'Boo!'

I drop my phone in response to my friend's attempt at humour.

'I nearly had a heart attack, Em.'

Picking up my mobile, I continue the video tour of the flat. Emma received instructions not to tell Ben I've got the heebie-jeebies. Pride will always be my downfall. Besides, he'd belt down the motorway to rescue me if he knew about Louise's death. Much as I want to see Ben, it won't help me to be more courageous.

'Not sure about those curtains.' Emma wrinkles her nose.

I assess the garish geometric pattern of the material. Circles, diamonds, and squares clash and vie for space on the fabric.

THE WATCHER

What was once considered outdated is now retro. Living through a fashion once leads to understanding it's never acceptable the second time around.

Training my mobile around the flat, I share the gadgets on offer. 'Bloody love this kitchen, though,' I say. 'Bekstar certainly doesn't buy cheap tat.'

'If my throat didn't feel like sandpaper, I'd be salivating over the coffee machine. The pizza oven is heaven on Earth. They're at least five hundred quid. To think I could've been living there.'

I lean against the fridge. 'How are you feeling?'

'Like a slightly warmed-up corpse.'

As Emma rubs her eyes, I admire her spectacular bed head. She must be sick. Emma doesn't even answer the door without make-up on and her hair styled.

'Didn't Bekstar know about this Louise woman?' I ask.

'She's never mentioned it. Remember, Bekstar's hardly ever there as she travels so much. I've tried phoning, but she's in the rainforest and difficult to contact.'

I approach the lounge and scan my mobile across the room. 'Where do you reckon the cabinet was that Louise hit her head on?'

Emma leans into shot as if she can tumble into the flat.

'Woah, too much cleavage,' I tease.

She jiggles her boobs. 'I have to leave the buttons open on my PJs. I'm burning up. At least you've got Bekstar's furniture. Having a dead person's stuff would be creepy. Focus the phone on the floor.'

I hold the screen face down and take measured strides. Despite myself, I count each step. Habits really do die hard. Order still dominates my thinking.

'Lower,' Emma says. 'I can't see it.'

'What?'

'Kneel down and I'll tell you.' My kneecaps creak in protest at the hardness of the oak flooring.

'Stop!' Emma shouts as I'm set to collide with the wall. 'Reverse up and zoom in.'

The hessian rug scratches through my dungarees. Instinct rather than discomfort makes me move away. Like ripping off a plaster, I fling the rug back.

'Shit.'

'Indeed.' Emma's eyes are in full-on, frog-bulging mode.

'I didn't think it would be that bad,' I say. An indelible brown stain eats into the floor. The mark is making its own circle within the wood. Louise is gone. Her blood remains.

'Blood's a bugger to get out of wood,' Emma says.

'How the hell would you know?'

'Just do.'

I turn the screen towards me. 'I don't need this. Can I go somewhere else around here?'

'Not at this short notice.' Emma musters a smile. 'I understand it's unpleasant. Put the rug back and you won't see it.'

But I'll know it's there. A dead woman's blood taints my new home.

CHAPTER 14
The Watcher

For a warden, Adam Foster can seem remarkably unobservant. Some attribute this to prolonged grieving. He's claimed bereavement as a reason for being, having never recovered from his wife's death. Occasional outbursts of anger take over when he considers a denied future.

At night, Adam talks to a photograph placed on what should have been his spouse's side of the bed. The besotted look of a bride, high on the buzz of getting married, exudes from Tina. Her smile outshines the silver frame. Adam shares the details of another mundane day with his photograph wife.

When he arrived in Harmony House, Adam remarked upon the compactness of the building. The landlord misconstrued it as snobbery and said if it wasn't good enough, he could find employment elsewhere. The matter was cleared up when Adam declared its size was perfect. He likes to give the impression of a small-town man who doesn't dare to think big. The grizzled, world-weary recluse persona suits his purposes. Mastering the territory offers purpose. People who threaten Adam's dominance soon learn of their error. The warden is a jealous ruler of his self-created kingdom. Having a flat at the front of Harmony House means never missing anything. All the residents have to pass his home to enter and exit the building.

Moving to Harmony House was a necessary upheaval. The family home changed from paradise to prison. Memories sparked by places his wife sat, laughed, slept, ate, and cried, attacked him. The Victorian house's enormity expanded with grief until Adam exploded with despair. He needed an enclosing escape. Harmony House offered this with its small spaces and a chance to hide.

Despite moving, Adam brought the past with him. Tightly packed in furniture feels claustrophobic to visitors. Adam doesn't want space. He can't afford to fall through the gaps of a painful past. Units, shelves, and display cabinets form a barrier against the world and darker memories.

Elevating to a better place, Adam fixates on photograph Tina. When dusting the shepherdess ornaments, he tells them they're a beauty to behold. He has an eye for details.

Wherever Adam goes, his anguished heart is constant. It makes him objectionable. The grieving widower act always garners sympathy, though. People excuse his oddities on the basis of mourning.

Since he started working as a warden, Adam's made many mistakes. I know them all: the extra money tenants are charged for maintenance already part of their rent; backhanders for sub-letting; shortcuts taken with the building's upkeep; and ignoring residents' calls and knocks on the door.

The warden position is perfect for a watcher. Adam supervises Harmony House. Am I him? Think of the opportunities a warden has.

Not yet, dear listener. It's too soon for the final reveal. Teasing this narrative is proving to be most enjoyable. You'll have the answer when I give you these recordings. Can you hear my smile? I'm considering the delicious revelations awaiting you, including Adam's.

What's most interesting about the warden was the fixation on Louise. When he saw her bloodied corpse, his expression wasn't one of shock. Adam deserved to feel guilty for what he did to Louise.

CHAPTER 15

Sophie

Upon waking this morning, I decided to give Harmony House a chance. Someone dying here is terrible. Louise's death is a tragedy, but I can't let it define this space. People die all the time. I expect the percentage of deaths in the home is high. I can't keep freaking out about Louise dying in this flat for a whole month. This is a fresh start, not a memorial.

Last night I laid a single flower on the rug, covering Louise's blood, to pay my respects. In hindsight, the bloom may have been a weed plucked from the garden. It's a hardy specimen against the winter. Maybe the weed can teach me about triumphing through adversity. I removed the floral memorial this morning. The act signifies a new era. The flat can be whatever I want. Home might be here for a while, as well as in Oxford, although being without Ben for too long won't happen.

Still, my steps over the rug concealing the bloodstain are cautious. I'm playing the adult version of avoiding pavement cracks to dodge Louise's misfortune.

Ben phoned while he was driving to work. I could tell he was forcing the cheeriness. Every joke died on its arse, but I didn't want the call to end. No one says my name quite like my husband.

I wish we could find a way to be together that doesn't hurt us. I'm working on it.

Outside, it's heartening to see a friendly "face" in Vera. She's still holding on and has blended in with a coating of seagull crap deposited on the icy windscreen. Those rats with wings are hardcore, coming out to shit in any weather. The possible offender glares at me from their spot on the wall, laying claim to Gull Lane. We engage in a staring contest. Menacing yellow eyes invite me to take the bird on. Pinprick pupils expand with the light. Crossing my arms, I root myself to the pavement. My avian enemy flaps their wings in a bird's version of a hissy fit. Sticking out my tongue in response is juvenile and apparently not acceptable. The gull swoops towards me.

'Okay, you win,' say to my attacker as I cover my head with my arms. 'Piss off and migrate.'

I scan the sky, looking for the gull's mates to turn up while catching my breath. I can hear the little buggers squawking in the distance. Despite the threat of re-enacting Hitchcock's *The Birds*, the scenery wins.

'Not too shabby, eh, Vera?' I lean against the car and take in the view of Harmony House.

The confident sun defeats the winter chill, piercing the azure sky and warming unshaded spots along the pavement. Briny sea air reignites the child within me who ran across the beach on summer holidays. The lure of distant crashing waves draws me in. Southbourne offers a welcome.

Seeking the light I saw in the original photos above Harmony House, I look up. A petite woman leans against the steel balcony rail outside an upstairs flat. Despite the temperature, she's wearing a wispy negligée. After tossing away her mane of brown hair, she closes her eyes, allowing wintry rays to touch her skin. I study the upturned nose and elfin face. Her ethereal quality conjures an image of a fairy queen presiding over her kingdom. She'd be a perfect model to sketch for Emma's novels. Maybe I'll ask this fantasy figure to sit for me. Sensing my watching, the woman looks down and scowls. As if shooing away vermin, she flicks her hands. Perhaps I won't request her modelling services.

THE WATCHER

I turn to my only friend in Southbourne. 'Let's hope they're not all as unfriendly as her, Vera.'

'Do you often talk to yourself?'

A man appears from crouching behind my car.

My pencils clatter as they hit the concrete. Each strike derails my attempts not to consider the expensive lead shattering.

'You gave me a fright,' I say to my stalker. 'Why are you hiding?' I move away from the man, hoping my anger's a deterrent to getting closer. 'If you're trying to nick my car, good luck. You'll be lucky to get Vera out of Bournemouth.'

The man mumbles something into a scarf wrapped several times around his mouth.

'What did you say?' I ask. 'I can't hear you.'

He yanks the scarf down. 'You've named your car *Vera*? Excellent. I thought I'm the only person who names inanimate objects.'

The man steps forward while pushing glasses up the bridge of his nose. I retreat. While keeping an eye on the man, I try to pick up the art equipment. Pastels slide from my gloved hands.

'Sorry.' He fixates on scuffing his foot along the edge of the kerb. 'Mother keeps telling me to say *hello* before launching into conversation. I often forget. Hello.'

'Er, hello.'

He continues scraping his tatty trainers, exposing a hole already formed in the toe box. I hold my bag in front of me as a shield, while waiting for a polite moment to leave. Manners will be the death of me. Ben says I'd probably check if a murderer wants a cuppa before they kill me.

'And you are?' I'm guessing he's not going anywhere until we've completed our introductions.

He affects exaggerated shock while hitting the side of his head. 'Silly me. Mother told me to say who I am when greeting others.'

Who the hell am I dealing with here? Norman Bates reincarnated? The mother complex is freaky. Note to self: always check behind the shower curtain and be glad Harmony House isn't a motel.

'I'm Tobias Alfred Peters.' He holds out a hand.

Accepting it's the best way to speed up this awkward process, I shake his hand with the tips of my fingers. There's no way I'm letting him get a grip on me.

'Hello, Tobias Alfred Peters. Do you live around here?'

'Yes, I thought you knew already. I rent one of the flats above yours. My flat is at the back of the building. Since Adam said you're moving in for a while, I've been desperate to see you. It's important to meet the people I watch.'

I assess Tobias while considering how to escape. Difficult considering he's a stocky bloke who could knock me over with a poke of his finger.

'You watch people?' I take a step away.

'Oh yes.' He claps in a clumsy, childlike manner. 'Mother says it's good for me to have a hobby. It helps keep my mind off horrible things. I like to observe people. They're fascinating. You mustn't tell Mother about this, though. She'll be furious.'

'Right.' I turn to show my intention to leave.

'Wait!' Tobias grasps my forearm.

Despite my small stature, I can be forceful when provoked. I shove Tobias away. He retreats and resumes destroying his trainers against the kerb.

'So sorry. I wasn't going to hurt you. Honest, I'm friendly. I only want to chat, Sophie.'

'How do you know my name?'

'Adam told me.'

Choosing a random direction, I leave before he grabs me again. If I don't end up at the beach, at least it will be safer than being near Tobias. I try not to think about how I can't avoid him forever considering he lives in Harmony House, too.

As I hurtle away, I cast a glimpse back.

Tobias shields his eyes from the sun to get a better look at me.

CHAPTER 16
The Watcher

Sophie's already proving to be an interesting project. I wondered if she'd be weak, particularly as Emma didn't come due to illness.

Women leaving their spouses behind under the illusion of improving their lives are often pathetic. Louise proved it. Despite the apparent bravado of people forging their own way ahead, many crumble when faced with loneliness.

Still, I had such hopes for Louise, even daring to believe she could be my listener. Upon arrival, Louise was fragile but defiant. My favourite type of person. They make for interesting studies. Intricacy is a fascinating puzzle I need to solve.

My listener must be more than a one-dimensional cardboard cut-out of a human. They must question my motivations and wrestle with their impulses. To be my listener is the ultimate accolade. They are the chosen vessel for transporting my interpretations beyond these walls.

When Louise first entered Harmony House, the nibbling of her lip indicated nervousness. The transformation in her expression when she stepped into the flat was a sight to behold. With the gradual dropping of hunched shoulders, I could almost hear exhalations of concern leaving her body. Louise hugged herself, as if offering self-congratulations for finding such a place. Whenever returning home, she always smiled. It didn't last. The clichéd wiping the smile off someone's face comes to mind. I'm proud to have been part of erasing it. Smugness isn't a great look.

Louise's descent made me feel murderous. Thinking about it always makes my fingers twitch. No one lets me down. There are consequences for those who deviate from my expectations. They must learn to be better. If Louise had made more suitable choices, she might still be alive. I make no guarantees, though.

Sophie has a spirit that's almost admirable. However, I'll never elevate anyone to a higher position than mine. Sophie's an artist, dreamer, and a tortured soul. I'm a clinician, a scientist, and an observer. I keep my distance while zooming in on others' lives.

Love is the kryptonite of the human race. Consider how many have died in its name or lost so much in the pursuit of love. Emotions make humans do ridiculous things. My actions are always considered, careful, and controlled.

Love cannot infiltrate my barricaded heart. When I was younger, I thought my inability to care was a weakness. I sought my identity in devotion. Parents are allegedly the first people to show unconditional love. My childhood always had conditions, the main one being love didn't feature. Don't you dare pity me. My parents trained me well. Unburdened by love, I can do or say the deeds and words you'd never contemplate.

Someone once tried to love me. They laboured under the misapprehension their devotion had the power to change me. Nonsense. I allowed them to get close because it suits the purpose. If you're loved, others believe you're loveable. It's the ultimate disguise.

Sophie oozes affection. Even at this early stage, I can tell her capacity to love is boundless. The way she talks to her husband and friend displays it. Adoration and kindness might get Sophie into trouble. I must work on her. Sophie's face softens when she sees the underdog, Tobias, despite the initial fear of someone watching her from behind her car.

Tobias' idiot role can be somewhat tedious, but there's genius in the performance. The hapless fool act either makes others ignore him or evokes sympathy. It's obvious Tobias is different. He asks to be looked over and looked after.

Sophie's interaction with Tobias indicates an inquisitive mind. She's right to be wary. Tobias Alfred Peters is a hidden threat in Harmony House.

CHAPTER 17
Sophie

My screaming thighs protest at the walk I've taken from Harmony House to the beach. I have a word with myself that it shouldn't be an issue. Southbourne will make a walker of me yet and not because my car is a scrapheap. Still, I cringe at the steep slope I've walked down, knowing the only way back is up.

A few dog walkers and an elderly couple sitting on a bench are my only beach companions. Getting an early start was a good idea. I hope winter weekdays are always this quiet. Solace is often my medicine. When the tourists descend, I expect it's chaotic. Tabloid newspaper images of beaches teeming with sun seekers and hardly a spare patch of sand come to mind. Thankfully, this happens more on Bournemouth beach, from what I've learned. Despite being so close, Southbourne remains more a province of the locals. Where does this place me? I'm caught between being a resident and a grockle; the disparaging term those who live in seaside places call tourists.

Today I'm going to sketch and enjoy the scenery. Hypnotic sounds of the sea ebbing and flowing reflect in my relaxing muscles. Tension unknots. Limbs loosen. The stress of dealing with the strange Tobias disappears with the waves.

A cacophony of colour splashes across the line of beach huts. Their shadows cast away from me, helping the sun compete

THE WATCHER

against the arctic wind to tickle my skin. The confrontational breeze nips at my fingers.

A brass plaque on the bench is engraved, *In loving memory of my beloved wife, Kay Cross*. I touch the metal, imagining the widower who created this memorial. Despite the abrasive salty air, the metal gleams. Love's hand has polished it. It must be devastating to lose love. Death or a partner's decision to leave separates us. Does love end when you're apart? Not for me. If anything, my devotion to Ben is increasing.

As always, art will rescue me from sadness. I lay the sketchbook on my lap and forage through my bag, discovering only one pencil. While trying to escape from Tobias, I didn't pick up all of them. Pastels will suffice. Ben usually carries my art equipment. I bring everything with me, ready to capture a scene. Where others use cameras, my hands and mind, along with art materials, portray what I see. I record my perspective, not life through a detached lens.

The soothing sound of the calm sea lulls me into a sleepy haze. Sulphurous seaweed tinges the air. Seagulls sing in a discordant choir. A boat motors along the water, severing a line between the similar blues of sea and sky. Glints of sun upon the waves leap from the water and onto my page. Fogginess makes my mind as fuzzy as the chalky pastels. I didn't sleep well last night. Being in a place where someone died results in insomnia. Maybe I could doze for a moment.

A threat looms. Intuition ignited, I flick my eyes open.

The sunlight streaming behind the figure is blinding. A silhouette shades the person from identification.

'I picked up your pencils,' a newly familiar voice says. 'They're an expensive brand. You might miss them.'

I edge away from the strange man. 'Did you follow me?'

Tobias steps closer. 'I walk this way to work. When I saw you sitting here, I thought I'd give these back.'

Sweat trickles down his nose, making his glasses slide. I close my sketchbook and take the pencils Tobias offers. He moves away and removes the ridiculously long scarf, then unzips his coat.

Underneath is another jacket. He unbuttons it to reveal a flannel checked shirt.

'You must be boiling.' I try not to laugh. 'I'm all for bundling up, but you're somewhat over prepared.'

Perspiration breaks out on Tobias' forehead. As he wrestles out of the coat, his glasses hit the ground. Poised to pick them up, my attempt is thwarted by a seagull swooping in, probably attracted by light reflecting off the lens.

Tobias laughs as he moves the gull aside with far more gentleness than it deserves. They stare at each other in a standoff.

'Why aren't you picking up your glasses?' I ask.

'You're obviously not au fait with seagulls,' Tobias says. 'He won't steal them. Gulls are charming once you get to know them. They have their own kind of majestic beauty.'

The bird gives a distinctive yellow-eyed glare. Despite my fear of its pickaxe beak, I look closer. Our "guest" rests on Tobias' feet like a devoted puppy. I cast aside preconceptions of sky terrorists to study the creature. It transforms into a melding palette of virgin white, nestling into chromium grey, tipped by a natty black and white polka dotted rear.

'I never knew they could be trained.'

I approach, wanting in on the affectionate action. It flaps a wing out at me before retreating behind the bench. Tobias sits next to his feathered friend. The bird tries to strut, undermined by its propensity to walk lopsided.

'He's called Stanley.' Tobias pats the creature on the head. 'You'll get used to seeing him around Harmony House, too. Sometimes he follows me when I walk to work.'

Despite holding a fist against my mouth, I can't suppress my laughter. 'There's no way you can tell one of those from another.'

'See how this leg is twisted and his foot points more to the side than forward?'

'Yes.'

'Stanley's been in the wars. Poor old chap's leg is gnarled, but he still keeps on going.' Tobias gives his friend a pat on the head.

'Broken, but soldiering on,' I muse. 'Don't birds migrate at this time of year?'

THE WATCHER

Tobias waggles a finger. 'A common misconception, but gulls are rather hardy. It's true many go further inland where it's warmer, but some, like Stanley, prefer their coastal home.'

'Are you a bird expert?'

'No. I love learning. When I find something fascinating, I learn all I can about it.'

Stanley hops away, craps next to Tobias' glasses, and then flies off.

'Charming,' I say. 'Your mate could do with learning some manners.' I hand Tobias' glasses to him. 'They're not damaged. How you can see through the smudges is baffling, though.'

He wipes them on the hem of his shirt and puts them on. 'They need tightening. Louise used to tend to my optical needs. She was so kind.'

'Did you know her well?' I ask. Although I'm cautious of the man who's confessed he watches others, finding out more about Louise feels important.

'Louise was nice to me.' Tobias takes off his jacket, creating a pile of clothing hanging over his arm. 'Some people aren't. They call me strange.'

'I expect Louise's death was upsetting.'

'Such a sad day. I should've helped her.'

'Wasn't it an accident? I'm sure there's nothing you could've done to prevent it.'

He slaps a palm against his temple. Connecting the action to when this happens, I'm guessing it's an anger and stress tic.

'Don't you understand? I need to make sure people are okay. When others are safe, I am too.' Tobias unbuttons his shirt.

'Careful,' I say. 'You'll catch a chill if you strip off too much. Cool T-shirt, by the way. Lord Retribution, right?'

Despite my wariness, Tobias' enormous grin makes me smile.

'Do you play *Warrior Wrath*?' he asks.

'My husband paints and plays it.'

'Would he like a game with me some time?' Tobias bounces from foot to foot. 'Dorset has a great gaming community.'

I take a breath. 'Ben's in Oxford, so he won't be able to.'

'Why's he not here?'

I debate how much information I want to share with a stranger. Less than an hour ago, I thought this man was a crazy stalker. My gut says he's more a blend of literal and quirky.

'Long story,' I say. 'Maybe I could look at your models sometime. I'm an artist.'

Steamed lenses obscure Tobias' eyes. 'Come to my shop. I'm the assistant manager of Game On. It's a gaming store near here.'

His enthusiasm is infectious.

'Why not? Give me the address and I'll pop by later.'

The distraction might be good, although there's no way I'll trust him yet. Still, he could prove useful for settling in. I expect Tobias knows a lot about the residents.

He's certainly a watcher.

CHAPTER 18
The Watcher

Sophie's smile makes me zoom out. Happiness is repulsive. Cheerful people make for mundane viewing. Sometimes I must erase their smiles.

Since childhood, I've enjoyed making joy turn to despair. I recall story- time sessions at school. The teacher closed the book, the signal for children to lie on the carpet to sleep. I never settled, always needing more of the story. Sleep happened when I dictated. Flailing limbs of restless sleepers touching my skin made me nauseous.

Nap time was more for the teacher than for the students. Every morning, a cake box from a local bakery appeared. My cretin of a teacher tried to hide it from my keen eyes. As the class slept, she retreated to a corner of the classroom, overwhelming her flabby body with more food. Glutinous cream smothered her mouth as she crammed more in. The binging made my stomach roil. The elation on my teacher's face deserved punishment. Hurting an adult wasn't possible. I understood frustrating childhood limitations. Sleeping children were fair game, though. My teacher had taken her eye off her obligations. Their distress would be the penalty she paid.

Back then, my underdeveloped brain didn't know the intricacies of subterfuge. Unleashing a box crawling with ants to terrorise the dreamers was obvious and yet, the image still gives me chills. Collecting ants and hiding their new home was genius. When I foraged at break times, the teachers smiled at the inquisitive child, enjoying nature.

Children's noses twitching as insects homed into their nostrils and mouths were delightful. Observing infants pulled from sleep by creatures crawling over their bodies was a new watching high. Across the decades, the children's screams of terror reverberate.

The teacher put down her cake long enough to console children the class. While she dealt harsh words, knowing only I would be capable of such a heinous deed, I remarked upon her cream coated chin. I wasn't punished. No one wants to be outed for gluttony. My capacity to steal someone's happiness began so young.

I now zoom in on a far too content Sophie. Dancing around the kitchen, the new tenant sings along to tinny music playing from her phone. Like the person, Sophie's musical tastes are eclectic. Once again, I question why I'm drawn to such a strange being. The purple streaked hair and a penchant for dark and quirky clothing aren't my thing. Maybe it's because she's not afraid to be herself that I feel an affinity with her. She's the difference inside me others misunderstand. My identity defies convention. Perhaps Sophie is similar.

Her haphazard stacking of the dishwasher makes me shudder. Mugs balance precariously on top of bowls. The wash cycle will bring forth a crashing of crockery I refuse to listen to. There is a correct method which Sophie doesn't follow. Order comes from precision. Mistakes cannot be made. If Sophie isn't organised, I'll work on her. Carelessness won't destroy my empire. Years of planning and training have gone into this.

My earlier projects lacked the auditory dimension. The combination of watching and listening is sublime. Everything else I did in other buildings was merely practise. The Listener must display discipline. Sophie needs work.

THE WATCHER

The domestic goddess glides around the flat, owning the space. As her feet rest on the sofa, I imagine an axe lopping them off. This mundanity will not do. Complacency never bodes well. Someone could come along and upset everything.

Look out, Sophie. There are some surprises heading your way.

CHAPTER 19

Sophie

Emma gives a weak wave as she comes into view for our video call. 'Hello there. How's it going in sunny Southbourne?'

I regard the drizzle spritzing against the window. 'Not so bright today, but still lovely. Even on a grey day, you can't beat being near the seaside.'

'Oh, I do like to be beside the seaside…' Emma splutters and falls back onto her pillows.

'Still tone deaf as well as ill. Hey, I went to the beach yesterday. It's lovely. There was hardly anyone around, and it was so peaceful. I could get used to this.'

'Not too much, for Ben's sake.'

'Trust you to bring me crashing back to reality. Ben's always first in everything I think, say, or do. I'm missing him more than I can describe, but I have to try this.'

'Sorry.' Her voice takes on a more delicate tone. 'I know you'd never leave Gentle Ben behind. I was just teasing. Remember, I'm the one who suggested going to Southbourne. So, what's been happening?'

'Well, I met a bloke called Tobias. He lives in one of the flats upstairs.'

Emma's eyes widen. 'Is he hot? Should I visit?'

THE WATCHER

'Er, no.' I laugh. 'For one, you look like crap. Also, Tobias isn't your type and not because he's a bit of an odd-bod. I met him watching me, hiding behind Vera.'

'Is he a stalker? Do you need to leave? Should I call the police? I knew I shouldn't have let you go alone.' Emma's sentences trip over each other.

'Chill your boots.' I hold up a hand. 'Despite the weirdness of how we met, he seems okay. Tobias is one of life's characters. He thinks by watching people he's protecting them. Strange, but once you get to know him, it makes sense. I'll admit I wasn't convinced at first Tobias wasn't going to murder me in my bed. After visiting his shop, I feel more comfortable around him.'

'What kind of shop is it?'

'He helps run a gaming store. The kind of stuff Ben's into.'

'Geeky boys' toys.'

I nod. 'Seeing the people painting and gaming in the shop being friendly with Tobias set my mind at ease. Their painting skills are amazing. It's given me some great ideas for your cover.'

Emma rubs her hands together. 'Ooh, goody. I can't wait to see it.'

'Patience.' I smile at my friend's habitual impatience. 'While I'm a little cautious, Tobias could become a friend. You should have seen it. When Tobias chatted with the customers, his awkwardness vanished.'

'He's a lucky fella to have you on his side. You've always been one for championing underdogs.'

'To a degree, I can relate to the messed-up relationship he has with his mum. Tobias said she labels him as "normal" to others while secretly seeking a diagnosis for his quirks. Tobias moved from Birmingham to escape her. I didn't think it fair to say he isn't free, considering his mum's paying the rent and how often he talks about her.'

'Make sure you don't take on his issues.' Emma waggles a finger at me. 'Don't lose sight of why you're there. This is time for you, not sorting out everyone else.'

I give her a salute. 'Yes, sir.'

'Boss Bitch to you.' Emma winks.

'By the way, I spoke to Ben this morning. He sounded so choked up. I nearly got in the car to come home. He was so lovely, reminding me that wherever I go, he's with me.'

'Don't worry. I've called him a few times and some of the gang are planning to go round and see him. I'm rooting for you both. A world where Ben and Sophie Walters aren't together is unimaginable. It would be like cheese without extra cheese.'

We join in laughter at my habit of adding cheese to almost anything.

Emma continues. 'Seriously though, as jealous as I am, I'm glad you're settling in. This could be what you need.'

'Have you heard from Bekstar yet? Does she know about Louise's death?' I have to ask. Despite my good mood, it's still troubling.

'Damn, I forgot to say. Bekstar says she was told, but it didn't put her off the flat. She apologises for not telling us.'

I take a glimpse at the rug, trying not to visualise the bloom of blood underneath. It's forbidden fruit calling to be consumed by fear.

'I'm determined to make this work. No more Sophie scaredy-cat.'

Emma gives the thumbs up signal. 'That's my girl. Got to go. I need to sleep. Speak soon. Love ya.'

'Love you too.'

I dare to lean back on the sofa. Years of dealing with a mother who complained about dirtying the "good furniture" is ingrained. The problem was every stick of furniture in the family home was the decent stuff. The childhood terror of staining, wrinkling, or breaking something remains. It's taken years not to feel naughty for leaving my shoes on in my own house.

A thump on the door startles me. I won't be a bundle of nerves. I'm not going to fall over, hit my head, and die undiscovered because no one knows me or cares. I'm not Louise.

After opening the door, I look into the hallway and check the stairs. No one's there. An envelope lies on the floor. It's probably marketing rubbish. How did the delivery person get through the main entrance, though? I have a feeling Adam would've seen them approaching the building before they had a chance to enter.

Inside the envelope are a couple of pages. One is typed. The other is a photocopy of someone's handwriting. I read the note first.

Welcome to Harmony House, Sophie.

It's best to know what you're facing. Maybe this extract from Louise Penrose's diary will satisfy your curiosity or ignite your fear. Your choice.

A friend.

CHAPTER 20

Louise's Diary

All I wanted was to make a fresh start. Why is it too much to ask for? When will I learn? I'm an educated woman who's a moron when it comes to matters of the heart.

After leaving Karl, I thought I was done with making foolish decisions. As I drove away from our home, I believed the cheating and deceit ended with my husband. Turns out I was wrong.

Evil lurks within these flats, sneaking into the crevices and creeping into the cracks. It's nonsense to believe in the stuff of horror films and yet, I'm living in one. A monster is stalking me.

Every night someone tries to break into my home. Barely audible knocks on the front door play with my mind. Did I hear it or not? Looking through the spyhole suggests I didn't. I know the truth. The monster is invisible.

Some of my belongings are missing, too. Adam says it's silly to be concerned about a hairbrush, ornament, book, lipstick, and my favourite mug. He said I'm forgetful. The thefts are happening subtly to make me second guess myself. Despite others' opinions on my drinking, my mind's still sharp.

Footprints cleaved into the mud outside my window cannot be denied. Tobias questioned why I was measuring them and taking photos. He said it would be Iris doing a spot of gardening.

THE WATCHER

The treads are too big for her dainty feet. Besides, Iris doesn't tend to the front garden in the winter. Even in the summer, there's little to work with. Sometimes I wish I'd taken a flat at the rear of the building for a more scenic view of the back garden.

Someone's trying to get to me. The monster is out there.

The GP says I'm under stress. When I listed what's been happening, he gave an exaggerated frown. He tried to palm me off with tablets, but I won't take them. Someone wants me dead. I refuse to exist in a drugged haze, waiting to be killed off. Alcohol numbs the pain, but it also blunts my senses. The drinking must stop.

Maybe I deserve fear. Reckless choices have led to me living in peril. The knife slips out. I slide it back into the pocket sewn into the underside of the pillow slip. Can I use it? Will I have a choice? Does the monster know I have a weapon? Of course, they do.

The monster sees everything. They're always watching. Their power is in knowing all. The monster's knowledge could be the death of me.

CHAPTER 21

Sophie

While running through events in Harmony House with Ben, I didn't mention Louise's diary. Ben sounds strained enough throughout our phone call without adding to his worries. I can tell it's taking all his strength not to comment on us being apart.

I try to get comfortable on the sofa. It's a tiny two-seater and no match for the giant version my husband's reclining on at home.

I continue describing Tobias. 'He's certainly an interesting character. Tobias' Warrior Wrath models are incredible. The shop Tobias runs is brilliant, too. Everyone was so friendly when I popped in. You'd love it there.'

'I can't go, though, can I?'

'How's work?' I skirt over my mistake.

'Same old. Lots of making numbers work and dealing with execs who only speak in acronyms.'

We join in laughing at the idiosyncrasies of his role as a finance manager in a marketing company. Ben's a mathematical genius; the logical to my creative. We complement each other. No wonder I feel unbalanced without him.

'I better go,' I say, caught between wanting to keep talking forever and understanding why we need time apart.

'Okay.' Ben draws out the word.

THE WATCHER

'Speak tomorrow?'

'Of course. Love you more than ever.'

I gulp against a knot in my throat. 'Love you even more than that.'

After the call ends, I stare at my mobile, wishing Ben could teleport through the screen. My heart feels too big for my chest. Seeking a distraction, I type a message to Emma.

The ceiling rumbles. A thud reverberates. Crashing ripples in the aftermath. Someone's probably doing DIY upstairs. Determined to be an understanding neighbour, I decide to focus on making dinner. On the way to the kitchen, thumps come from the flat above me. Smashes sound against walls. A female scream terminates the noise.

I clutch the edge of my open door, assessing the options. Lingering here won't help a woman in distress. Adam didn't open his door when I knocked. Time to decide: check what's happening or leave it.

I have to act. If someone's hurt, they need help. I've never turned away from a person in need and I'm not going to start now. The distress of the cry was unmistakable. How would I feel if nobody helped me in a similar situation? I wouldn't feel anything at all. I'd probably be dead. Stop it. Think. Move. Act.

I grab the amethyst in my pocket and stroke its cool surface. Whenever my thoughts spiral, I touch something to focus. Anxious thoughts are a twilight zone. The rock brings me back to Earth.

With concentrated treads, I make my way up the stairs. I summon the courage to knock. If I don't help, I'm complicit. Still, I wonder if Tobias is in his flat next to this one. Strange as he is, having someone with me would help.

As I approach, a woman unleashes a volley of shrieks, accompanied by a man bellowing in Italian. Most likely he thinks even if they can be heard, no one can interpret. Unlucky for him, my Italian boss at the restaurant favoured swear words over any other form of vocabulary. I'm almost fluent in normal Italian, too.

My fist forms, braced to knock. A door creaks behind me from one of the two flats opposite. The sliver of a woman's face is barely visible within the crack.

'Hi, I'm Sophie. I'm looking after one of the flats downstairs. Do you know what's going on?'

'Don't get involved, dear,' her quivering voice replies. 'They won't thank you for it.'

The old woman shuts her door. Locks slide into place. What have I got myself in to? I'm alone outside the home of a couple having a domestic. I can't walk away. If either of them is hurt, I'll be partly to blame.

Before tapping on the door, I take a breath. A man roars in what sounds like Italian that they need to be quiet. The woman screams again as if beckoning rescue. My knuckles smart from more assured knocks.

The door bursts open, held by a shovel of a hand. An Adonis lurks behind the dismissive woman I saw out on the balcony when I arrived. The man circles an arm around her neck. She offers a Cheshire cat grin.

Betraying my courageous attempt, heat flushes my cheeks. 'Hi. I'm Sophie. I'm looking after the flat below you.'

'We know.' The man's words dart at me.

'Anyway,' I continue, willing confidence to remain my companion, 'I thought it best to check you're okay. It sounded like there might have been an accident or something up here.'

The woman removes her partner's choke hold. 'So sorry, *Tesoro*, we were having a discussion.' Her laugh is acrid. 'Italians tend to express themselves at full volume.'

'Sure.' My reply is barely above a whisper. 'Are you sure you're both all right?'

The man pushes in front of the woman. 'So kind of you to check on us, Sophie. It's comforting to know our neighbours care. We are fine, just full of Latin passion.' He offers a handshake. 'I am Federico Gallo. This is my wife, Aurora Gallo.'

My fingers threaten to crack under Federico's vice grip. Aurora nods.

THE WATCHER

'Interesting,' I address Aurora. 'I thought Italian women couldn't take their husband's surnames.'

'We married in this country,' Federico replies on his wife's behalf. 'Aurora enjoys being a Gallo, right, *cara*?'

She slinks away from her husband's shadow. 'Of course. It's an honour.' Aurora's last word is muffled by her husband's booming voice.

'Apologies, Sophie, for the noise we've made. Unlike the British, we're not repressed. Italians release their fire. You will soon get used to it. For you, though, we'll be quieter. We mustn't scare our new neighbour away.'

'We'd hate for you to leave on our account,' Aurora adds. 'Our fellow residents are important to us.' Her keen stare is loaded with an indecipherable message.

Federico extends a hand into his home. 'Please come in and have a glass of wine.'

'Thank you, but I'm getting an early night. Maybe another time.'

'Of course,' he replies. 'Sleep well, Sophie. Thank you for looking out for us. It's good to know someone's keeping watch.'

CHAPTER 22
The Watcher

The Gallos are a covert couple. Others have tried to intervene in their domestic life and learned not to try penetrating the barriers. The sparring Italians can't keep me out. As with all the tenants, I know everything about the Gallos.

Tempestuousness underpins Aurora's and Federico's union. One moment they're fighting, the next they're in bed. Their relationship may be precarious, but it's never boring. They've given me enough material to last a lifetime.

I'll never forget these two, particularly Aurora. Her beauty makes others literally stop in their tracks. Aurora isn't an imbecile. She uses her looks to get what she wants. A swish of her glossy locks and a flicker of those spidery eyelashes weaken women and men. Looks are deceptive, though. Life with her husband isn't all it seems. Neighbours skirt around the matter. Some dare to ask questions. The more inquisitive are drip-fed answers as a challenge to work it out. They never do. It's disappointing to witness. The truth about the Gallos isn't as complex as people think. Maybe Sophie will crack their code.

The Italians are a picture-perfect couple. When they met in an English nightclub, it was more than physical attraction that brought them together. Electricity pulsated through their bodies.

THE WATCHER

They sparked and set each other alight. Since then, their fuses are short, alternating between attraction and giving each other shocks.

Federico was a bartender in a dingy nightclub, earning paltry wages and scraping by in a bedsit. Leaving Italy for England was supposed to be a great adventure. Aurora swept in, the Princess Charming to Federico's Cinderfella, whisking him away into wealth. Before he met Aurora, Federico rode the waves of uncertainty. He thought life would be smoother after they married. Never has it been more turbulent.

The Gallos' shows of deceit never disappoint me as an audience. Sophie would do well to keep an eye on them, too. She is getting nearer to the truth. The walls of Harmony House are drawing in, bringing us all closer than ever before.

CHAPTER 23

Sophie

Another night of little sleep. Even covering the digital alarm clock display and stuffing my ears with cotton wool didn't help. I guess it's not surprising considering what's happened here in the space of a few days. Meeting Rory, Adam, and Tobias is enough to keep anyone's mind occupied. Adding Louise's diary entry, the ominous note, and the Gallos' domestic incident to the mix is over firing my imagination. A session of rhythmic squeaking bedsprings confirms the Italians have resolved their argument. Sound certainly travels in Harmony House. Maybe eight flats in one building aren't as quiet as I'd thought.

I roll over to the bedside cabinet and open the drawer. Reading Louise's diary again won't help with settling in here, but somebody wanted me to have it. I keep trying to unearth the message it has for me. How did someone get hold of a dead woman's diary? Someone must be watching me. Anyone else doing the looking makes me twitchy. I am the watcher. I cast my eye over people and scenes to interpret them within an artistic vision. Being captured by another's stare freaks me out.

As I draw back the curtain, a clear and crisp day beckons. I open the window a fraction, seeking invigoration. I swear the air here is different from Oxford's. Southbourne's breeze gives me an energy I haven't felt in months. The beach is calling.

THE WATCHER

A tapping against the windowpane demands my attention. A seagull pushes its beak into the open crack. Braced to shoo the bird away, my hand hesitates. The gull hobbles towards me, dragging a twisted leg.

'Well, what do you know? Tobias was right. You really are a fixture around here. Good morning, Stanley.'

* * *

I wiggle the key, my fingers growing numb with trying to lock the door. The teasing lock gives a little and then stops. Adam said he'd changed the lock as per procedure for whenever a new person moves in. I wanted to believe him, but Adam has a habit of turning away and mumbling. What other reason would he have to use a locksmith?

My wrist smarts as I twist the key. 'Pissing thing.' As if powered by profanity, the lock turns.

A gust of wind travels inside as the main entrance door opens. The timid woman I saw last night, who lives upstairs across from Tobias and the Gallos, shuffles past. A Michelin Man-style padded coat wears her rather than the other way round. Her eyes peek above the collar.

'Apologies for swearing,' I say.

'Not to worry, dear. I've heard worse.'

She regards the bottom step of the stairs and then looks to her feet, as if assessing how to negotiate the climb. Multiple carrier bags sway while she corrects her balance. I'm impressed she's managed to carry so many bags. I'd struggle with them. Stringy scouring pad grey hair shields her face as she bends to hoist her shopping up.

I place my bag and art equipment on the floor. 'Let me help.'

'I've got it. I'm not a weakling.' Her voice is porcelain.

With a decisive lift of her shopping, a string-thin handle splits. Oranges and apples break free and roll across the carpet. I rush to collect the fruit while the woman stands. When she unzips her coat, I notice her down-turned mouth. Is it sadness or is her face set like that? My mum said my frowns would become permanent if the wind blew past. I'd scowl back in spite.

While we transfer the woman's groceries into linen bags I always carry, I try to make conversation. 'I'm Sophie, by the way. I think I told you last night.'

The woman tries to force a smile against the sullenness. Deep wrinkles stretch across her skin, like subsidence creeping up a wall. The smile lacks the genuine substance of revealed teeth.

'Iris.' She speaks into her hair, half-covering her face.

'What a beautiful name. My gran's favourite flower was the iris.'

'My uncle named me. When I was born, he said I was as pretty as a flower.'

'That's a lovely story.'

With a grip on the banister, Iris rises from the step. 'Not really. He wasn't a pleasant man. Not many of them are.'

She gathers her shopping and walks up the stairs. Conversation over.

'Nice meeting you,' I call after her.

Iris retreats to her flat. The slam of the door ends our socialising. I can relate to needing a place of solitude and safety. Iris and I might be kindred spirits.

CHAPTER 24
The Watcher

Iris Scott's life is ordered by the clock. Spontaneity is an enemy. Surprises and uninvited guests aren't welcome. I can relate.

At 7am, Iris wakes without the need of an alarm. Decades have ingrained the waking hour. Even though she's retired, Iris rises early. There's much to do on a seemingly monotonous day. From sliding her feet into slippers waiting by the bed, to feeding the cats the usual brand of food, she's a slave to routine.

At 8am, Iris catches a bus from the stop on the corner of Gull Lane. Regular travellers know her seat is on the right, directly behind the driver. Before sitting, she will inspect the chair and dust it off. Throughout the journey, Iris watches the passing scenery as if witnessing a new scene. Passengers note how invested she is in looking.

The bus drivers are often the same few people. Friendliness induces them to chat about the weather and the news. They're rewarded with a head movement or a mumbled reply. Iris' need of a bus for the short journey to the Grove has people scratching their heads. Her guardedness leads some to disbelieve she could enjoy a bus ride surrounded by people. Choosing peak travelling time defies logic. It is because there are others around that she catches the bus. She shares with her cats what she witnessed on the journey. The felines hear assessments of her fellow travellers. Regulars don't know Iris' name, but she knows theirs.

The bus alights near a café where she'll have the usual cappuccino and eggs Benedict. A creature of habit, not even snow is a deterrent. Busy staff plying workers with their caffeine fixes still makes time for Iris. Upon her entering, they're already preparing her breakfast. The woman doesn't engage in conversation, but the servers let it slide. Frequent generous tips ensure silence.

One bus ride a day is enough. Walking keeps Iris fit. She can walk for miles. The ravages of time will not take all of her body. Intuitive feet pace the high street and lead her to the beach. Beginning the walk, she stretches her arms above her head as if warming up. For those she recognises, Iris offers nods of acknowledgement. Despite her guardedness, civility doesn't go astray.

Upon returning to Gull Lane, it's almost lunchtime. She'll pop into the convenience shop for a newspaper reserved by the owners. The cashier knows to only make polite statements and allow their regular customer to shop without distraction.

Once a week, Iris goes to a supermarket in Bournemouth. She makes a morning of trawling through the aisles and selecting treats. The special day concludes with a taxi for the journey home. Living in an area where having a car isn't necessary is perfect. Her needs are simple. All she requires is nearby.

Afternoon activities comprise of reading, doing a crossword, or crocheting. A blanket she made lies across her lap, the riot of colour jarring with her introversion. Radio 4 is a steadfast companion. Safe in solace, she speaks back to the talk shows, offering vehement opinions.

In better weather, Iris works with nature. Harmony House's garden is her refuge and exercise. The earth on her hands makes her feel alive. Digging makes Iris aware of muscles demanding movement. The tree outside her window captures her attention with its cycle of the branches bearing and shedding leaves. Afternoons blend into evenings. Sometimes Iris becomes so consumed with activities she only notices the darkness with the need to turn on a light. At night, she only leaves her flat when necessary. She's not afraid of the dark. Her concerns are more complicated than conventional fears.

In matters of the heart, Iris doesn't revert to stock standard love. An endless connection gives her life. Whenever thinking of it, she's young again. Despite this, the intensity of Iris' obsession is alarming. No one has ever been as devoted as this. It would kill a lesser person to have to endure it.

CHAPTER 25

Sophie

I cover my ears as Emma's shrieking reaches a deafening pitch.

'My publisher loved your designs, Soph!'

'Calm down, you'll make yourself even more ill.' I swish a hand across my forehead. 'Phew. At least I don't only have to eat baked beans while I'm here now.'

The joke masks my continual concerns about money. Ben understands how I stress over our savings dropping sometimes. Anxiety makes me want to be in control of things. Ben's job has always been our safety net. Working freelance is a precarious existence for someone like me. When we have to live off Ben's wages, it's not easy for me to accept, no matter how often he says we share our money. Now I'm contributing, my pride has returned. Commissions for one-off pieces are coming in and the publisher is using more of my book covers. After some false starts and failures, I'm making money doing something I love.

'I'm still amazed by how you encapsulate my characters,' Emma says. 'It's like you're inside my head.'

I give an exaggerated shudder. 'No thanks. That's a scary place to be.'

'Cheeky. Found out any more info about Louise?'

'No. The diary entry's playing on my mind, though. Hear me out, as I know it sounds a little crazy. I'm wondering if Louise's death wasn't an accident. Maybe the "monster" she describes killed her. Perhaps they took the diary as a trophy.'

'You know me,' Emma begins. 'I'm always searching for a dastardly deed in everything. It's why the pixies in my novels are so evil. But the coroner confirmed Louise's death was an accident. From that entry, it sounds like she was easily spooked. Perhaps Louise was losing it. Although, I'll admit I'm as intrigued as you are. I'll find out if Bekstar knows anything. That's if I can get hold of her.'

'Thanks.'

It helps to have someone sharing the burden of the note and Louise's diary entry. Not telling Ben evokes guilt, but he's worried enough about me as it is.

'Met anyone else from the other flats recently?' Emma asks.

'I have a new friend in Stanley, the seagull. He's a bird with a twisted foot and has taken a shine to me.' I spot my friend's mouth curling into a smile. 'Don't judge. It's hard trying to get to know people around here. Adam's a crotchety enigma and the Gallos are a no-go area. Dealing with Federico was excruciating.'

'From what you've said, it sounds like they made up after the argument.' Emma sniggers.

'And every flaming night since. Aurora can really hit the high notes when she's having a good time. As you're aware, some Italians are all about the extremes.'

My mind goes back once again to waitressing at Luigi's. They were halcyon days of laughter, planning the future, and endless nights of socialising. Occasionally, Emma and I take that era out of the memory box. Neither of us wants to return, though. We're too knackered and jaded. If someone spoke to me the way they did when I was a waitress, I wouldn't be responsible for my actions.

'Better go,' I say. 'Someone's knocking at the door. Take care of yourself.'

'Speak soon.'

After opening the door, I'm greeted by a tall stick insect, sporting a mass of coloured curls, along with slug eyebrows. She pushes past me into my flat.

'All right there, Soph? About time we met. I've been looking out for you.'

CHAPTER 26
The Watcher

Conversations are my favourite part of observation. The residents' guests are oblivious teachers. Observing people when they're alone can be illuminating, but when they engage with others, I discover so much more. Tobias' mother always provides insightful watching and listening fodder.

We all hide in plain sight. A friend asks how we're doing. Politeness dictates we must reply that everything's fine. We won't confess drowning in tears last night, fighting the fear of loneliness. In company, we try to mask the truth.

As a watcher, I peel away the veneer to reveal true selves. Sometimes I use this against my subjects. People are most compliant when faced with the evidence of their transgressions. Playing back misdeeds on the screen makes people pliable. I've lost track of the amount of memory sticks I've purchased, recorded on, and sent.

Today, Nancy Peters is paying a fortnightly visit. She has a presence; holding everyone to account. Nobody escapes her inspection, least of all her son. The scheduled visits are to accommodate Tobias' need for routine. He knows she's there to satisfy her nosiness and desire to control. He could do without his mother's interaction. No one else is allowed into his sanctuary.

Paying the rent allows Nancy access, but there's one place she'll never be permitted to enter.

Nancy pinches her fingers together. 'How's the little shop going?'

She visited once and swore never again. Within minutes of appearing, Nancy wrinkled her nose and left. She returned, armed with cans of deodorant, handing them to those she deemed in need of a spray. It's not good enough that her son manages a gaming store. Reminding Tobias of his wasted IQ is one of Nancy's favourite activities.

'The shop is fine, Mother.'

The slaps against Tobias' temples will come soon. They always do.

Nancy patrols the property. After skimming a finger along the surfaces, as usual, she inspects the absence of dust rather than its presence.

'Are you bleaching again?' she sniffs her hand. 'Do you need a reminder of what the doctor said?'

Tobias must rein in the compulsive sanitisation. His attempts at erasure only cast a spotlight on his mysterious inner life. Within his home, nearly everything is sanitised. An antibacterial soap dispenser, mounted by the front door, is the first form of defence. Germs aren't his concern. It's the contagion from the residents. Nancy wouldn't understand his terror of contracting others' filthy habits and misdoings. After witnessing their acts, he feels unclean and tainted. Outside the home, Tobias has adapted. He's reconciled with his inability to control all environments. Inside, he's the king of cleanliness. Scaly hands betray fastidious hand washing. A monthly bulk order of sanitiser and hand cream takes a financial toll. It's worth it to create a clinical fortress against Harmony House's impurity.

Tobias harbours other secrets, too. His mother edges closer to them. With the usual habit, she tugs the door handle of the second bedroom. A grimace smacks across her face at the audacity of something resisting her will.

'Have you still not found the key?' Nancy rubs the top of her nose; the sign of another migraine brewing. 'That warden will sort this out right now. Why am I paying premium rent when you don't have full access to this flat?'

Tobias splays his arms across the front door. 'No. I've sorted it. Adam's located the key. He'll bring it round later.' Tobias won't tell his mother he had the lock installed himself, not Adam.

Nancy's piggy eyes disappear into slits. She'll undoubtedly test her son next time. He must consider a new excuse for the locked room. Such a small space harbours an enormous enigma. If Nancy discovered it, she'd send Tobias back home. She might even get the police involved.

After all, what lies behind the door is criminal.

CHAPTER 27

Sophie

I'm annoyed at myself for being apologetically British. So far, I've watched a woman barge into the flat without asking her any questions. No more.

'Er, I'm sorry, but who are you?'

She offers a hand in greeting. 'Hi, Soph, I'm Zara. I live across the hall from you, next to Adam.'

'How do you know my name already?' I ask.

'Adam told me about you, the mardy old bugger.' A snake-hiss snigger rattles from her mouth. 'I had to extract the details from him. Love your streaks, by the way.' She points at my hair. 'Bold choice.'

I compare my purple dye job to Zara's peroxide and black skunk curls. Despite trying to be kind and a feminist, sometimes I fail. Nobody's perfect.

'When you need your bonce doing go to my hairdresser, Yoshiro. Rhianna at Eye Eye keeps these beauts in shape.' Zara smooths her slanted comma eyebrows. 'Your caterpillar brows could do with shaping, hun.'

'I'll bear it in mind.'

I stay standing as a message to my uninvited guest not to get too comfortable. I was looking forward to a quiet night. Zara crosses one impossibly long leg over the other.

THE WATCHER

'I'm such a dozy tart.' She unzips her humongous designer handbag. 'Nearly forgot this. I've bought champagne as a welcome gift. Get the glasses out, girl, and let's have a drink.'

In the kitchen, I open cupboards, seeking something resembling flutes. Bekstar isn't a champagne drinker. It makes me like her even more. Tumblers will have to do. I'm not the champers swilling type either. A pint of bitter or a drop of whisky is more my style. Before rejoining Zara, I summon patience. This is going to be a long night.

CHAPTER 28
The Watcher

Zara's back in action after another hangover. Her misbehaviour is always guaranteed to stir the Harmony House pot.

The good-time party girl finds acceptance in socialising. Daddy issues are such a cliché, but many suffer from the affliction. Parents have so much to answer for. Daddy gives his princess whatever she wants until she abuses the credit cards. Zara has paid her penance and promised not to max out the plastic again. As ever, it's a lie.

After her father's irate phone call, she ranted at the walls about his selfishness. Then she purchased a new wardrobe online. Her father will loosen the financial reins for a while. He always does. Guilt at ignoring his daughter's emotional needs since childhood guarantees it. Playing poor-little-rich-girl is one of Zara's favourite pastimes. Watching others battle with loathing an indulged woman while pitying her lack of love brings such pleasure.

Shaking off the dregs of annoyance with Daddy, Zara focused upon meeting Sophie. Common conceptions state girls must have each other's backs until they become competition. Friends are overrated. I tried it once and didn't care for it. You give so much and get so little back. Where's the benefit of that?

THE WATCHER

Friendship is an elusive concept for Zara. Whenever she's around other women, Zara's spiteful vibes unleash. She assesses them against her own body: are they as tall, toned, and preened as her? So far, no one's realised the spite is a test. She pushes people away, while awaiting their worthy return.

Since her mother left when Zara was a teenager, assessing other's loyalty forms part of her armour. Sybil, Zara's mother, regularly sends lavish gifts from an everlasting world tour. High-end cosmetics, designer scents, and one-off pieces from fashion houses placate Zara. She would only miss Sybil if the presents ceased.

Mother and daughter understand the necessity of their geographical distance. The last time they saw each other was in Paris for Zara's eighteenth birthday. It was a disaster. Neither will admit to their similarities. Throughout the weekend, they sparred, mainly about where to go. Both are driven by a compulsion to be seen and admired by others.

Whenever Sybil extracts her catty claws, Zara reminds her mother she's ageing. Sybil inhales, as if shooting up power, and exhales vitriol back. Their screen time is an event certain to entertain. The verbal tennis, played by a daughter who demands attention and a mother jealous of her protégé, is great sport. Sybil's rivalry ensures Zara will never trust females.

Wealthy women have mocked Zara's lack of class. For them, New Money cannot match lineage and good breeding. Zara always takes revenge for the humiliations. Husbands are stolen and reputations sullied. After one too many reports of Zara's misbehaviour, her father made her move to Southbourne. She craved a beach lifestyle, but St Tropez was more her line of thinking. Ever adaptable, she accepted the challenge. Good behaviour for a while means she will prosper.

From the first day, Zara could see Harmony House's possibilities. A new opportunity opened up. Her father believes he coerced her into coming here. Swearing in the emptiness of her flat helps to assert her dominance. Daddy hasn't won this time, even though he doesn't know it yet.

After closing the blinds, Zara slips into pyjamas, wipes off the make-up, and lets go. Loathing and outrage snap and bite. The timer ticks away twenty minutes of indulgence. We all need to rant sometimes, even me.

When the cutting loose time is up, Zara returns to her version of normality. Make-up and a skimpy dress draped over a year-round tan are her uniform. Once again, she's ready to take on the world.

Am I Zara, lurking in Sophie's domain? Wouldn't that be quite something? Am I in Sophie's home, testing her suitability for my needs? It's far too soon for the final revelation. Zara still has work to do.

The public façade continues.

CHAPTER 29

Sophie

Champagne is magic. My tolerance for Zara's outrageous behaviour has increased after drinking half a bottle. We're now on the decent whisky; the one I only buy at Christmas and decided to bring as a comfort. While I savour each sip, my companion downs it, shots-style.

'Thirty-five?' Zara continues, trying to guess my age.

'Nope. Add seven years.'

Zara's eyes roll towards the ceiling. 'You're pulling my leg. Seriously, you're forty-two?' She slaps my knee and gives another donkey laugh. I swear she hee-haws.

'This whisky's older than you, too,' I say. 'Vintages are the best.'

'Know what you mean, sweetness. I've got a fab Chanel vintage dress in my wardrobe.'

As Zara squishes my cheeks, I no longer startle at her touch. It's in a long list of inappropriate, unsolicited gestures she's made this evening. Alcohol lowers my defences.

Zara sweeps a thumb across my jaw line. 'You have a lovely bone structure. Not many wrinkles either. What's your secret?'

'Soap and water.'

The donkey brays again. 'You're too much. I bet you use night cream at least. My mum trowels it on. I'm not being rude, hun. Older people can be cool. They're wise and stuff. Well, some of them. Perhaps you could join the bowling club at Seafield Gardens. Plenty of old 'uns there.'

'What a great idea!' Sarcasm drips from my lips. 'I'm shit hot at bowling. I was Oxfordshire champion last year.'

I've not set foot on a bowling green in my life. If Zara wants to test me, I'll play the game. It's obvious she's insecure, masquerading as brash. We won't be the BFFs she's pledged we're becoming, but for now she's good entertainment.

'So, you've left the hubster,' Zara begins. 'Getting back out there on the scene?'

'As I said earlier, I'm still with Ben. I'm flat-sitting for Bekstar.'

I haven't mentioned the miscarriage. It's obvious this woman doesn't have the sensitivity to discuss it.

'I've been in this area for a while.' Zara pushes up her balconied boobs. 'Worked my way through most of the local blokes. It's been dead around here lately. Summer's better when the tourists drop. Great for a one-night stand.' She nudges me with her elbow.

To move on from her over sharing, I decide to find out more about Harmony House. 'What are the people like who live in this building?'

Zara leans in closer. 'Right bunch of weirdos here, mate. Adam's crap at his job. If you ask him to do something, add on a few extra days to what he says. Then there's Una in the flat next to you. Old bird. Hardly ever see her.'

'I've knocked on her door a few times to introduce myself,' I say. 'No answer, though.'

'Una's probably hiding. Maybe she's plotting something. Una could be a secret serial killer.' Zara blasts out more loud laughter. Stamping sounds from upstairs. 'Piss off, we live here, too,' she shouts at the ceiling.

'Probably best to keep it down,' I say. 'The Gallos seem annoyed enough with me as it is.'

THE WATCHER

Zara knocks back another double whisky. 'Italians are unpredictable. Daddy deals with them all the time in his business. So, you've met those two.' She points upwards.

'Yes. Not all Italians are the same, although the Gallos are certainly a fiery pair.'

I tell her about my incident with Federico and Aurora. Zara's eyes widen throughout. The telling takes longer than it should. Her arching slug eyebrows are mesmerising.

'Federico's a bit of a sort.' Zara's tongue flicks over her top lip. 'I like a dangerous boy, but he's too weird for me. Totally under the thumb, too. As for Aurora, she can jog on, thinking she's all that with her natural beauty.' The green-eyed monster seethes on my sofa.

'Tobias is nice once you get to know him,' I add.

'He's a freak. No one who plays with toy soldiers is right in the head.'

I push out my chest to show off the Warrior Wrath T-shirt Tobias gave me. My companion fixates on her manicure.

'Where were we?' Zara continues. 'Iris is so boring; same thing with her, day in, day out. I'm going to sleep just talking about her.'

'That leaves us with Rory.'

Zara's smile disappears. 'Rory's dodgy. Stay away from him. You'll regret it if you don't.'

CHAPTER 30

Sophie

I am dead.

Why did we crack open a bottle of tequila? With every shot, Zara raised various toasts to becoming lifelong friends.

Drool glues the pillow to my cheek. My eyes struggle to adjust and push away the blurriness. An express train of pain speeds through my skull. A lightweight like me should never drink shots. After too many incidents in my youth, with Ben holding back my hair as I puked, I was happy to leave partying behind. Oh, Ben. Whenever I think of you, my chest tightens. Or it might be…

I grab the cereal bowl left by the side of the bed from early morning munchies. Classiness disappears along with the contents of my stomach. I definitely need more sleep.

* * *

My brain bangs to the beat of a bass drum. I clench my skull. The drumming intensifies. It takes a while to realise someone's knocking on the front door. Despite trying to move faster, my legs and mind won't cooperate. The visitor continues playing bongos on the woodwork. I swing open the door.

'You've left your key in the lock, dear,' Iris says, pointing to the problem.

THE WATCHER

I groan as I remember trekking to an off-licence with Zara to get the ill-fated tequila. It felt like we'd walked for miles, trying to find a place still open. No wonder my feet are throbbing. How Zara managed in spiky heels is a secret known only by fashionistas. She's practically half a person taller than me in them. Why do tall women wear heels? It's not fair on us smaller people.

When we returned from getting booze, I must have been rat-arsed. I always make sure I've got my keys. Security is my thing. It's a source of amusement for Ben how many times I push a door to check it's locked.

'Thanks so much,' I call to Iris, who's already halfway up the stairs. I shove my fingers in my hair, forcing them through the tangles. 'Sorry, I must look a terrible sight.'

Iris faces me. 'Nothing I haven't seen before, dear.'

CHAPTER 31
The Watcher

Goosebumps form on Sophie's skin as she steps into the shower. For me, nakedness is a fact, not a source of visual excitement. Sophie's body is a map of her life so far. I begin at the mole on her shoulder, travelling to the silvery suggestion of former stretch marks on her hips, moving down to a scar on her knee. Blemishes tell stories.

Hopefully, the cascading water will sharpen Sophie's senses. Keep the door locked. Don't let anyone else enter. You'll never stop me from sneaking in, though. I'm already here. No invitation required.

Sophie made a mistake in opening up her home to Zara. The master manipulator latched onto Sophie's obvious kindness. It's no accident Zara turned up when she did. Giving the new resident time to settle in made her more relaxed. Zara enjoys unnerving people. From the moment of arrival, she won't allow you to forget her.

Stay alert, Sophie. Stop wallowing in regrets and a hangover. Tidy up the flat and give it the respect it demands. Living in Harmony House is a privilege. Being watched by me is an honour. Earn it. Maybe you're not worthy of this great responsibility. Why am I talking directly to you when you might not be my listener? Don't ever waste my time and effort. If you fail me, you'll regret it. Sophie, you could be the one, my one, if you'd get your act together. You failed the test with Zara by letting down your guard. You're lucky, though. Another assessment of your worthiness to be The Watcher's accomplice is coming.

I'm not a lame villain in a trashy crime novel revealing my deeds because I'm about to be exposed. You are not the hero. We are subverting the narrative. I am the protagonist in this story. I make it happen.

By going to the police with these recordings, you'll place my ventures in the spotlight. I can see you shaking your head, considering silence. If by some freakish turn of events you kept these recordings to yourself, I still prosper. What I saw and why I watched won't ever leave your mind. You'll never feel safe or private ever again. It will always seem like someone's watching. That's because someone always is.

CHAPTER 32

Sophie

After a shower, fry up, and painkillers, I'm feeling more human. I can't blame Iris for wanting to get away from me. After seeing her, I looked in the mirror and recoiled from my sticking up hair, panda eyes, and deathly pallor. Thank goodness for industrial strength make-up remover and feel-good clothes. When it comes to confidence, sometimes you have to fake it to make it. The silver, sparkly DMs are on, along with my favourite jeans and a Bauhaus T-shirt. All is right in my world. Well, my appearance at least.

Today I'm going to explore the area. Dorset is more than beaches. I'm going to take a stroll and sketch whatever catches my eye. Sometimes the best pieces happen this way. I relish the prospect of a scene, an object or a person snatching my attention, and gripping my twitchy hands to unleash the vision on the page. The creative surge is the only high I need. It doesn't end in hangovers either. I must be careful with my alcohol consumption. It doesn't always agree with me and can lead to a plummeting mood the next day. When I see Tobias tonight, I'll stick to soft drinks. We're going for dinner at a restaurant near his shop. It's a good opportunity to discover more of his interesting character. That man certainly has layers.

THE WATCHER

After opening the main door, I check both ways. The pavements are empty. Zara's well-meaning, but I can't cope with the donkey laugh and incessant questions today. She'd mentioned coming round for breakfast. I'm hoping Zara's forgotten or is sleeping off last night. The heavy door slips from my hold. Banging reverberates around the hallway. Adam appears.

'Can you be quieter, please?' Leaning against his door frame, Adam folds his arms. 'It's disrespectful to the neighbours.'

'You practically leapt out of your flat. Are you watching me?'

'Why... er... why would you ask that?'

'I'm only joking.'

'Well, I don't find it funny.'

Adam's door crashes behind him. Apparently, the warden can do what he likes, while the rest of us must obey.

'Ignore him.' A melodious voice carries from the top of the stairs.

Aurora emulates a movie-star entrance with each step. In dagger-sharp heels and swishy fabrics, she exudes grace. I'm comfortable with it. Looking that good requires effort I can't be bothered with attempting.

'Adam's such a grouch sometimes.' As if inciting an argument, Aurora raises her voice when she nears his flat.

This composed woman is far removed from the one I previously met. When I went to check on the argument with Federico, she was cowering.

As I open the main door, frigid air snaps at my nose and cheeks. Aurora walks ahead. I hold the door, wondering how she cast me as concierge. With practised ease, she flicks the sunglasses resting from the top of her head onto her face. It's a gloomy day that doesn't warrant shades, but Aurora's star quality makes it acceptable.

'How are you settling in?' Aurora asks while beckoning me forward with a hand.

'Fine, thanks. You know what it's like, getting used to a new place.'

'Because I'm Italian and don't belong in your country?'

I assess if she's being antagonistic or joking. A neutral face denies me a reading. The tinkling laugh catches me unaware. Even that's beautiful. She's a real-life Disney princess with an underlying touch of an aloof villain. Isn't *Aurora* the name of Sleeping Beauty? This version seems constantly alert and not the napping type. Despite my aversion to her snootiness, I find her fascinating.

Aurora taps my arm. 'Stop looking so intense. I'm teasing. I've been here for a few years, so I'm almost native. Although, I understand what you mean about settling in. Until I came here, I travelled a lot.' She stares across the road, deep in contemplation, and then snaps her fingers in front of her face to focus. 'After Federico and I met around here, we stayed. It's strange how I found my Italian husband in another country, don't you think?'

'Yes,' is all I can manage in response.

Ben and I have been together for such a long time. We met locally. Aurora's wealthy lifestyle is far removed from mine. She's not perfect, though. No matter how much she wants to cast her marriage as a fairy-tale, it sounds more like a tragedy.

'Your English is brilliant,' I say, seeking a way to keep the conversation going.

'I'm fluent in many languages. My father values education.'

When Aurora reaches for the sketchbook nestling under my arm, I move away. No one's allowed to look at my work until I'm satisfied it's complete. Not even Ben. Aurora's scowl morphs into my mum's disapproving pursed mouth. I don't recognise myself as I hand over the book and study Aurora's expressions as she flicks through. The reward of approval is absent as she snaps the sketchbook shut.

'You will draw me.'

It's not a request. I decide to play it cool and not jump to her instructions.

'I'd love to,' comes from my mouth.

Nice one. That's how you *don't* do carefree.

'Now.' Aurora waggles a summoning finger.

I follow the leader.

CHAPTER 33
The Watcher

Maybe I was wrong. How can Sophie be my listener when she continues to be such a disappointment? I thought she'd have more fight, more resilience. Watching her succumb to Aurora's charms was excruciating. It's fair to say Aurora has a knack for making others obey, although I hoped Sophie would resist. I guess beauty and confidence demand compliance.

Aurora is more than a diva. No one knows what goes on behind her closed door. Within her home, she lives a different life, which always offers a fascinating perspective. She's made Harmony House her own. When the Gallos arrived, they instantly belonged. Up on high in their top-floor flat, they look down on those who dare to judge. Even those living in the other three flats on their floor know the Gallos have superiority. The neighbours used to complain about their noise. Nobody protests anymore. Federico's macho bravado makes others retreat. Icy-cool disdain is Aurora's signature. With a glance, she can render you useless.

With the burden of being a warden, Adam dreads intervening on behalf of the residents. Whenever he has to speak to the Gallos, it's clear he wishes he'd never taken the job. Antipathy towards the couple pounds against each stair as Adam approaches their home. He rehearses his lines, opting for a charade of civility.

He always leaves, making promises to Aurora. What she possesses goes beyond feminine wiles felling men. An undefinable strength keeps her in Harmony House and a questionable marriage.

Aurora's confidence is a public show. Does she display it inside her home? Does she crumble when faced with a husband who promised so much and deceived her? Only Aurora and I know the truth. I respect her enigmatic persona. She rewards it with occasional shows behind the veneer.

Federico never looks away from his wife. He has a mission to watch over Aurora, no matter the cost.

CHAPTER 34
Sophie

Keeping up with Aurora's commands for how to pose her is tiring. Dealing with a diva on a day when I'm sweating tequila isn't great. Aurora's idea to sketch her on the beach usurped my plan to discover more of the area. I only have myself to blame. I could have said we'd do this another time.

The star of the show reclines under a parasol. The way she secured it was quite something. Aurora gave the man cleaning tables outside the promenade café a sultry look, commented on sand getting in her eyes, and he took a parasol out of the table fixing. The servant even set it up on the beach and laid a tablecloth for her to sit on. She lowered her sunglasses to give the man a reward of a seductive gaze. He simpered, jabbered in response, and shuffled away. I swear he walked backwards so he didn't have to look away from the beauty on the beach.

Sodden sand soaks into my jeans. No tablecloth or parasol for me. Aurora's fan didn't even register me while pandering to her whims. Trussed up in velvet and fake fur, easily mistaken as real - I checked - Aurora oozes class. When she's around, everyone else is invisible.

Finally, the starlet has found a position she likes: chest out; lips pouting; and a lithe leg draped over the other. If I tried that, I'd face-plant into the sand. I'm not questioning it, though. After forty-five minutes of waiting, I can start sketching.

Drawing people is an intense and connecting experience. Looking deep into someone's eyes and reading body language helps understand a person on a deeper level. My subjects often remark on how I've captured their essence. Some are embarrassed at feeling exposed. Others are grateful to be recognised. Aurora's the first individual I can't interpret.

'Could you remove your glasses, please?' I ask, trying to search for a glint of something in her eyes.

She flings the designer shades aside and resumes position. As Aurora cradles her waist, her sleeve falls away. A circular line of bruises dot her wrist, displaying someone's forceful hold. She assesses the marks, gives a shrug, and adjusts her coat.

'Just an accident,' Aurora says.

'Are you sure?'

The stare could slice ice. 'Please don't question me. I hope you're not calling me a liar.'

'Not at all.'

While I wish she'd confide in me, I know I can't force it. I'll spend more time with Aurora, earn her trust, and then I can find out more.

The day so far has been long and unproductive. Passers-by often stop to appreciate the model. Despite trying to shield the sketch, they look over my shoulder, assessing my ability to encapsulate such beauty. Disapproval tinges their polite comments. Aurora has an essence I can't immediately capture. Eventually, I'll figure her out. I never give up on a project.

Inky clouds settling behind my subject kiss the shoreline. The breeze increases in tempo, licking at the pages of my sketchbook. As I place a hand upon it, a shadow creeps over my shoulder.

'This is where you are.' Federico steps in front of me, blocking the view. He's wearing ridiculously tiny shorts, barely covering his backside. Hairs standing to attention on his legs make me shiver.

THE WATCHER

Aurora scrabbles to stand. Discarded glasses crunch under her foot. I expect she'll leave them behind. Material possessions don't matter to people like the Gallos.

I turn away as the couple greet each other with a passionate kiss. Unfortunately, there's no escaping the slurping sounds. Ben would make vomiting noises at this public display of affection. How I wish he was here.

'*Amore mio*, you didn't mention you're running today.' Aurora looks at me while squeezing Federico's bicep. 'My husband's so strong and handsome, don't you think?'

Sarcasm clings to the tip of my tongue. I swallow it down. After scraping sand from my soggy backside, I begin packing away. Neither of the Gallos offers to help. A gust attacks the beach. Sand stings my eyes and drifts into my mouth. At least with a gob full of sand, I don't have to respond to Aurora's question. Saying I believe Federico is possibly a wife-beating brute wouldn't go down well. I need proof and resolve to keep more of an eye on the Gallos. I know how to do it.

'Can I sketch you again?' I ask Aurora. 'It's nowhere near finished and I'd love to do more.'

Federico grabs my sketchpad and flicks through it.

'Of course, she will continue,' he says, handing back my book. 'As long as my darling doesn't die from the cold.'

Aurora doesn't connect with his stare.

'Such beauty must be captured for posterity,' Federico adds. 'Although from what I see of the sketch, Sophie, you have much work to do. It's somewhat basic.'

'Thanks for the feedback. I didn't realise you're an expert in art. Aurora is beautiful, but she's her own woman.'

'Nothing is ever as it seems.' Aurora offers.

Federico seizes his wife's arm. 'Time to go home, *bella*.'

As they take the slope leading away from the beach, Aurora clings to her husband. Instead of holding her hand, he clamps her wrist where the bruises lie.

Aurora looks back at me. Pleading is in her eyes. She's asking me to watch over her. I can and I will.

CHAPTER 35
Sophie

The wooden front door of the flat chills my cheek as I lean my ear against it. My habitually nosey mother would be proud. Many childhood memories include tugging on Mum's sleeve and being told not to bother her. Watching the neighbours' antics through our net curtains was more important. Determined not to be like my mum, I swore I'd never have twitchy curtain- pulling fingers. Awkwardness has put me in this position. The draught slipping through the gap at the bottom of the door makes my toes cramp. I miss my slipper boots. There's always something I forget to pack when going away.

I was preparing to leave as I'm meeting Tobias at a restaurant in the Grove. Then I heard people arguing outside my flat. Being near the main entrance is a pain sometimes. Residents like chatting out here, either with each other or on their phones. Why don't they do it in their flats? Doesn't anyone value privacy around here? My hypocrisy of listening at the door confirms they don't. Initially, I thought it was the Gallos, bringing their domestics outside. When I looked through the spyhole, the sight of Rory and Zara was unexpected. The other night Zara said he wasn't to be trusted. After meeting him and being subjected to the ropey chat-up lines, I agree.

'I've told you, I'm in charge.' Rory's voice rises in volume.

Zara jabs him in the chest. 'Considering what I know, you can't tell me what to do.'

Rory thumbs hook into his pockets and he tilts his pelvis towards Zara. The man's permanently on heat.

'Don't take me on, sweetness. It won't go well. Stay on my good side.'

I await Zara's returning volley of abuse. Instead, her donkey laugh brays. The sound makes me crash into the shoe rack. While swearing at the throbbing in my shin, I realise there's no choice but to leave. My neighbours mustn't think I'm spying on them. Damn, I really am turning into my mum. I grab a jacket from the hook and slam the door behind me.

'Oh, hello.' Rubbish acting skills make me sound more strangled than surprised.

Caught in an act she obviously doesn't want me to see, Zara removes her hand from Rory's forearm.

'Hi there, babes,' she says. 'Glad you're here, as I've got news. You and I are going out tomorrow night. Cheeky's awaits.'

'What's Cheeky's?' I ask.

'Only Dorset's most bangin' nightclub. We've got VIP passes. It's time to celebrate you being a newbie to the area.'

'Didn't we do that the other night?' I try not to groan at the memory of tequila and bad choices.

Rory sneers. 'Nice welcoming gift. VIP in Cheeky's is a bottle of pomagne and a table away from the sticky patches of carpet. Who wants to go there?'

'Hun, you should know.' Zara's tone could cut glass. 'You're there often enough, putting it about.'

'Not so much nowadays. I take the hunt further afield.' Rory winks at me. 'Maybe I'll make an exception for you, Sophie.'

Maybe I'll see you in a frozen version of hell.

'Have either of you seen Una?' I ask, seeking a change of subject. 'Isn't it strange how she never goes out?' I look at the door to the flat next to mine.

'Don't worry about Una,' Rory replies. 'She's probably snoozing.'

As he saunters up the stairs, Zara watches.

'Rory may be a letch, but he's got a lovely arse,' she whispers.

I shudder. She must be half Rory's age and he's a total sleaze. I wonder if Zara's had sex with him. Before I disrupted them, there was a moment of connection.

'Forgotten something?' Zara points to my feet.

In the rush to leave, I didn't put on my boots.

'Careful with your snooping,' Zara says, approaching her flat. 'Unless you're an expert, you'll only get half the story. Rory and me? Let's just say it's complicated.'

CHAPTER 36
The Watcher

From a young age, Rory's had an eye for the opposite sex. His conquests often hear about his early sexual start. It forms part of the seduction. Their lipsticked mouths form into surprise O's as he describes the older woman who took fourteen-year-old Rory to bed. The excitement is tangible as he transports back to an experienced woman's touch. Some question the moral implications. He assures them it was the best thing that ever happened to him.

Fourteen was Rory's seminal year. His father left to be with another woman. Vince was an absent parent who found fatherly affection abhorrent. Rory's mother took her husband's deception hard, went to bed, and hardly got out of it. The depth of her devotion was alien to Rory. He'd never known love, not even a teenage crush. Suffocating village life meant knowing each other's business. Rory couldn't approach a girl for fear of being allied with his childhood mishaps. Trying to get a date was impossible when you were remembered as the boy who wet himself in assembly.

An older woman felt natural as the catalyst for Rory's sexual awakening. The fourteen years symmetry in their age gap made it perfect. He would tell anyone who labelled it abuse they have no right to judge. How could they if they haven't tried it? What the woman didn't have in her sexual repertoire wasn't worth knowing. Rory extended the learning to teach other women. He maintains a man has needs. One partner isn't always enough.

Sex alone isn't enough either. Observing is where the thrill is found. The female form in its various guises is a thing to behold. Rory appraises every curve, roll, angle, and dip. He couldn't stop watching if he tried. He'd rather go blind, which is somewhat apt, as it can get dark. Chosen women are thrust into his depraved fantasies. He awakens from a hypnotic trance to the harsh reality of female fear staring back at him.

Rory must not shut his eyes. He has to stay alert. People can die on his watch.

CHAPTER 37
Sophie

Ever the gentleman, Tobias holds the door of Harmony House open for me. His solid frame leaves only a gap underneath his outstretched arm to get through. Missing my intention, he leans towards the door frame, jamming me against it.

Tobias jumps away. 'I'm so very sorry. I wasn't trying to touch you.' While wrapping his arms around his stomach, Tobias lowers his head.

'Don't worry. No harm done. I should've said what I was doing.' After spending the evening together, I've learned he needs clarity. 'Thanks for a lovely meal. I'm surprised I can still move after stuffing myself with pasta.'

Tobias releases his arms to linger by his sides. 'I'm glad you enjoyed it and we can be friends.'

'I hope I didn't show you up by joining in with the singing waiter. No one should ever have to sing "That's Amore" alone. Italian restaurant rules well, the ones that have me in them.'

'I found it amusing. You're funny.'

'Funny in the head, as my husband says, even if he's usually my singing partner in crime.'

'Did you leave Ben because he said mean things?' Tobias frowns.

'I haven't left Ben. Remember, I'm looking after Bekstar's place while she's away. Ben is a kind man. Sometimes our humour is a bit silly and inappropriate.'

'Right, of course.'

It's obvious Tobias doesn't understand sarcasm at all. I'm too tired to explain, but my manners are still intact.

'We'll definitely go to see something at the theatre,' I say. 'It sounds great. Let me know when you've checked the listings which you're interested in.'

Tobias claps. 'I'd love that.'

I place the key in the lock. 'Goodnight.'

'Shall I check inside before you enter?'

Tobias' hand lingers near his forehead, probably preparing to engage in the slapping tic.

'I'll be fine,' I reply. 'Thanks for looking out for me, though. See you soon.'

As I go inside, I can feel Tobias' eyes on me. Through the spyhole, I watch him fixating on the door. He mumbles something, shakes his head, and then moves away.

Despite the coolness of the flat after the heating timer has gone off, a sense of warmth rises within. I've made a new friend. Maybe I can fit in for the short while I'm here. Sheets of paper lying on the floor soon extinguish the glow. It's another of Louise's diary entries, along with a note.

Go home, Sophie. You're not welcome in Harmony House. Terrible things happen to those who don't belong here.

CHAPTER 38
Louise's Diary

My stresses loosen with the sound of the fountain's flow. The unseasonably warm day was an invitation to go to Fisherman's Walk. When I first discovered this trail in Southbourne, it felt like it was made for me. Stepping through the archway to be greeted by a pond and its fountain is like entering a magical kingdom. This is my peaceful place and only a short walk away from Harmony House. When the Gallos' weekend wars begin, I often retreat here. A stroll through Fisherman's Walk, leading into the Grove for a look around the shops, helps takes my mind off things.

I try not to get involved with a mother, pulling her child away from the pond and bellowing obscenities. The mother's words are a fleeting fear with the potential to form permanent hurt. The child's wounded expression bears the evidence.

Karl's spiteful words remain with me. Every man I chose after my husband was meant to heal my abused psyche. It's true some people always repeat their mistakes. I've drifted from one abuser to another. Not all of them have hit me, but they've taken so much: my confidence; resilience; and sanity. This is why I must move on. If I stay in Southbourne, he will break me; the man who wants to have it all.

My handwriting is descending into a scrawl. Watching the upset child makes me fall away from the lines. I wonder if she'll slip away, too. I hope she has a better life than mine. Maybe my diary could be a cautionary tale to the girl. Keeping a record has helped me survive. I should have started it when I moved into Harmony House. There would be more evidence. My memory isn't so reliable nowadays.

It will take courage to let someone read this. Can I tell those secrets? They reveal my ugly truths: the cover-ups; ill judgement; and others' criminal behaviour. My words will bring him down to where he belongs.

The thought of leaving always gives me strength. A fresh start here was once shiny and new. Now it's tarnished and rotten. Harmony House is over. Before I go, I'm determined to make better memories of this area. He won't have everything of mine.

I'm daring to sit in the middle of the bandstand where strollers can see me from all angles. At university, when I played Truth or Dare, I never refused a risk. That woman is long gone. Sitting under a roof where musicians entertain seems harmless. Not for me. Experience states I must not stand out. The threat of the eyes always on me usually makes me hide. Not today.

Surrounding trees are a canopy of security. Twisted trunks delve deep into the earth. Like them, I stand solidly in the centre of Fisherman's Walk. Can you believe I just span around, arms wide open? I expected judgement. I received only smiles. Not everyone has an agenda. Even in Harmony House I've found friends in Tobias and Una.

Una's such a sweetheart. She never mentions what she hears travelling through the walls. Popping in next door to see her is my favourite part of the day. The stories of her years as a tailor are fascinating, particularly the dresses Una created for celebrities and royalty. When I asked if a rich benefactor's paying her rent, she gave a girlish giggle.

Last night, Una confided she wants to write her memoirs. She knows so much about the private lives of those we idol worship. I've spent many cosy afternoons with her, sharing salacious tales.

THE WATCHER

I'm like a child enjoying a bedtime story. Despite not having her own children, Una makes me feel mothered.

Maybe I'll become Una; alone, without a family. When I witness her content, it doesn't seem such a bad life. We are alike. Una's confided she had an eye for the men, too. She talks wistfully of the one who got away. I can't relate. I'm the one who needs to get away.

Tonight, we said our goodbyes. Una promised to keep my secrets. I trust she will take them to the grave.

CHAPTER 39

Sophie

Courage makes me knock on Una's door. I don't know her, but after reading Louise's diary entry from when she was preparing to leave here, something's niggling at me. Una has to go outside eventually. I'd love to meet my next-door neighbour and the woman Louise cared about. Who else is looking out for the old lady since Louise died? Tobias says he's tried knocking on Una's door, but he doesn't get an answer, either. I'd hate her to think no one cares.

The second note sent to me confirms someone doesn't want me to live here. Perhaps a resident's annoyed at an outsider living in the building. I may not fit their notion of the ideal tenant in a wealthy playground, but I won't be intimidated. Instead, I'll be a model neighbour, starting with checking on Una.

Zara said Una is spritely, despite having asthma. Zara mimicked drawing upon an inhaler as if it's a joke. A healthy young woman has the luxury of mocking the elderly.

I wait outside Una's flat. No reply. How many times can you knock before it becomes overbearing? Remembering Ben's gran when she had a fall, my anxiety rears.

'Hello, are you in there?' I call. 'I'm Sophie. I'm looking after Bekstar's flat while she's away.'

THE WATCHER

A stranger might be alarming, but I'm hoping curiosity will make Una come to the door. I place my ear against it, cringing at the continual descent into becoming like my mum. Listening at doors seems to be my default position in this building.

A soft scratching sound increases in intensity.

'Who's there?' I ask, shaking my head at the ridiculous question. The animal inside the flat can't reply.

I tap my fingers against the bottom of the door. A cat gives a pitiful cry. I can't walk away now.

'What do you want?' Adam asks upon opening his door.

While he needs a lesson in manners, we must concentrate on more important matters.

'I'm worried about Una. She isn't answering and the cat's going nuts in there trying to get out.'

'She's fine.' Adam prepares to shut the door.

Mid-slam, I catch the door.

'Please check on her,' I say. 'It's not right to leave an elderly person alone like this.'

Adam stares at me, probably judging what he's dealing with. I hold my foot in the doorway as Adam retreats. With a jangling of jailer type keys, he reappears.

'This is a waste of time,' he grumbles. 'Tenants are entitled to privacy.'

'I'm sure if it was one of your loved ones in there, possibly hurt, you'd want someone to check.'

Adam's face whitens. 'I came home to find my wife dead on the kitchen floor after she'd had a heart attack.'

I reach for his shoulder. 'I'm so sorry. I didn't mean to remind you of it.'

Shrugging me off, Adam knocks on the door.

'Una, it's Adam. Are you in?'

The cat's scratching is frantic, matched by plaintive mewing.

'Bloody animal,' Adam mutters. 'I'll have to go in or he'll shred it to pieces. The landlord won't be happy.'

Adam pushes open the door. Concern for Una makes me bold. I forge ahead into the gloom. Stagnancy surrounds us. Stifling air thickens in my throat.

Then it hits.
Decay.

CHAPTER 40
The Watcher

How wonderful! Sophie's finally proving to be an asset. Her kindness might not be the weakness I feared. Sophie's detection skills are improving by opening the door to death.

Finding Una's body has taken far too long. So much for Harmony House's sense of community. From the moment Una struck the floor, I've waited for someone to find her. While witnessing the stages of decomposition, my patience wore thin at such a delectable sight not being shared. I needed the horror of another's discovery of death. Thank you, Sophie and Adam, for giving me my prize.

Usually, my patience is unsurpassed. Passivity frustrates me, though. Waiting for others to take action is excruciating. I try not to force matters ahead. Spontaneity has no place in survival. Vanity would lead to my capture. This project will not fail. Every second of watching has led to Harmony House.

Sometimes a watcher must become a player in the observational game. When I get involved, things happen, often ominous events. In my rookie years, I was discovered a few times. No matter. Mistakes are a fertile learning ground. Using a handheld camcorder was clunky and far too obvious. It led to fleeing previous abodes. The early days were based upon trial and error. Young boys tell their parents when they realise they're being videoed. The culprits omitted the part where they were coercing girls into showing their genitals behind a garden shed. Irate women also blast threats when they discover tapes of them sleeping.

Now I'm more accomplished, mistakes never happen. I'll get it right when choosing the correct listener. Sophie's shaping up nicely. One day The Listener and The Watcher will unite. When my Listener hears what I saw and did, their life will never be the same.

CHAPTER 41
Sophie

'I don't want to die alone.' My breathing catches on the sobs.

'I'll always be here for you, right until the end.'

Hearing Ben's soothing words helps me focus. The embarrassment at the paramedics dealing with my panic attack while they were removing Una's body won't go. I believed I'd got it under control. The shame of others seeing my anxiety was almost more terrifying than the incident itself. At least back in my flat, I can hide.

My husband was the first person I called. I must not shield him so much, but it's difficult. This is the man who will stay up all night to help me problem solve. Why on Earth did I try to get pregnant without telling him? All I had to do was talk it through. Pride and shame are my answers. I thought if I told Ben how much I wanted a child, he'd look at me differently and not like what he saw. My heart knows he doesn't view me any other way than the woman he's always loved. How did I get it so wrong? How do I fix this and climb over this mountain of grief? One issue at a time. My neighbour is dead, and I've just seen a corpse.

'How did she die?' Ben asks.

'They think it was an asthma attack. The body looked like she'd been there for a while. That poor woman. No one checked on her. The smell…'

I can't finish the sentence. There's no way to describe it. I don't want to.

'Soph.' Ben's tender voice is a balm to my whirring mind.

'The cat kept returning to Una, even as I tried to let him out,' I continue. 'He seemed to be guarding her.'

I cry again, unable to repeat my fear of a lonely death. The husband I've chosen to leave behind doesn't need to hear it.

Ben sighs. I know he's frustrated at not being able to hold me.

'Does she have any family?' he asks.

'Adam said Una never married or had children.'

We're both silent. Maybe he's thinking the same thing as me; without offspring, who will mourn us? Is it a selfish reason to want children?

'Calling this place *Harmony House* is a joke.' I can't disguise my bitterness at the blighting of my refuge. 'There's too much death here.'

'Who else has died?' Suspicion loads his words.

Damn. I haven't mentioned Louise. Ben knows living where someone died would spook me. I share the details of Louise's demise, but not the diary entries someone's sending me, along with poisonous notes. Ben has enough to contend with from a distance. My husband is broken, too.

'Two "accidents" in one place,' Ben replies. 'Never trust coincidences.'

As a man of numbers, he always looks for logical patterns. Coincidence and fate never feature in his thinking.

'Please don't worry me anymore than I already am,' I say.

'Sorry. As you've said, they're accidents.' He couldn't sound less convincing if he tried. 'Be careful. I'm concerned about you. You can come home at any time.'

'I know. I miss you so much, but there's so much work I need to do. I haven't even started on my beach sketches yet. I'll be fine. It's unfortunate these things have happened, but I'm not at risk.'

THE WATCHER

As I say it, I'm not convinced. Am I safe in Harmony House?

CHAPTER 42

The Watcher

Una Jacobs' last and biggest mistake was looking out her window at that moment. Usually, she kept to her own affairs. Many don't around here. I often have to hide from scrutiny. When The Watcher is the watched, I'm forced to self-protect. It's such a rarity for me to be at risk of discovery, though. Genius defies detection.

Fate, bad luck - call it what you will - led Una to witness something shocking. The beloved cat was the death of her. If she hadn't been looking out the patio door, trying to find the errant feline, Una might still be alive. Coaxing the moggy away from the building was worth the deathly outcome.

Una had to go. She'd witnessed a revealing view in the back garden, way beyond the dramatic plots of her favoured soap operas. Harmony House harbours a damning secret which brought disharmony for the old woman.

Narrating her death scene after the event is one of my favourite recordings. I'll add it to this collection for you, The Listener. There's an extra element to not only watching a death happen in real time but also narrating it in a god-like fashion. As I described the actions that brought about Una's death, my voice masterminded her demise.

THE WATCHER

To think Sophie might hear of the story of Una's end, frame-by-frame. Not only will a decaying corpse haunt Sophie, she'll know how it happened.

Don't feel sorry for Una. Her death was her own doing. A naïve lady, with her home always open to others, was asking for trouble. Louise seemed to be in Una's flat more than her own. The neighbour's loneliness compromised Louise's safety. She mistook a painted-on smile for friendship and let her murderer in.

Studying life ebbing from Una's body is quite something. Clawed hands gripped her collar, trying to make way for air. Kicking away the inhaler she dropped was a dastardly manoeuvre. Her body lowered to the ground by degrees, each faint breath diminishing strength.

Words killed Una. Threats of what would happen to her mangy moggy created panic. Stress exacerbated asthma. Throughout her life, she avoided stressors. This time, she didn't have a choice. I'm not a monster. I made sure the cat kept her corpse company.

In a way, it's a pity Sophie and Adam discovered the body. Returning to the scene of the crime is one of my favourite views. Whenever I saw Una's body, something stirred inside me: excitement.

CHAPTER 43
Sophie

I hand the letter to Iris. 'This was delivered to my flat by mistake.'

As part of his warden's role, Adam sorts our post from the main postal box attached outside. Let's just say he doesn't give it all his attention.

'Thanks for bringing this,' Iris says. 'Don't hang around in the draughty hallway. Come in, dear.'

Since I've moved in, Iris avoids eye contact and scurries away whenever we're near each other. I won't decline an invitation to learn more about her. It's friendliness, not nosiness. Ben calls me "inquisitively curious" rather than nosey. We always aim to boost each other's ego, figuring the world does a good enough job of dragging people down.

The heater in the lounge is roaring on all bars. Cloying heat singes the air. If you were to imagine the stereotypical home of an elderly, reclusive woman, this could be it. Bookshelves line the walls, groaning under the weight of various genres. The sofa's jacquard floral material loses its pattern within worn patches. A crossword puzzle book and pen lie on the arm of a chair.

'Take a seat.' Iris shoves three sleeping cats off the sofa. One gives her a haughty glare while taking its sweet time to move. 'Meet Mary, Howard, and Edgar.'

'Horror fiction fan?'

THE WATCHER

'One of my guilty pleasures.' Her sullen mouth attempts a smile and fails.

'Let's see if I can get this right,' I begin. 'You named them after Mary Shelley, Howard Lovecraft, and Edgar Poe.'

'Smart lady.'

Despite myself, I blush. For some reason, her approval matters. Strange, as I'm not usually a people pleaser. First Aurora, now Iris. Settling into Harmony House is more important than I thought. Getting along with the residents is part of it.

'I'll get the tea ready,' Iris says. 'Make yourself at home.'

I scan the room, searching for more clues regarding the person who lives here. My artist's vision imagines Iris in the armchair, flanked by cats. It would make a brilliant cover for my next fantasy novel commission. Iris epitomises the Lady of Cats, although Emma's character is three hundred years-old. While Iris seems elderly, she moves with a youthful vigour.

Jesus stares at me from above the television. The Sacred Heart picture denotes a religious person, family tradition, or someone with Catholic guilt. Ben's aunt is a lapsed Catholic. She says she keeps a Sacred Heart picture in the bedrooms, just in case. I'm not sure what she thinks might happen if Jesus's image isn't nearby. It's unsettling trying to get intimate with your husband when Jesus is watching. We discovered this after a weekend spent in the aunt's home.

A shelving unit is filled with folders stacked to the ceiling. Blank labels on the spines capture my curiosity. What does Iris file? Perhaps she's like my nan, who tore anything she found interesting out of newspapers and magazines. After Nan died and we were emptying her house, the yellowed, crisp paper made me cry. As I touched birth notices, recipes, and handy hints, I connected with Nan's smudged fingerprints.

A photograph, partially hidden by a stack of books, draws my attention. I take a closer look. Younger Iris was stunning. Long and thinning grey hair was once lustrous gold. Her down-turned mouth used to grin with such enthusiasm her face could barely contain it. She still has those hypnotic eyes. Now, faded vibrancy vies against aloofness.

Younger Iris cradles an arm around a boy. His adoring gaze towards her hints they might be related. Their features aren't similar, but the child's hold is one of trusting in a parent or guardian.

Iris returns with a tray laden with a tea pot, cups, milk jug, biscuits, and a bowl of sugar cubes. After thumping it on the table, she rushes to take the photo. Territorial hands clutch it against her chest.

'Apologies,' I say. 'I shouldn't be looking at your personal items. Is that your son?'

'No.' She flings the photograph into a drawer and slams it shut. 'I don't have children. Do you?'

'I recently had a miscarriage.'

My statement catches me unaware. I don't talk about it with strangers. Maybe saying it out loud is part of my healing.

Iris takes a seat. 'Sorry to hear that. It must have been devastating. I couldn't have children. Enough said.'

I won't pursue it any further. The subject is obviously a delicate one.

'Sorry for my snappiness,' Iris says as she pours the tea. 'I'm feeling a little edgy. Una's passing has shaken me, and it's confirmed my suspicions. Calling this building *Harmony House* is ironic. It's anything but.'

I shift around in my seat. No one wants to be told their place of retreat isn't a refuge.

'Have you lived here long?' I ask.

'A fair few years. Seen and heard many things.'

'Bet you have.'

I scoot further back into the sofa, waiting for more juicy information. Iris is silent. I won't give up on finding out more. Who knows if she'll be this sociable again?

'Did you know Una well?'

'Well enough. She mostly tended to her own business, as it should be.'

I heed the hint not to pry too much into Iris' affairs.

THE WATCHER

'How are you bearing up, dear? It must've been such a shock discovering Una in that manner.' She raises a napkin to her mouth and holds it there.

'I can't believe Una was there so long, with no one raising concerns. Tobias is devastated and says he should've checked on her sooner.'

Iris removes the napkin and spreads it across her lap. 'Terrible business. I hope when I go someone cares enough to notice my absence. It's all we want really, isn't it? To be loved.'

Once again, she struggles to form a smile. One of my customary random thoughts enters my mind. Does this woman have teeth?

I consider my luck in having Ben's love. Tea forces its way past the lump in my throat. Being without Ben isn't something I could ever get used to. I remind myself every day that I'll be going home to him soon.

'Despite the asthma, Una was as fit as a fiddle,' Iris begins. 'She went for daily walks along the seafront. We regularly bumped into each other. Una moved near to the sea for the air. Poor old soul. I'm confused about why she didn't have an inhaler when she had the attack. Una always carried one.'

'Sounds like you knew her well.'

'I remember things others tell me. I take everything in.' Iris' eyes narrow as she leans towards me. 'Reading crime novels is a great education for spotting clues. Una's death wasn't an accident. She was killed.'

CHAPTER 44
The Watcher

Occasionally, I leave observing until night-time. While others sleep, I watch their lives on the screen. Studying people while they obliviously snooze feels decadent. As you descend into dreams, I fall into the day you've left behind.

I've accepted I need people. What else would I analyse? I'm not the bird watching type and I'm no David Attenborough. Don't ever think this gives you leverage over me. I choose to scrutinise how you operate. I choose to imitate your humanity, so I blend in. I choose to let some of my quirks show so you may see I'm a little different. I chose to progress, despite my parents neglecting to teach me how to be a functioning member of society. My best choice of all was to be a watcher.

Some nights, I prowl the Harmony House building. I tiptoe up and down the stairs. My feet know the depth of each step between two floors. Daring hands touch the residents' doors. Fatalism whispers to knock. I won't create my own downfall. Taking risks is energising. I could self-protect and not share my work. So far I haven't, which has led to years of safe viewing.

Boredom is my nemesis. I won't live unknown, unrecognised, and unappreciated. Somebody else must acknowledge and applaud the magnitude of my project. What's the point of living if you don't leave a legacy? Someone else believed *they* were creating

THE WATCHER

a legacy when helping set up my watching projects. They never take risks while I thrive on danger, always certain I can subdue it. I let the other person think they have an equal footing in watching. Their lack of confidence in my ability to avoid detection has consequences. This time I'm going it alone. Their fury when they discover my deceit keeps me motivated.

These recordings are stacking up. When The Listener is right, I'll be heard. Show me, Sophie, with Iris' revelations of murder, your worthiness. Respond with your moralistic, enquiring nature I'm beginning to see. Now is the time, Sophie, for you to shine in The Watcher's eyes.

CHAPTER 45

Sophie

'Somebody killed Una.' Iris' glare feels like a challenge to refute her claim.

A betraying gasp escapes from my mouth.

'Why do you think that?'

'Una knew more than others believed she did. As you get older, people view us as harmless and weak. Ageing makes you invisible. Looks fade and so do you, as a person. The invisible are powerful, though. If you can't see someone, you don't realise they're watching you.'

The cat skulking around my legs doesn't help the rising nerves. 'How do you know Una was watching people?'

The cat wriggles in her grip as she manhandles it outside.

'Where was I before that pest got in the way?'

Iris grunts in frustration or it could be the effort of lowering into the chair. Her physicality is confusing. One moment she seems fragile. Then she'll walk with an assured posture and carry multiple bags of shopping. I guess the body becomes confused as it negotiates into the latter years. Goodness knows, my knees never know if they're going to be creaky from one day to the next.

THE WATCHER

Iris finds her thread again. 'When tending to the front garden, I often caught Una looking out the window. More of a curtain-twitcher than she let on. If we're honest, we all are.'

Recalling my recent snooping habits, I concentrate on drinking tea.

'No shame in it,' Iris adds, as if giving me absolution. 'How else can we learn what's around us without paying attention? It's harmless enough, unless someone takes exception.'

She's no longer the woman I met with the quivering voice. The more time we spend together, the more confident she's becoming.

'What do you reckon Una saw that could've led to her being killed?'

My question sounds ridiculous. The paramedics said an asthma attack was the most likely cause of death. Much as I don't want to recall the sight, Una's body didn't show any signs of violence.

'I can't be certain what happened, but I'm monitoring things.'

Iris pours more tea into her cup and then offers the pot to me. I decline. All this talk of murder has jellified my stomach.

'As for Louise, I know she was murdered.' Iris rubs her hands together, warming up to another deadly subject. 'She was killed by a man who got too close.'

I consider whether it's a good idea to keep this conversation going. I've had suspicions about Louise's death, but I have to live where she died. Is ignorance bliss? Whenever I step over the rug in my flat concealing blood, I try to think of other things.

'How do you know Louise was killed?' I ask. As ever, curiosity wins.

'I don't have proof. She was rather free with her affections. When I was coming in or out of the building, I often saw different men leaving her home.'

'It doesn't mean Louise deserved to die.'

Iris flings a hand to her heart. 'Of course not, dear. I wasn't saying that. Live and let live. Women deserve to have an exciting sex life, as much as men do.'

Sex talk doesn't seem to fit this prim woman's territory. She has embroidered covers on the chair arms and lace doilies on the coffee table. Iris isn't all she seems to be, though, and I should respect it. Being older doesn't mean she's dead inside.

'I worry one of those men got a bit rough.' Iris swipes a finger at the corner of her eye. 'She had a habit of picking the wrong ones. Even from up here, you could hear the arguments coming from Louise's flat. If a nice chap had come along, she might still be alive.'

'What do you reckon happened to her?'

'It's just an idea. Perhaps someone pushed Louise on purpose, so she'd hit her head.' Iris takes a tissue from her cardigan pocket and blows her nose. 'I told the police I don't believe it was an accident. They wouldn't listen.'

'As awful as it is, let's hope it was a fall,' I say, hoping these fanciful ideas are the product of too much time alone and reading detective fiction.

'Stay aware,' Iris says. 'Gull Lane will gain a terrible reputation if all this business continues. A lot has happened around here. Things you wouldn't believe. There's trouble in Harmony House and I fear it's not over yet.'

CHAPTER 46

Sophie

Iris' suspicions about Una's and Louise's deaths whirl around my mind. What have I got into by coming here? Do I believe someone who might have an overactive imagination, or should I trust both deaths were unfortunate?

'Earth to Sophie.'

'Sorry. This death in Harmony House business is getting to me.'

Emma's eyes widen. She picks up a notebook and begins scribbling. '*Death in Harmony House* is a brilliant book title. Not my usual genre, but as you know, I've been toying with writing crime.'

'When you do, don't kill me off. If there's a killer in this building, they'll get there first, anyway.'

Emma flicks a dismissive hand. 'Stop it. You don't know for sure Una or Louise died, other than how it was pronounced. Since when did your head go to dark places?'

I raise an eyebrow.

'Of course.' My friend chuckles. 'I forgot who I was dealing with.'

'Someone sending Louise's diary entries isn't helping me to settle. Why give them to me?'

'Maybe they want you to learn more about the woman who lived in the flat.'

'But why do they have the diary? The notes they're adding aren't friendly either.'

'True,' Emma says. 'Keep alert and you'll be all right. Try to focus on why you're there and not on Jessica Fletcher upstairs. It sounds like Iris has too much time on her hands and a vivid imagination. Granted, the diary entries and having two deaths in one building are peculiar. I reckon it's an odd-bod who nicked Louise's diary and has issues with the neighbours. Every place has a resident weirdo, but it doesn't mean they're a threat.'

Emma knows I need sensible advice. If I discussed this with Ben, he'd be driven by love and a desire to protect me. I don't want saving. It's not Ben's fault. For too long, I've allowed him to play the chivalrous knight when I could've saved myself. This time the princess must go it alone.

Emma's phone buzzes. 'Better go. My editor's calling. Only so many times I can pretend to be working on my novel when she phones. She doesn't understand the concept of being ill. Speak soon.'

After finishing the call, I swing my feet up on the coffee table. The force tips over my glass. Orange juice spills onto the floor. It soaks the rug and aims for the floorboards. I grab a tea towel from the kitchen to mop up the mess.

In a pronounced crack between the boards, a silvery glint catches my eye. Using scissors, I hook the item out, holding it up for inspection. A cufflink was caught in the gap. The owner is seriously lacking in class. Written in diamantes is the word, *Sexy*. Iris is right about Louise's dubious choice of men, unless it's connected to Bekstar.

Urgent knocking rumbles against the door. Upon opening, I'm greeted by Adam's puce face.

'What the hell are you doing?' he yells.

Spittle lands on my nose from his venomous verbal attack.

'What do you mean?' I ask, backing away.

THE WATCHER

Adam barrels towards me like a prop forward. 'Stop meddling in Louise's affairs. Let her rest in peace! Do you want to get hurt?'

CHAPTER 47
The Watcher

It's not often Adam loses his temper. It begins with a gnawing nugget of discontent pulsating in the gut. Indignation travels upwards, burgeoning against his ribs. Explosive anger rockets from his throat.

A persona of grouchiness is a tactic for keeping others away. Adam won't risk getting close to anyone again. He tells his photograph wife he doesn't want to be a shell of the man he once was. When Tina was alive, she'd help to laugh his furrowed brow away. A tickle or a kiss dispelled the melancholy.

While he has memories and the cherished photo, Adam and Tina will never be parted. Sometimes he wonders if he's losing his mind. Adam asks his son if chatting to a picture is a sign of madness. They agree it's a necessary channel for grief. For a while, there's consolation in being a widow seeking solace. Later, he'll question his sanity again, pondering on how marriage subdued the darker part of himself. Tina softened her husband with her love. Sometimes he hates her as much as he mourns.

Adam makes it through the days by doing chores and appearing to be a warden. When the sun sets, darkness descends as a weighted blanket of futility. To silence the cries of the head demons, he goes to bed early. In fitful sleep, Adam barters with his judges, protesting he did all he could for Tina and Louise.

THE WATCHER

When the wakening devils drag him into reality, he clutches photograph Tina and begs for forgiveness.

Adam can't let go of the past. When remembrance is threatened, he forgets propriety and unleashes the inner beast we all try to conceal.

Louise suspected Adam was a watcher. The lingering looks gave her pause. Moments stacked up where Louise opened her door to find the warden standing outside with a ready excuse. Louise understood he took the role of overseer seriously. Whether he was guarding over her or concealing malicious intent wasn't answered in Louise's lifetime.

Louise did Adam a favour by dying. No one wants their watching to be exposed. Adam's last look at Louise's corpse ended months of viewing.

CHAPTER 48

Sophie

Brandishing an orange juice-stained tea towel at an irate man isn't the best form of defence. Adam's sudden entrance into my flat didn't give me a chance to prepare.

'Please leave,' I say with a calmness I don't feel.

Adam stands solid. His glare is a challenge.

'Do you have any idea how much trouble you're causing, asking the residents questions about Louise?'

'I'm only taking an interest. Besides, I have a right to know what happened, considering I'm living in this flat at the moment. Who told you I was asking questions, anyway?'

Heat flushes his cheeks. 'None of your business.'

His body trembles with increasing rage. Will he gain a superhuman strength nothing can deter? Am I dealing with the Hulk? I assess the suitability of an open window for escape. My erratic anxiety wheel of thinking is interrupted by a cry. Adam gasps as his neck is placed in a chokehold.

'Leave her alone!' Tobias yells.

As the grip tightens, Adam wheezes.

'Let go, Tobias,' I say. 'We don't need another death around here.'

Tobias' arm drops.

THE WATCHER

Adam rubs his throat and turns to his attacker. 'I wasn't going to hurt her.'

'A likely story.' Tobias adopts a karate pose. 'I'm ready if you try to attack her. Sophie's my friend.'

'Why would I want to harm anyone?' Adam asks. 'Did you seriously believe I'd attack you, you idiotic woman?'

'Barging into my home and threatening me is unacceptable. You're not allowed in here without prior notice. Also, I'm not poking my nose into Louise's affairs. Considering I'm in what was her flat, I can't escape her death.'

Tobias blocks Adam's exit as he tries to leave.

'Stand aside,' I say. 'That's the point. I want him to go.'

'Not until he explains his obsession with Louise.'

'I haven't got a clue what you're talking about.' Adam's chin dips to his chest.

Tobias folds his arms. 'Why were you stalking Louise?'

* * *

Adam insisted he'd only tell his side of the story in his flat. Being in his territory probably feels safer. It suits me. I don't want him in my home. I'm glad Tobias is here, too. Adam's moods are changeable, although Tobias' chokehold was unexpected. These men aren't all they seem.

Adam passes a framed picture to me. 'Remember this photo of my wife?'

'Yes, of course.' I rub my thumb over the raised filigree patterning on the frame.

Tobias leans over and regards the photo. 'Oh.' He slaps the side of his head. 'How could I be so stupid?'

I catch his hand as it aims for another bash. 'Calm down. You'll hurt yourself.'

'Worked it out, Tobias?' Adam blasts. 'Perhaps we should ask how you're aware I was following Louise. You must've been watching, too. Guess it's okay for you, though.'

'I was protecting her,' Tobias whispers.

I place the photo on the table.

'Don't you realise he likes looking after people?' I say. 'He has to check on those he views as vulnerable.'

'Bloody odd,' Adam mutters.

'How did you find out I've been asking around about Louise?'

'I heard you mention it to someone on the phone.'

The photo frame rattles as I slap my hand on the table. 'That's an invasion of my privacy!'

'I was bringing in the post and I overheard you.'

'At any point, you could've walked away. You lingered long enough to eavesdrop.'

The shame of hypocrisy creeps back in. I've done similar things. I'll never get answers if we keep arguing. Asking Tobias questions will be more helpful.

'What's the relevance of the photo?' I address him.

Tobias scrolls through photos on his mobile. He turns the screen around. Adam's intake of breath is audible. I take a closer look at the picture. Tobias is smiling alongside a familiar-looking woman.

'How come you've got a photo of Adam's wife on your phone?' I ask.

'It's not,' Adam says. 'That's Louise. She was the double of Tina.'

CHAPTER 49

Sophie

Tobias paces around the lounge. If he didn't look so tortured, a long-legged man constantly turning around in a small space would be comical.

'I should've checked all sources!' he cries. 'Evidence is important. Facts must always come before opinions.'

'You weren't to know Louise looked like Adam's wife.'

I beckon him over to the sofa by patting the cushion. He continues marching.

Adam circles his thumbs around his knees. 'Suppose I'd better explain myself. I can see how it might appear, me keeping tabs on a woman who lived in this building.'

'Not to mention finding her body,' I add.

Adam flinches. 'Please sit down, Tobias. You're making me nervous.'

'What have you got to be nervous about?' I ask.

My newfound interrogator role is surprising. Iris and her amateur detective ways are rubbing off on me.

Tobias sits next to me. Twitching legs must be another of his coping strategies.

'When Louise moved in, I almost had a heart attack,' Adam begins. 'Bad choice of phrase, considering that's how Tina died.

Anyway, a woman knocked on my door and I nearly collapsed when I opened it. Louise was the spitting image of Tina in her forties. They say we all have a double out there. In this case, it's true.'

'Did you tell Louise?' I ask.

'I couldn't at first. Telling someone they remind you of your deceased wife would be strange, wouldn't it?'

'No less weird than keeping tabs on her. Following people isn't cool.'

Adam addresses Tobias. 'You know how you want to protect others?'

'Yes.'

Tobias' leg shaking increases. Can you get motion sickness on a static sofa? I'm approaching it.

'I had an instinct to look out for Louise,' Adam continues. 'And not how you might think. It was completely innocent. Eventually, I showed her a photo of Tina. We laughed it off as one of life's strange coincidences. If I'm honest, neither of us was comfortable with it. I tried to get over the likeness to Tina by staying away from Louise. Then the men started appearing. For an intelligent woman, Louise had a habit of picking up the bad sort. I stepped in a few times when I heard the rows and things crashing around the flat.

'Of a fashion, we became friends. Louise viewed me as a fatherly figure. It made me consider how she could've been my daughter. Not literally, of course, but in the way she resembled my wife. This sounds odd and I'm not making much sense. Our first child was stillborn. She was such a precious girl.'

'Can I have some water, please?' I rasp as anxiety threatens to close my throat.

'I'll get it.' Tobias heads for the kitchen.

'Are you okay?' Concern rests on Adam's furrowed brow. 'Was I telling a familiar story about my deceased child?'

I nod while trying to keep my breaths even.

'Have you got a grounding item?' Adam asks.

I dig into my pocket for the amethyst.

'How did you know I'd have something to ground me?'

Adam raises an eyebrow. 'How do you think?' He pulls out a thimble from his pocket.

'You too?'

'Ever since I found my wife dead on the floor, anxiety's plagued me.' He rakes his fingers through the little hair he has left. 'You can imagine how I reacted at seeing Louise's body.'

My attempt to squeeze Adam's hand is rewarded. He allows my touch.

'Sorry you went through that,' I say, 'particularly as you cared so much for her.'

'I see both of them in my nightmares. Sometimes Tina turns into Louise. Other nights, it switches. The blood always creeps in.' Adam pulls out a handkerchief from his shirt pocket and dabs his eyes. 'I should've saved them. If I'd been more diligent, Louise wouldn't have been lying dead for days, just like poor old Una. Both of them were only across the hallway from me.'

'There's nothing you could've done for Tina,' Tobias replies. 'Heart attacks can kill fast. Once the flow of blood to a section of heart muscle becomes blocked and the heart can't get oxygen, a human can die quickly.'

Adam's mouth drops open.

'Don't mind him,' I say. 'He's often literal. You didn't mean to cause any offence, did you?'

Tobias' eyes widen. 'Never, not ever.'

'He's right though,' I address Adam. 'You're not responsible for Tina's death.'

A determined tear travels down his cheek. 'When Louise died, it felt like a punishment for what happened to my wife. If I'd done a better job of looking out for Louise, she might still be alive.'

'I watched over her too, and she still died,' Tobias says. 'A sudden blow to the head can be fatal. No measurable activity in the brain and the brainstem is called brain death and—'

'Quite enough information,' I say, 'but thanks for the science lesson.'

'Actually, it's anatomy.'

'Duly noted,' I reply, not having the energy for another long explanation.

Adam and I make eye contact and smile. I detect a hint of the man Tina loved.

'Do you believe Louise's death was an accident?' I ask Adam. Now we're on the subject, I might as well find out more.

'Of course I do. She kept dubious company, but I can't imagine anyone hurting her. Although, no… Don't worry about it.'

'What?' Tobias asks.

'The night Louise died - what the coroner concluded as her death date - I heard her shouting. It was a one-sided conversation, so I assumed she was on the phone. I was outside in the hallway and thought I'd better check.'

'What did she say?' I ask.

'I listened at the door for a while. A bit nosy of me, I confess. Louise told the caller they wouldn't get away with it. She said she was going to the police with evidence to stop them from watching anyone ever again.'

CHAPTER 50
Sophie

I tug the duvet up to my chin and tuck it in. Not one inch of my body must be exposed. Since I left Adam's, the chill inside me won't go, no matter how high I turn up the thermostat.

After the miscarriage, my bed was my sanctuary. It seemed easier to disappear within the sheets. Days were lost in a blanket fort of despair and longing. When it became oppressive, I decided to get up and try living again. The first step out of bed, intending to stay out of it, was tough. I wondered if I was betraying my child by choosing to live.

'Now that you're in a cocoon, let's get into the details,' Emma says. On the screen, she wriggles in an armchair. 'Right, I'm comfortable. So, Adam didn't check on Louise the night she died?'

'He didn't want to interfere,' I reply. 'Considering Adam was eavesdropping, he felt awkward asking Louise about the phone conversation.'

'Being British will be the death of us. Can you imagine if the UK was involved in an apocalyptic disaster? We'd form an orderly queue to leave the country, rather than running the hell for our lives. Well, the decent people would. There are some selfish bastards who'd use your corpse as a springboard.'

'With Ben by my side, no one would stand a chance against us.'

'Aw, so lovely.' Emma's voice falters. 'I've got to find a fella to get me through an apocalypse.'

She plays the opening bars of Bonnie Tyler's "I Need a Hero" on her phone.

'I bloody miss you,' I say when she stops the music. 'Even though we talk every day, I'm pining for Ben too.'

'You're doing the right thing. This will strengthen your relationship.'

I clear my throat. 'Let's hope so. For now, I'll make do with Stanley seagull. He's got into the habit of rapping on the window when he wants attention. I'm even allowed to touch his head.'

'I think you might be lonelier than you're making out, if your new bestie is a bird.'

'Are you feeling threatened by a seagull, you daft mare?'

'Not at all.' Emma gives me a wink.

'Here's something else you'll find hilarious. Remember the lothario I mentioned who lives upstairs?'

'Rory? Dodgy cowboy man?'

'That's the one. He put a note through my letterbox, asking me out on a date.'

'As if.' Her laugh is deafening. 'What did he write?'

I grab the piece of paper from the table and read it aloud. 'Hey, Sophie babes. Hope you're finding Harmony House harmonious. Lol. How about making it even sweeter by having a drinky with me? I'll give you a night to remember. Apologies for writing rather than chatting. I keep looking for you, but you move so fast. All my love, Rory xxxx.'

I hold the note up to the phone for her to see the evidence.

Emma mimics vomiting. 'What a sleaze! Who the hell, apart from eleven-year-old girls dots the letter *i* with fat circles?'

'Rory.'

'Joking aside, though,' Emma adds. 'Keep an eye on him. The last thing you need is some weird bloke watching you.'

CHAPTER 51
The Watcher

Federico Gallo claims to have transformed since he met his wife. It's obviously not for the better. When he spotted Aurora Alunni dancing alone and not giving a damn, it transfixed him. It was obsession at first stare rather than love at first sight. They tell people the story of how they met, trying to capture one perfect moment before it all went wrong.

The Gallos are aware of their issues. Astute married couples often are. Most husbands and wives either let the problems fester or talk it through. The Gallos shout, strike, and have sex. They've never questioned the complexities. For them, this is their version of marriage.

As he moves around their home, Federico speaks his truths, unhindered by company. The monologue hints at his introspection. The opulence of the flat's decor gives no comfort. None of it belongs to him. He ponders on how to make an impact beyond the walls of the flat. Federico is Harmony House's ghost. Being invisible stirs a paradox of longings. He can harbour secrets if others look away, but being noticed is important. A perfect body deserves attention.

Aurora's sleeping, or so she says. Her husband knows better. When she shuts the door, he's certain it's because she can't bear to let him in. He tells himself while preparing coffee it's a fair punishment. He could blame the person he's become on Aurora, but maybe it was always lurking.

Federico used to pride himself on being strong. Strength isn't only physical. An emotionally robust man doesn't have such a tumultuous relationship. A decent man doesn't watch every move. A man of excellent character shouldn't need to observe to gain authority over others. Federico damns it all. He isn't a good man. The sooner he acknowledges it, the sooner he can take back power.

In the hazy past, Federico was a seemingly hard-working son. Years of growing up as one of eleven children to demanding parents left their mark. Aurora mocks the "hillbilly farmers" from which he's derived. Antagonistic Federico tries to defend the simpler life, while knowing it was an illusion. Why people who detest children insist on producing them like a factory line was a mystery. Now, he understands why his parents played the game of fitting in. In their area, large families were standard. Father-provider and mother feeding her family from a permanent place at the stove were the norm. Federico's mother never cooked a meal in her life. His sisters picked up the domestic slack while their mother napped and gossiped. When their father returned from a day's graft, the bellowing at his lazy wife began. Images of his father often feature a raised belt and a sneer.

Whenever Federico tried to leave home, his father always brought him back. Gallos belong on the farm. The escape to England offered freedom. Until he married Aurora, Federico cut off contact with his family. On the night of the wedding, he rang his father, boasting of the wealthy family he'd married in to. Parental approval came for the first time. It was enough. Federico didn't need them anymore. He had Aurora.

The disconnection remains between Federico and his family. When his parents ask for financial help, he does the dutiful thing while enjoying having dominance over them. With each line of jealous praise in their emails at him wanting for nothing, Federico chokes on the lies. His fingers hammered out disgust at what his upbringing made him do. He tells his parents illusion is better than the reality. Federico always deletes his truths. They are one indulgence he cannot have.

As the espresso jolts through his veins, he resolves to be more watchful. It's the only way to survive. Others will learn this. There will be more casualties. This is the pact Federico made and must keep paying for. When you strike a deal with a devil, they always collect what you owe.

CHAPTER 52
Sophie

Four glasses of prosecco earlier, I swore I wasn't going to a nightclub. Now I'm preparing myself for Cheeky's. Damn my life.

In Zara's bathroom, I'm trying to shoehorn into a skintight dress. I'm thankful it belongs to Zara. It's longer on me than the bum-skimming length it probably is on her. My shoulder protests as I contort to reach the zipper at the back. A stray elbow smacks into a shelf covered with high-end products. The room resembles a department store beauty counter. Spotlights above the mirror highlight an obsession with shining bright. I tried standing under them and soon leapt away. The bags under my eyes are collecting extra luggage. I could do with sleeping rather than going out.

Zara's persuasive skills are unsurpassed. I'd prepared for a chat with Ben and then an early night when she showed up. She formed a pout and offered a sob story about needing a night out. Devastation at a broken nail that can't be fixed by the salon until tomorrow can only be alleviated by clubbing. I insisted on drinks in her flat only. At the drama queen's insistence, I put a plaster on the "wound" after blowing a kiss on it, like her grandmother did. I wasn't sure if I should be offended at being likened to a much older woman. With Zara, one moment you're her best friend, and the next, you're tugging at the knife lodged between your shoulder blades.

'Hurry up, hun,' Zara calls from outside. 'I'm dying for a slash.'

I open the door to be greeted by her, wearing only a risqué scarlet underwear set.

'You're not even ready,' I say.

'Won't take me long to get dressed.' She holds up a slip of material that would only cover one of my bum cheeks.

'Give us a twirl, then.'

I oblige while dying inside. Emma and Ben would piss themselves laughing at this Bacofoil abomination.

'Looking fabuloustastic!' As Zara jumps up and down, I turn away. Her bra's losing the battle to contain her boobs.

Catching my reflection is nightmare stuff of the hall of mirrors. 'I resemble a Christmas turkey roasting in the oven. No way am I going out like this. I haven't worn a dress since the nineties and it's Baltic out there.'

'Babes, if I look that bangin' at forty-seven, I'd walk around in a bikini, whatever the season.'

'I'm forty-two, thanks very much.'

'Whatevs.' She ushers me out of the bathroom. 'Gotta pee.'

I pick up a half-full glass of prosecco and neck it for courage. Glitter from the stem of the flute flakes onto my fingers. All this glitz isn't me, but perhaps I should try something new. Coming to Southbourne is about self-discovery. Perhaps I'm the type who secretly likes tight clothing. I tug at the hem, trying to cover my thighs. Maybe not. I remind myself I wore dresses like this a few decades ago. It doesn't help. I take my jacket from the coat hook. Thank goodness for my trusty old parka.

Zara appears. The material drapes across her honed body in the shape of an X, barely covering her breasts and crotch.

'You'll catch your death.' I cringe at the echo of one of Mum's favourite sayings.

'Get a grip, Soph. I don't do all the exercise for nothing. Gotta put the goods on show.' Zara picks up a bag the size of my wallet. She points at my feet. 'You can't wear those.'

'Why not?' I ask, inspecting the silver DMs. 'They're my best boots.'

'I've got a bangin' pair of Louboutins to go with your outfit.'

I claw back some of my confidence. 'No thanks. Not being rude, but your feet look bigger than mine. Besides, my boots match the dress.' I don't add my coat isn't coming off to show what's underneath.

'Your fashion funeral.' Zara shrugs. 'Come on, let's party.'

CHAPTER 53
Sophie

Cheeky's is everything and less than I expected. Tackiness has vomited pink everywhere. You can't move for candy pink pompoms hanging from the ceiling, flashing cerise lights, and multitudes of love hearts. This is a teenage girl's domain, not one for cynical forty-something women.

The nightclub is nestled in the heart of Bournemouth's student social scene. This would've deterred me if Zara had bothered to share this information. When I read the poster at the door, welcoming all students, I wanted to strangle my companion. Not only do I feel like mutton trussed up in a spring lamb's clothes, but I'm also probably the oldest person here.

A thundering bass line ripping across the club makes my teeth rattle. Lasers flash on the dance floor, giving a second-rate light show. Neon flashing signs above the bar repeat *This is Cheeky's*, in case you weren't aware.

After arguing with the door staff that DMs aren't trainers and I wasn't flouting the rules, I needed a drink. I'm set on one glass of whisky and then soft drinks for the rest of the night. I nestle into my coat; glad I didn't have to fight the bouncer on wearing this as well. He'd have to prise it from my cold dead hands, particularly as there's a pert young woman wearing the same dress.

When we arrived, Zara headed for the toilets. I received orders to get the bevvies in. It's not a hardship. Whisky can't come soon enough. My arm bears the strain of holding it up, trying to be served. Fluffy blondes with gargantuan breasts shove in front of me. Their drinks arrive in minutes. Instead of protesting, I check out what the kids call entertainment nowadays. This will be my only opportunity.

A bloke with a comb-over and John Travolta's *Saturday Night Fever* cast-offs can't fail to catch my eye. He's sharking around women dancing in a group. The closed sisterhood circle should be a sign. Throwing his arms up like he's having an electric shock won't get him a girlfriend. I mentally thank the man for being more embarrassing than me. A further scan of the room confirms I'm surrounded by a tribe. Desperate faces of people on the pull make me more than happy with my married status.

As a willowy brunette slinks past to the bar, the glittery butterfly spanning across the back of her dress catches my eye. I remember being freaked out at butterflies mounted on a museum board. On a school trip, I showed up my teachers by banging the case, trying to set the insects free. Even as a kid, I knew the oppressiveness of feeling trapped. *I* was a butterfly encased in my parents' ridiculous notions of perfection. They've never forgiven me for removing the pin they stuck in, trying to hold me in perfect place.

Apprehension's fingers drums along my neck to the top of my spine. Despite the stickiness of body heat from the crowd waiting at the bar, I shiver. I glance behind to see if someone's too close. I'm still alone at the rear of the queue. Assessing eyes evaluate me somewhere in the room. Once more, I'm a butterfly. Only this time I'm trapped in a jar labelled *Cheeky's*.

I stare into the gloom of the booths at the back of the club. They are the domain of fumbles, deals, and those who want to be alone. Does my stalker dwell there? I try to decipher shapes in the dark. Stillness. Maybe this Louise business is making me edgy. As I look away, a light flashes. Did someone take my picture?

'What can I get you, love?' the bartender, a man who's all biceps and ZZ Top beard, asks.

THE WATCHER

'The best whisky you have and a pornstar martini, please.'

While the man makes a ceremony of preparing the drinks, I concentrate on the back booths. Glitter balls hanging above catch the strobe lights. That explains what the flash was. I'm in a club full of nubile women whose boobs don't aim for their navel when their bra comes off. No one here wants to take my photo.

I carry our drinks over to the area Zara's reserved. Cheeky's VIPs are only worthy of velour sofas riddled with stained and worn smooth patches. A ratty sheepskin rug reeks of wet dog. Zara reclines, possibly awaiting the peeling of grapes.

'Did you put the bevvies on my tab?' she asks.

'No,' I reply, while trying to sit like a lady. No mean feat when you're used to wearing trousers. 'I didn't know you have a tab. Besides, I like to pay my own way.'

I won't share how I'll have to re-mortgage our house in Oxford to buy another round.

Zara's donkey laugh competes with the music blasting from a speaker above us.

'You're so old-school. Keeping it retro. Bet you paid cash.'

Zara stands to adjust her dress, although there isn't much to work with. She parades in front of the mirrors set on the walls. After gathering an audience, she stretches out her arms to reveal plenty of side-boob. A woman walking past knocks into her.

'Watch where you're going, clumsy cow!' Zara shouts.

The icy-cool blonde stops. 'Are you talking to me?'

Zara makes a show of looking the woman up and down. 'Not unless you've got someone hidden behind that fat arse.'

I slink further down the sofa, trying to avoid questionable stains, while hoping it will swallow me up.

The blonde advances towards Zara. 'Say that again and I'll rip your face to shreds. I'm ready for you.'

Zara lunges from her seat. A man grabs her middle. She rises into the air, legs kicking out. I turn away. Her underwear isn't offering the best coverage.

'Get the hell off me!' Zara yells.

The blonde smirks. 'Is he your boyfriend or your dad?'

Rory gives the woman a hard stare. She scurries away. I would too. Trouble is written all over him.

* * *

Zara sways as another potent cocktail takes effect. 'I had the situation under control,' she slurs.

Rory insisted on getting us a drink and shows no signs of leaving. I haven't touched mine. Being alert around him is wise.

'I was only looking after you,' Rory replies. 'Of course, you were always on top of it.'

Zara rewards him with a beauty queen grin.

'Why are you here?' I ask Rory.

His spider fingers crawl along the back of the sofa until they're skirting my neck. I shift away.

'That's not very welcoming,' Rory says. 'I've made a terrible impression on you so far, haven't I?'

'Were you watching me from over there?' I point at the gloomy back booths.

'I've only just got here, sweetheart. Do I have a rival for your attention?'

My silence signifies a refusal to inflate his machismo. I want to go home wherever that may be. Anywhere that's not here. I don't belong in Cheeky's. Perhaps I don't belong in this area. I imagine Ben, asleep and cuddling his pillow in my absence.

'Stop trying to get into Soph's pants, you old lech.' Zara giggles. 'Come and dance with me.'

I send a series of SOS messages to Emma. She doesn't reply. It's approaching midnight and I'm a reluctant Cinderella in an outrageous dress. Make me Sophie again, someone, please.

Taking another look at the back of the club, I notice movement. Dare I go over there? What if I see something happening in the darkness I shouldn't? I stare at the shadowy figure. Light flashes again. It's not a disco ball. I spring to my feet. A boy barricades my path. He's wearing what he probably thinks is an ironic "Kiss Me Quick" hat. As he sidles up to me, I try to dodge past.

'Get out of my way!' I shout.

THE WATCHER

The shadow in the booth is moving away. The boy squeezes my backside. I pick up his hand and hold it. Thinking his luck's in, he winks.

I stare into his unfocused eyes. 'It's best to warn you I'm a serial killer who dismembers young men. I start with their penis and then decapitate the head. Would you like to be next on my list?'

Drunken boy can't escape soon enough. He scoots to the bar and his jeering mates who are demanding payment. Nice to know I was a bet.

I check the back of the room. The booths are all empty. The prickling sensation on my skin of being watched hasn't gone. They're still here, somewhere. I return to the VIP area and huddle over my mobile, reeling off texts to Emma. My trembling hands lose purchase of the phone. Leaning under the table, I stretch to retrieve it. A hand grasps my shoulder. I prepare to face my watcher.

CHAPTER 54

Sophie

'Is this woman bothering you?' A female bouncer asks. 'Do you want to report it?'

I turn away from the crowd Rory and I have attracted. My hand tingles, punishing me for the punch I landed on him. Being watched brought out my fight rather than flight instinct.

Rory shoos the bystanders with his hands. 'Nothing to see here, just a lovers' tiff. Disperse.'

People obey, finding their places back on the dance floor or at the bar. How does Rory have such gravitas? He's a joke of a man. Perhaps this is his stomping ground. He mentioned how often he comes here. Still, don't these people see what I do?

'He's not my partner!' I shout at the bouncer.

There's no way I'm allowing anyone to think I'd touch him with a bargepole, let alone my body.

Rory turns to me and whispers. 'Do you want to land up at the police station? Play nicely, Soph.'

Rory draws the bouncer aside for a chat. He's practically twice her height and age. I wait for her to remark on his sleaziness. Instead, they exchange telephone numbers. After giving her a kiss on the cheek, he joins me.

THE WATCHER

'Stop watching me.' I say. 'Hiding in the dark, taking photos of me isn't right.' Despite trying to be confrontational with my words, his intense stare weakens my voice.

'You're pretty hot, but I've got better things to do than play voyeur. I've been dancing with Zara. Ask her.'

'Where is she?'

'Gone to powder her nose, if you know what I mean.' He mimics sniffing a line.

Great. Not only am I being stalked and in a club where the most retro song they've played is from last month, Zara's abandoned me to take drugs.

'Weren't you aware Zara's keen on the marching powder?' Rory spreads his legs across the sofa. 'She's full of surprises. So are you. I didn't expect you to wear such a sexy dress.'

I secure the top button. 'How the hell do you know what I'm wearing under my parka?'

'Your coat fell open when the security guard pulled you away from belting me. I can't understand why you're hiding such lovely assets. Give us another peek.'

He reaches for me.

'Get your bloody hands off me!'

'Louise used to cover up, too. She shouldn't have. Her body was amazing. I guess some women are bashful. I soon gave Louise the confidence to be naked, though.'

'You were involved with her?'

'I prefer to call it hooking up.' Rory's hand cups his crotch.

'Didn't your mother tell you if you keep playing with your knob it'll fall off?'

He grins. 'Thinking about my penis, are you?'

'Nope, I don't sweat the small stuff. I have no doubt you're a big-headed man with tiny dick syndrome.'

'Louise never had any complaints.'

'Were you upset at her death?' I ask, trying to make Rory hurt, or at least show some humanity.

He shrugs. 'Not especially. We weren't close. Well, I wasn't. Louise was in love with me. It became awkward.'

'You really are an absolute bastard.'

He grips my wrist. 'Only if you want me to be, darling.'

I push him away. As Rory holds up his hands in mock surrender, his cufflinks catch the nightclub's flashing lights. He notices me looking.

'Do you like them?' Rory strokes his cuffs. 'I had to get a replacement pair. One went missing in a scuffle. I'm still annoyed that bitch provoked me to fight back. These are custom made and expensive.'

The word *Sexy* is written on them in diamantes. They're the same as the cufflink I found in my flat. Rory fought with Louise. I'm sitting with a man who hurts women.

CHAPTER 55

Sophie

I'm saved from Rory's scrutiny by a woman who joins us. She roots her heels into the carpet and places her hands on her hips. It's the first time I've seen Rory flustered. I already like this woman.

'Didn't think you'd ever come in here again.' Her acerbic tone matches a mean mouth.

'If I'd known you were here, I'd have turned up sooner.' Despite his trembling voice, Rory tries to turn on the charm.

She leans in, her face inches from Rory's. 'After what happened last time, I don't think so. You're lucky I didn't go to the police.'

He edges away. The juvenile mocking is obviously a front for his ebbing confidence. 'Gabrielle, we both know that's a foolish idea. We're two consenting adults.'

Tears form in her eyes. 'That's a complete lie! You've had the last penny from me.'

'Silly girl.' He shakes his head. 'You owe me. Seeing as I'm in a good mood, I'll give you an extra few days. Next instalment's due on Monday.'

She addresses me. 'Run away, sweetheart, while you can. If you don't, you'll regret it for the rest of your life.'

'Gabs, you love me really,' Rory says. 'I'm only getting my investment back.'

I use the moment where he's focusing on Gabrielle to escape. Leaving a vulnerable woman with a predator makes me feel compromised, but Gabrielle's friends are standing nearby. I'm still not convinced it wasn't Rory taking photos of me earlier. The further away I am from him, the better. One problem, though. He lives in the same building.

Wings of apprehension flutter from my chest and into my throat. The eyes are on me again. Determined to stare courage back at him, I try to locate Rory. He's at the bar, waving cash around. His attention is on the blonde bar steward, not me.

Clubbers cram the dance floor. The surge of bodies offers a shield against my predator. Zara's still missing. She's probably snorting drugs or found another pushover to manipulate. I'm such an idiot. This isn't my world. I send Zara a message to say I'm leaving and to check she's safe. As I near the main door, my phone rings.

'Ben, I'm so glad it's you.'

'Are you okay? You sound scared.' His voice is thick with tiredness.

'It's so good to speak to you.'

'Where are you?' he asks.

I pause, wondering how to tell him why I'm here and everything that's happened tonight. He has to know. Keeping things from Ben to stop him from worrying must end. I need my husband.

'The music's flaming loud. Are you in a nightclub?' Ben's annoyance creeps through the phone. 'You don't even like clubs.'

'Hear me out—'

'While I'm missing you so much it hurts, you're out on the razzle.'

'No, I'm not!' I yell.

Someone grabs my mobile from my hand.

'Piss off, Ben. If you gave your wife what she wanted, she wouldn't be on the pull.'

CHAPTER 56
The Watcher

Sometimes I take my watching outside. There's only so much to see within the confines of Harmony House. Eight flats aren't enough entertainment. A mobile phone is a powerful tool for recording audio, photos, and video. Over the years, as technology has improved, I've embraced everything on offer.

Whenever I find an interesting study, I also observe their behaviour in the wild. A whole new dimension opens up before my eyes. Being so close that I might be seen is part of the game. They never spot me. I don't wear a disguise. That's for amateurs. If anyone saw me, I'd have a plausible explanation. No one would question my motives.

If Sophie had discovered me spying on her tonight, it wouldn't have been an issue. Blending into the background of the nightclub was the challenge. My target didn't make it any easier by starting an argument. Cheeky's and I have a tangled history. It was risky being there, but no one keeps me from watching. If Sophie is to become The Listener, it's worth my threatened exposure. The cajoling to get her to come here was rewarded. I'll confess it surprised me she agreed to go. Loneliness can make people do unpredictable things.

Taking photos of her was a dicey move, but playing it safe is miserable. The booths at the back of Cheeky's were made for people like me. Dark deeds happen in dark places. The game of cat and mouse with Sophie tonight was fun. The woman's intuition at being watched is something I've never encountered. She's my first subject who's shown alertness at being observed. Her insight will make or break me. Nervous goosebumps forming on the back of her neck as she detected my scrutiny was delicious.

At a distance, I trail behind as Sophie walks unknown streets. The choice of a wrong turn is infuriating. Her shoulders convulse as she sobs out her woes. There are plenty of them: Rory's suspicious connection with Louise and his intentions for Sophie; Ben's mistrust; and Zara's abandonment.

Zara always wins. The staff at Cheeky's are loyal to one of their biggest spenders. After Zara cut off Ben's call and told Sophie she's too much under his control, no one intervened. Instead, Sophie was ejected for causing a nuisance. The female bouncer who had her eye on Rory relished pushing what she perceived as competition out the door.

As Sophie misses the road where the taxi office is situated, I wonder why emotional women often behave irrationally. Louise is a prime example. When I consider how she allowed me to believe she could be The Listener, Louise's death is justified.

If Sophie stood still and ceased snivelling, she'd realise she's only a phone call away from getting a taxi. Please don't let this be another sign of her ineptitude. My listener must be smart. Only an astute mind will know what to do with my recordings.

Sophie glances behind.

I lower the hood over my face.

She takes a closer look.

Has curiosity killed this cat's project?

I freeze.

Is The Watcher now the watched?

CHAPTER 57
Sophie

Where the hell am I? Allowing emotions to guide my decision making can lead to trouble. Here I am, standing in the centre of it. I'm lost. Ben's annoyed with me. I'm pissed off with him for having a go at me. Maybe, though, he's missing me and thinking I'm out on the town hurts. I'd always rather be with Ben. Loneliness seeps into me along with the progressive drizzle of the rain.

Trying to place my location, I look around. Repetitive cross sections of residential roads are disorienting. Even the names are similar. Harmony House feels a million miles away. This wouldn't happen in Oxford. I could be anywhere in my hometown and guaranteed to find the way back to my house.

Footsteps behind me increase in momentum. In the last few minutes, I've become aware I'm not alone. I tighten the hold on the strap of my bag, repeating the mantra, "I'm safe. I'm okay". The person following me won't be rewarded with my fear, if that's what they're aiming for.

I take a glimpse. A figure halts and then shifts into the shadows. The butterfly pushes against my lungs and spreads. Is this who was watching me in the club? Think. Move. Act.

The footsteps retreat. I surge forward, seeking light in this bleak night. Don't stop, Sophie. Get to a safe place and phone for a taxi. Why didn't I do it when leaving Cheeky's? Anger at Zara clouded my thought processes. Think. Move. Act.

Fumbling with my mobile, I pick up the pace. Heavier rain hitting the screen makes my fingers clumsy as I try to find a cab company.

The sense of being watched returns. An ominous presence draws closer. I raise my hood against the downpour. A movement swishes out of the corner of my eye as I cover my head.

A hand grips my arm, pulling me into an alleyway. My feet slide over slick concrete. Narrow walls seem to decrease. I try to break free from my attacker's firm hold. On the ground, our limbs tangle. My opponent's strength and build beats mine. The reek of rotting food from the bins competes with the weight of violence in crushing me.

'Get off,' I garble. 'You can have my purse.'

A panic signal surges to my brain. Welcome rain pelts against my face, keeping me alert.

'I don't want your money,' a man replies.

Please, no. If he doesn't want cash, then he must want… No. Don't go there, mind. Do I recognise the voice? Can't think. Can't move. Can't act. Treacle air coats my lungs. A light shines in my eyes.

'Keep breathing!' he shouts.

A tender touch cradles my jaw.

'Don't die on me, Sophie. I need you alive.'

CHAPTER 58

The Watcher

Stop being so weak, Sophie!

If you were more observant, you wouldn't be lying in an alleyway, fighting for air.

Stupid, stupid woman! How dare you try to dupe me into believing you could be my listener? No one deceives me.

Sophie's face turns grey. Her fingers uncurl and lay flat on the concrete.

Die.

See if I care.

CHAPTER 59

Sophie

I try to shake off the fuzziness after almost passing out in the alleyway. My former potential attacker, turned companion, remains silent. Throughout our walk, he hasn't looked at me once. Counting steps demands all of his attention. Gull Lane is in view. I'm closer to Harmony House than I thought. Being lost always makes you feel like you're a hundred miles away from your destination.

'You can't keep following people,' I say. 'While I understand you believe it's for protection, I was terrified when you grabbed me and pulled me into the alley. You could've done some serious damage.' I touch my chest. The burden of his bulk upon it remains.

Tobias drags the soles of his shoes along the kerb.

'Stop doing that!' I shout.

'I said I'm sorry.' He becomes a chastised child. 'I didn't mean to make you fall. Sometimes I'm a bit clumsy.'

'It's not good enough. You're lucky I didn't brain you.' My threat is weak, considering Tobias' comparable height and build. 'I'm getting fed up with defending you when you behave like this. Were you in Cheeky's earlier?'

'No way. I can't stand nightclubs. They're full of drunken people behaving irrationally.'

THE WATCHER

'Why are you following me?' I ask.

'I was out for a stroll. When I spotted you, I was about to approach when I saw the stalker. I thought if I made them aware I was here too, they'd back off.'

I stand still. 'Someone else was following me? Are you sure? Did you see them?'

'Not fully.' Tobias hits the side of his head.

'Are you lying?'

'No!' he yells.

The force of his cry makes me widen the distance between us.

'Okay.' I hold out my hands in a stop gesture. Tobias responds better to visual cues. 'Calm down. I needed to ask. You must understand why I'm wary after what you just did.'

I wince against a fresh sting of pain in my knee. Looking down, I assess the rest of the damage. Zara's dress is probably ruined.

'You're bleeding,' Tobias says. 'Sorry I caused that.'

'Well, you should be.'

'I'm only protecting you!' The head hitting habit begins.

'Stop that right now, Tobias Alfred Peters.'

Reciting full names is a parenting trick. Tobias' mother terrifies him. I go for it. Tobias told me the middle name comes from his dad's Batman obsession. I expect Mr Peters initiated his son into geekdom.

'Do you know who was following me?' I ask. 'Have you seen them before?'

'No.'

'Where did they go?'

'Don't know.' His eyes roam, looking everywhere but at me. 'Can we go home now?'

'Yes.'

I pick up the pace. Sparse street lighting makes it difficult to read his expressions, but the faltering voice betrays him. Tobias is lying.

CHAPTER 60
Louise's Diary

Tobias has just left. Once again, his glasses are broken. We've discussed controlling the tics. When Tobias slaps the side of his head, his fingers often catch the frame and damage it. When I mentioned having therapy, it took hours to calm him. I forgot the treadmill of doctors and therapies his mother has made him endure.

Before leaving, Tobias checked all the rooms in my flat in the usual order. Initially, I found the scrupulous inventory disconcerting. Now I let him do it. Considering the circumstances, his compulsion to protect others is understandable. Tobias is hiding something from me, though. When he pulled out books from the top shelf of my bookcase, I asked what he was doing. He became flustered, claiming it was nothing. His poker face needs work.

After Tobias left, I checked what he'd seen. There's just a vent there. Maybe Tobias is being cautious. Blocking the airflow isn't helpful, so I moved the books even further aside.

The Gallos are fighting once more. I wish they'd give me one night of peace, free of their yelling and the ceiling rumbling from stomping. I won't miss hearing the eruptions. It's too close to my past. When I came here, I thought I'd never know violence again. Now, I have a front seat.

THE WATCHER

At the weekend, the Gallos' arguments escalate. On Fridays, they kick off and then keep at it. I've tried to intervene, but knocking on their door is terrifying. Federico glares. Aurora shies behind him with haunted eyes I recognise. They were mine. I was once her.

Yesterday I caught up with Aurora. She's trying to avoid me since I last asked if she needed help. This time I was ready, watching and waiting for her return.

Attempting to hold her hand was a mistake. Comfort always helps me. I received it at the beginning of my marriage when friends tried to understand. After too many nights of calling for help, my friendship circled dwindled. They couldn't comprehend why I stayed with Karl. I couldn't explain why either, although it's simply one thing: fear.

When I reached for Aurora, she pulled away as if I'd set her on fire. A ferocity flared in her I didn't believe she possessed. As she demanded I never touch her again, I realised my error. A sudden movement or unsolicited touches are a threat for women like us. Overwhelmed by my mistake, I could only watch Aurora going upstairs, back into danger.

CHAPTER 61
Sophie

Aurora's request to have another sitting for her portrait was initially something I welcomed. I need to get out of Harmony House for a while and I can get some beach sketches in, too. Even the low temperature outside isn't a deterrent. I'll take braving the elements over facing Zara, Rory, or Tobias.

Ben's on my shit-list, too. I can't reply to his messages at the moment. Let him consider the impact of ranting at me for being in a nightclub. If he'd bothered to listen, Ben would've known how much I needed him. It's fair to say we didn't get a chance to chat after Zara told Ben to piss off and ended the call. Annoyance builds inside me at the thought of seeing her.

After reading the latest offering from Louise's diary, sent to me overnight, Aurora's suffering and how Louise couldn't help her feels like my burden. I have to show Aurora there's a way out. Louise's concerns about Tobias lying to her don't help either. Was it only Tobias who followed me last night? That alone is odd, but explained by his protective instinct. If someone else was there, why won't Tobias say who? Is he scared? Should I be, too?

Today didn't start well. Aurora darted a dirty look at me when I bought a chocolate bar at the corner shop. The skinny goddess probably thinks its chances of travelling straight to my hips are likely. Rebellious as ever, I shoved a mouthful in. A seagull swooped in and had the rest of the chocolate away from my hand. As I watched the bastard nosh on my treat, I checked its legs for deformities. Thankfully, it wasn't Stanley, or we'd be having words. Aurora gave a sly "Told you so" smirk while I swore about greedy shite hawks the size of cats. Then we finally settled in for another portrait session.

I'm finding my groove and connecting with Aurora, although her shell is hard to penetrate. There are moments when I see beyond the aesthetically pleasing surface. Occasionally, a movement or an expression betrays what lies beneath. Aurora lowers her sunglasses and stares into my eyes. She winks. The spell is broken.

We relax back into business. Of course, my anticipated time of peace and reflection is ruined again. The threat's larger than an ill-mannered seagull. Federico's overseeing proceedings.

'Can you move away, please?' I say to him. 'You're blocking what little light there is.'

'Artists are so temperamental. I'll warm up for my run over here.'

Eyes never leaving Aurora, Federico stomps over to the beach huts. I stifle a laugh as Federico collides with a Yorkshire terrier. Federico mutters apologies for stepping on the dog's paw while admonishing the owner for having their dog off lead. Federico's smarm sits comfortably with severity.

Absorbed in being seen, Aurora's oblivious. Today she's reclining on a bamboo mat I had to carry. I drew the line at sourcing a parasol. Let her groupie from the café step up again. No matter how often I asked her to get into the same pose as last time, she wouldn't obey. This portrait's turning into a montage.

'We will pay you,' Federico calls from behind me. 'Everyone must be repaid for their efforts. Looking at my wife should be a reward in itself, though.' Federico is now beside me, performing squats. 'I heard you went to Cheeky's last night.'

'How do you know?'

'The walls are thin in Harmony House. The sooner you learn that the better.'

'I hear you often enough.'

Arrogance demands Federico isn't fazed by my dig at his dubious domestic circumstances. I shuffle away. The concrete promenade grinds against my jeans. No sitting on soggy sand this time. Aurora smiles, probably at herself. Despite her tempestuous relationship, self-satisfaction reigns.

'Federico used to work at Cheeky's.' Aurora's words are laboured, as if we are inconveniencing her. 'It's where we met.'

'I expected such fine people as you would go to more classy places.'

Their matching grimaces confirm my gentle teasing has spectacularly bombed.

'Not all of us are rich,' Federico blasts as he propels from a squat. 'I did what I could to make do. My family are workers. When I came to England, I needed a job.'

Aurora reclines and addresses the clouded sky. 'You should see my husband create a cocktail. It's most seductive. We don't go to Cheeky's anymore, though.'

'Why?' I ask.

'An incident,' Federico replies. 'Aurora deserves better.'

Federico spits on the ground. A lady passing by tuts at him. Federico begins his run. Slapping feet punish the concrete.

Aurora joins me to look at the sketch. I've learned she always gets what she wants, despite my hankering to keep a work in progress private.

'It's coming along.' she pats me on the shoulder. 'You have an observant eye.'

More than you think. I'll be keeping an eye on your husband.

CHAPTER 62
The Watcher

If I believed in fate, I'd swear Sophie came to Harmony House just for me. Her artist's eye connects with her hand to create an image. When she sketches, I'm enthralled. Creativity's ability to travel from the brain to paper is a thing of wonder. I do this in reverse. The picture is the beginning and then I decipher the meaning. As I watch Sophie flourishing a pencil across the page, I realise we're not so different. The camera is my pencil. My mind interprets and claims the images as mine.

My power play with Sophie is made more enticing by her not realising she's a player. Sophie thinks she is the one doing the watching. Being on the beach makes it even easier to observe her. We all come to the seaside to take in the view.

It's clear her sketching tries to pierce people's cores. Similarly, I penetrate the inner lives of Harmony House's residents. Cameras are paints laid upon my palette, ready to apply to the building's canvas. Each person is part of a communal masterpiece. Harmony House and Southbourne are the perfect settings for my work.

Location is everything to a watcher. This may not be the coveted Bournemouth, but it's a bonus. Southbourne has a haven of its own. My eyes aren't blinkered, though. I know of the nefarious deeds that happen at night. Beach life isn't the utopia many believe it to be.

Many hanker for retirement by the sea. The tempting pull offering an idyllic future keeps you going in the daily grind. One day, living near the seaside will come. For those who've lived in seaside towns for years, sea breezes become part of your breathing. You take it for granted. At the beginning of your new life, you'll regularly visit the beach. Before you know it, months have passed. The sea's still there, but its beckoning quietens to a whisper. You came to paradise and forgot it was there. Sand and crashing waves won't solve your problems. Occasionally, it lures you back with false promises. You remind yourself how lucky you are to be here and vow to make more of it. You soon forget.

This is you. Not me.

When I first arrived here, I never harboured such facile notions. This project could've happened anywhere. The shift from the city to the sea revived me somewhat. That's true. The lure of a new mission was more of an elixir than the sun emerging from the sea's horizon could ever be.

I admire the power the landscape has upon the swarming mosquito tourists. They are as predictable as they are prevalent. People believe they're individuals. They're wrong. Every single one of you reverts to a type. I can tell what a person likes to eat, drive, and wear within minutes of seeing them.

I understand you, Sophie. You have anxiety, but don't let it define you. You miss Ben intensely, and Emma's your constant. Purple-streaked hair and an eclectic wardrobe make you stand out while harbouring introvert tendencies. Most importantly, you view the world through a watcher's eyes. Keep impressing me by learning to listen, too. I will be your teacher. Harmony House's voices have so much to say.

CHAPTER 63
Sophie

My door bears the brunt of the hammering blows against it.

'Soph, open up! I saw you go in.'

'Is Zara still out there?' Emma asks in our phone chat. 'Tell her to do one. After leaving you last night with that Rory creep, she deserves it. I wish I'd seen your messages sooner. I'd have been there like a shot.'

'And this is why I love you,' I whisper. 'You're still too poorly to join me, though. Better go. I don't want the banshee outside to know I'm in. Speak soon. Bye.'

I hide behind the sofa, a ridiculous move as Zara can't see me. Ben and I took refuge like this whenever the landlord of our first flat knocked on the door. We were starting out and not prompt with the rent. Decency always made me cave in and face the landlord. I won't give in to Zara, though. We're not compatible as friends.

She knocks harder. 'I'm not going anywhere!'

'Stop making such a racket.' Adam's voice is barely audible.

'All sorted,' Zara says, 'As soon as Soph answers.'

'Maybe she's out.' Adam sounds clearer.

'Trust me, she's in.'

'Well, be a bit quieter,' Adam replies. 'Or even better, go back to your flat and wait.'

A door slams. It's likely Adam, exercising his perceived right to make as much noise as he wants.

There's a thump against my door. Something slides down it. I tiptoe across the room and look through the spyhole. Knowing Zara, she's probably given it one last kick before leaving. No one's there. She's finally got the message.

I grab my bag and coat, ready to pop to the shop for milk. Coffee needs to happen soon. Zara has held me captive. Add lack of caffeine to the mix and it makes for a tetchy Sophie. Upon opening the door, Zara tumbles backwards and lies on the floor.

'What on Earth are you doing?' I ask as she tries to stand.

'I'm staging a sit-in.'

Zara slaps her backside to brush off the dust. Claiming my space as her own again, she struts into the flat.

'Please leave. I've nothing to say to you.'

Zara laces her hands behind her neck as she gets comfortable on the sofa. 'But I have plenty to tell you. Starting with how you've got a stalker. I know who they are.' Her feet thump on the table. 'Do you have any painkillers? This headache is a banger.'

'I'm not surprised after how you behaved last night. Do you mind? I'll lose my deposit if you damage the furniture.'

I push her legs off the coffee table and check for stiletto scratches.

'Got your fighting claws out, Soph?'

'Only friends are allowed to call me, Soph.'

She raises her shoulders. 'Look, I'm sorry for abandoning you in Cheeky's and leaving you with Rory.'

Needing to get this over with, I sit in the armchair. 'Just tell me what you have to say about my alleged stalker.'

Zara assesses her surroundings. 'Bit dingy in here, ain't it? Bekstar must be one of those minimalists. I've got some fab flashing flamingo fairy lights you could put up. They'd look a right treat in that corner.'

'I'd rather keep it the way it is. After all, it's not my flat.'

She sniffs. 'I'm only trying to be friendly. You'd do worse than me for a mate. Be careful who you trust around here. I made the same mistake when I moved in and I'm still paying the price.'

'What happened?' I ask, chiding myself for sounding enthusiastic.

Zara smiles. 'Doesn't matter. Let's focus on you. Why do you trust Tobias?'

'Is this your way of saying you believe he's stalking me?'

She replies with a raised, razor-sharp eyebrow. The slugs have undergone a recent shaping process.

'Oh, come on.' Despite my own doubts, I feel a need to defend the man. 'Tobias follows people because in his mind it makes sense. He believes he's protecting them.'

'Has he fooled you into thinking he's got legitimate issues too?'

'Anyone can tell Tobias is different. There's nothing wrong with it.'

'Louise thought so, too. Look where she is; dead. You're next.' Zara yanks me up from the chair. 'I see you won't believe me until I show you.'

'Show me what?'

'Evidence of how Tobias stalks people.' Zara aims for the door, swinging her backside. 'Tobias has been stalking me, too. It has to stop.'

I dart in front of her. 'You're not seriously considering confronting him?'

'Of course not.'

'Good, because we need to talk about this rationally—'

'He's out. I checked before I came here. Let's hope he's not returned while we've been chatting.'

'Why?' I ask, even though I can guess the answer.

'I'm going to show you the secret room in Tobias' flat. Prepare to have your mind blown.'

CHAPTER 64
Sophie

Despite my protests, we're in Tobias' flat. I'm here to defend him. Zara wouldn't listen to reason. She's the type who refuses to understand anyone who isn't what she considers the "norm". I couldn't bear the thought of her violating Tobias' home.

Now we're here, I realise my mistake. If someone invaded my private space, I'd lose it. Tobias will be gutted if he finds out what I did. We've begun a friendship. Friends don't snoop on each other. Still, remembering him following me last night and dragging me into an alleyway makes me wonder.

While going up the stairs, Zara said she'd swiped the key from Adam when she went to his home with a fake emergency. She's proud of how she stole the key when he was making a drink.

While Zara marches around Tobias' flat, I follow with more stealthy treads. The B-movies posters make me smile. My geeky Ben would love this. Painted figures fill a display cabinet. Washes and intricate detailing denote a talented painter. The miniatures are organised into factions, along with name cards. This is my husband's idea of paradise. Invading someone's privacy is his notion of hell. The thought of Ben's disappointment twists in my stomach.

'Let's go.' I say. 'This isn't right.'

THE WATCHER

'Stop looking at those stupid toys. Focus on why we're here. I'm not leaving until you've seen it.'

I'll go along with Zara's mission for now. Even if I leave, she'll stay here. I imagine her taking photos of Tobias' belongings and mocking him on social media. At least if I'm here, I can stop that from happening.

Arrogance makes Zara bold as her heels tap on the floorboards. She's lucky we're above Una's old flat, so no one can hear below. The Gallos are next door, though. I've already told Zara several times to whisper.

'Keep it down.' She has the audacity to hiss at me as I trip over a cable.

The stench of bleach overpowers the flat. My eyes water at its potency. Zara heads straight for her target and produces another key to open the bedroom door.

'Where did you get that from?' I ask.

From what I've seen of my flat and of Tobias' so far, none of the rooms have keys. He must have installed the lock. This alone shouldn't be damning. If I had a meddling mother like Nancy, I'd lock things away, too.

Zara grins. 'A friend of mine came up here to get a copy of the bedroom key. It wasn't easy as Tobias always has it. My friend took an imprint while Tobias was in the shower. I had a copy cut.'

I head for the front door. 'You've taken this too far. I'm not being part of this anymore.'

She pulls me back. 'You won't want to miss this.' She flings open the unlocked door. 'Ta da! There is your evidence. Tobias is an obsessed nutter.'

Zara pushes me ahead of her into the room. There's no bed or any furniture lending to a domestic setting. Tall shelving covers the wall space and teems with notebooks. At a glance, each book appears to be the same. I smile at the notion of Tobias bulk buying the books. The quirks are endless.

I scan the room until my eyes settle on one thing. Terror renders me unable to do anything but stare.

Photographs cover a cork noticeboard. Every photo is of me. Above the collage, Tobias has pinned a handwritten note: *Target: Sophie Walters.*

CHAPTER 65
The Watcher

It's a thing of beauty to witness Sophie's horror. I wonder if she's ever sketched self-portraits. Her face is malleable, like clay. The way her expression shoots from contemplation to distress is something I've never witnessed.

Sometimes a watcher has to be seen for the next part of the plan to happen. Watchers will reveal parts of themselves if it benefits observation. Professional watchers adapt if discovered. When it happened to me, I used it to my advantage. If the moment of capture seems imminent, I escape. No project is wasted, though. I always leave a few mementoes. Residents receive notes detailing their secrets, crimes, and assignations. Not seeing their reactions to my final reveals is frustrating, but the lure of a new project helps in moving on.

Sophie's widened eyes cannot comprehend the shrine dedicated to her. A board of photographs display her trips to the beach, walking home from Cheeky's, and going to the shops. As she scans the gallery, Sophie's mouth opens and closes. Palpable confusion makes her mute. A hint of hurt lines her forehead. The skin of my bottom lip splits in retaliation at my over stretched smile. I lick the blood away.

The photographs are a testament to the observer's prowess. They've captured Sophie's essence, from cheeky smirks to a furrowed brow. Already, she's made an impact on Harmony House's residents, one in particular.

Tobias can't get enough of Sophie.

CHAPTER 66
Sophie

Despite the horror of a voyeur's collection dedicated to me, it's difficult to turn away. This is the product of a twisted mind. Why is Tobias preoccupied with me?

I was naïve to consider him as a potential friend. Many times I've defended him from others' judgement. I was so fixated on fitting in I became blind to what was happening. Soon after I arrived, Tobias hid behind my car to spy on me. The signs were there from the start.

'We have to get out of here!' I say to Zara. 'Tobias might turn up and I feel sick.'

Zara holds out an arm. 'Just a minute. You're not the only one he's stalking.' She leads me over to the shelves.

The notebooks are labelled with the residents' names on the spines. People who've lived here longer are the subjects of several books. I flick through one on Adam. Notes on his routines, likes, dislikes, and habits fill the pages. Other books on Una and Aurora are similar. The scrawl is hard to read in places, hinting at a chaotic mind.

My instinct for discovery demands satisfaction. I select one of the books based on Louise. This one's different. Tobias has added photos of her to the reports. They're like those he has of me on the noticeboard, caught in everyday life. Does he fixate on the women who live in my flat? Maybe he did this to Bekstar, too. Indignation rises. I came to Southbourne for refuge. How dare Tobias threaten it!

'Let's go,' I say. 'He could come home any minute.'

Zara fumbles with locking the door. 'I didn't know he took it this far. The bloke I got to sneak in here had a peek around when Tobias was in the shower. My mate saw photos of a woman matching your description, but he didn't mention this other stuff. This is some messed-up shit.'

'Hurry up!' I whisper.

A key turns in the front door. Tobias is home.

We rush to the only hiding place. The space between the back of the sofa and the wall is narrower than I expected. An exposed tack in the sofa's lining catches my hip. With her long limbs, Zara is also struggling. She shoves up against me as we hold on to each other for balance.

After Tobias shuts the door, I hear clicking sounds. He must be using the antibacterial dispenser. Footsteps sound across the lounge. He halts. I remind myself to breathe, but do it quietly. Under the gap between the floor and the bottom of the sofa, Tobias' feet appear. Waiting to be discovered, I close my eyes. Zara talons prick my bicep.

Tobias straightens a picture frame hanging on the wall to the right of the sofa. He lingers. I wait for him to expose us. He coughs and then walks away.

Cupboard doors creak open and slam shut. Chinking and clattering crockery and cutlery signifies food preparation. We could be here for a while. Perhaps we can slink out while he's in the kitchen. I shift to crouching on all fours. Working out my intentions, Zara shakes her head. She points towards the second bedroom. The key she used lies on the floor outside. In our urgency to hide, Zara dropped it.

The beginning of the microwave's cycle heralds another obstacle. The meal won't take long. It's time to think, move, and act. I'm closer to the bedroom than the front door. There's only one option: grab the key, hide, and hope Tobias goes out again.

THE WATCHER

As much as I want this to end, measured shuffles make less noise than darting. The tension of each movement is more excruciating than the unforgiving floorboards. I glimpse over my shoulder. There's no furniture in the middle of the room offering cover. I'm a slow-moving target. Worrying won't help. I must focus. The shining prize of the key glints.

Almost there. Got it. The key in my palm is like holding hope. I turn around to return to my hiding place.

Tobias coughs again. I freeze. Water from the kitchen taps gushes into the sink. I'm safe for now.

Zara's overenthusiastic hands beckon me to the safety of hiding. The space feels narrower. As I reach into the gap, the key drops from my hand, striking the wooden floor. Clanging echoes around the flat. Zara teeters on her heels and then falls onto her backside. She makes a hell of a thud as she hits the floor. Meerkat fashion, I bob my head over the top of the sofa. Hopefully, Tobias hasn't heard anything over the sound of rushing water.

The tap stops flowing. The microwave didn't ping.

'Why are you in my flat?'

CHAPTER 67
Sophie

Zara stumbles as she ejects from behind the sofa. She lands upon Tobias and sinks her nails into his face.

'Run!' Zara shouts. 'Call the police.'

I can't do it. She may not be likeable, but I won't leave her with this strange man. I know the pain of betrayal from what Tobias has done to me.

'Back off,' I say to him, brandishing the first thing to hand. A remote control won't save my life.

Zara's the female version of a crazed Edward Scissorhands. Later, she'll be wailing about broken fingernails. She sweeps Tobias' leg, and he crashes to the floor. He clenches his fists while remaining on the floor. Despite what he's done, I can't watch him being attacked.

'Come over here, Zara,' I say, injecting fake confidence into my tone. 'We're leaving. Don't you dare try to stop us.'

I aim the remote at Tobias, as if it can pause him into place. Clutching a spray bottle, he rises to kneel in the centre of the room. This isn't what I've envisaged stalkers doing, but it's not like I've had much experience of them. I need to expect the unexpected.

'Come on.' Zara shakes my arm. 'Let's get out of here.'

THE WATCHER

Tobias lowers his head. 'You've been in my home. It'll never be clean again.'

I notice the bleach label on the bottle he's holding.

'What are you doing with that?' I ask. 'Don't even think of spraying it at us.'

'I'd never do that.' His mouth drops open. 'I have this because I need it.'

The prevalent chlorine odour in the flat suddenly makes sense. I recognise a compulsion. How can I forget the fertility predictors and pregnancy tests that led to me coming to Southbourne?

'This isn't the time for cleaning tips.' Zara's nostrils flare. 'He should be explaining the contents of that room.'

'I'd never hurt anyone. They're only photos and notes.'

'You're a sick and twisted weirdo,' Zara blasts.

Tobias' shoulders tremor. 'I want to keep you all safe. I need to know where the residents are. If I don't, you'll die, just like she did.'

'See?' Zara flings her arms up. 'He's killed a woman, probably Louise. Shift your arse, Soph. You're next!'

Despite my reservations, I can't leave. This isn't as straightforward as she believes. She doesn't care enough to want to know Tobias' reasons. My justice-seeking instinct kicks in. He has one chance to explain himself.

'Who died?' I ask.

'My sister. It was my fault.'

'What happened to her?'

Zara lingers in the doorway. 'I'm not sticking around here listening to how he murdered his sister.'

'I didn't kill her.' Pain tinges his words. 'They pronounced it an accident, but if I'd been with Fiona, she would've lived.'

'Go on,' I say. 'Tell your story, but don't you dare lie to me again.'

Zara pulls the door open and bobs her head like a tennis spectator as she looks inside and out. She's not leaving, though. Her gossip-seeking need is still strong.

'Fiona was my younger sister. I loved her so much.'

Tobias stands and moves towards us.

'I'm warning you.' Zara raises her hands in a defensive stance.

He reaches for a frame, standing on a unit, and then offers it to me.

'This is Fiona.'

In the photo, a sandy-haired girl beams, not only in her smile but her entire demeanour. Her arms are locked around a boy I recognise as Tobias. It's sad to notice the younger version has a relaxed air the older one lacks. I recall the habit of dragging his shoes along the pavements. Regret and sorrow anchor him.

To look at the photo, Zara risks leaving her perceived place of safety.

'Wow, your haircuts haven't improved.'

He ignores the barb and takes the photograph from me. 'We were on a camping holiday. Fiona enjoyed swimming in the lake. Mother said not to go in without her or Father, as it was deeper than it appeared. Even though she was only eight, Fiona was rebellious. Despite me being older, I admired her. She stood up to Mother, whereas I couldn't. One night, Fiona sneaked out of her tent. Mother and Father were asleep, but I was awake, reading. I followed Fiona at a distance, thinking she was heading for the toilet block. Letting her go alone was out of the question, but I didn't get too near. It's not right to linger around ladies' toilets.'

Tobias tugs on his fringe as if it can conceal his blushing.

'It's the least of the strange things you've done,' Zara replies, fixing him with a flinty glare.

'For once, try to listen,' I say.

'Well, excuse me for existing.'

She slumps against the wall with a sulk plastered on her face.

Tobias continues. 'Fiona headed for the lake. When I called out, she darted through the woods. I couldn't keep up. My legs felt heavy and then I tripped over a tree root. It went a bit fuzzy for a while, longer than I had to spare.

'At the lake, Fiona had disappeared. Her shoes and nightdress were on the ground. The calmness of the water was eerie considering how it had consumed my sister.'

THE WATCHER

'What happened after you got to the lake?' Asking feels harsh, but he seems to need to let it all out.

'I couldn't save her.' Tobias hugs himself. 'I swam to the bottom, but there was too much area to cover.'

Zara comes closer. 'Was she found?'

The gossip queen can't resist drama.

'Yes,' he mumbles and then clears his throat. 'Police divers found Fiona's body at dawn. It was almost poetic, although as the sun rose, my heart plummeted. Mother still blames me. She says if I'd protected Fiona by making her stay in the tent, my sister would be alive.'

'Is this why you take photos and make notes on people?' I ask.

'I only took photos of Louise and you.'

'It doesn't make it any better!' Zara shouts. 'Some of those books are about me. I want one of them to see what's in it.'

'It won't help matters. He isn't going to hurt you.'

'I'd like to see him try,' she replies. 'I can handle myself.'

Tobias wipes his wet cheeks. 'There's nothing nasty or wrong in the books. They're only observations. I need to be sure everyone's safe. No one must ever die again because I wasn't looking.'

I have to ask a specific question that's been bugging me. 'Why do you have photos of Louise and me, but not the other residents?'

'Louise was a great friend. We're friends too, aren't we?'

I join Tobias, who's sitting cross-legged on the floor.

'We can be, but we need to discuss boundaries; yours and mine. I'm not comfortable with someone following me, taking photos, and writing notes on me. This has to stop. Do you understand?'

'Yes.' He looks at me. 'I'd never want to make you feel unsafe.'

'Let's work on a healthier friendship. Can I hug you?'

'No.' He flinches. 'But you may hold my hand. I like that. Fiona used to do it.'

I clasp his offered hand.

'What the hell are you doing?' Zara stamps her foot. 'One sob story and you believe he's innocent? Tobias probably made it all up. You saw the evidence. Ask him why it's behind a locked door if he's got nothing to hide.'

'It's a fair question,' I say to Tobias. 'You need to explain.'

'When I lived with Mother, she found my notes on the neighbours. She forced me to see the family doctor. He prescribed pills that made me sleepy, and I couldn't think properly.'

He smacks the side of his head with his free hand. I take it in mine, so I'm holding both.

'Did you lock the room so your mum won't make you go to the doctor again?' I ask.

'Mother will demand I return home if she finds out.'

'She won't know about this,' I say.

Zara marches over to us. 'Are you out of your tiny mind? This isn't normal.'

'Maybe not,' I reply, 'but define *normal*. Is it getting wasted every night? Is it judging others because they don't live up to your shallow standards?'

She inspects her damaged nails. 'Low blow. I thought we were mates.'

'After the way you treated me last night and Tobias today, it's obvious you and I will never be friends.'

'Your loss.'

'Not really.' Despite my annoyance, I muster compassion. 'I don't hate you. We're just different. I want to get along with you while I'm living here.'

'We'll see,' Zara huffs. 'He will pay for this.' She points at Tobias.

'I understand you're scared,' I begin, 'but there's no need. Don't go to the police. You've heard why he's like this and he promises not to do it again, right?'

Tobias looks up. 'Absolutely. Never ever.'

Zara prepares to leave. 'I won't get the police involved. I could do without them sniffing around here.' She turns towards us. 'Consider yourself lucky you got away with this, Tobias. I'll be watching your every move. You'll get what's coming to you.'

CHAPTER 68

Sophie

After leaving Tobias' flat, I called Emma. Ben isn't an option. In defiance of me ignoring his messages, Ben's gone silent. A marriage of two stubborn people can be hard work sometimes. An awkward breaking-the-ice phone call is coming next. I may be pig-headed, but I love my husband and hate not hearing from or seeing him.

'Please stop pacing,' Emma says, her furrowed brow evident on the screen. 'The camera bouncing all over your flat is making me dizzy.'

I sit on the sofa. 'This is hard to process. I'm right, though, in believing Tobias isn't a deranged stalker?'

'From what you've said about him, it sounds like he's taken the protection thing too far. He's been literal in needing to keep an eye on you by taking notes and photos. The bloke only wants to be your friend.'

'Zara doesn't view it that way,' I practically spit the words out. 'I'm worried she'll make Tobias' life difficult.'

'Lucky he's got you, then. I know how scrappy you can be when your mates are in trouble.'

'It must have taken Tobias ages to write so much on the residents,' I say. 'From flicking through a few books, I saw they are full of info. Reading Louise's could've been useful to find out more about her.'

'You should've nabbed one of the books when he wasn't looking.'

'It won't help with getting Tobias to trust me.'

Emma's smile drops. 'I'm concerned about how much has happened since you moved in there. Do you reckon it's time to come home?'

'No!' My alarm is unexpected. 'I'm determined not to give in. All my life I've been running scared of something, either because of anxiety or a situation. Now I want to be brave. I've relied on Ben and you for too long. After the miscarriage, I lost sight of who I really am. In a strange way, being here is helping me. Every time I come up against an issue, I'm discovering strength I didn't know I had. Perhaps I'm a masochist, wanting to deal with the stuff going on here. Do you understand why I have to stay a bit longer?'

She taps a pen against her chin. 'I'm strangely proud while also considering smacking some sense into you.'

'The dead woman who lived here, dead woman next door, pervy neighbour, feisty Italians, grumpy warden, shy old lady, spoiled princess, and a bloke who keeps tabs on the residents won't deter me.'

We laugh at my attempt at humour, both of us inevitably masking our fears. A sneeze blasts outside. The front door is ajar. In my haste to get back and speak to Emma, I must have left it open.

'Where are you going?' she asks. 'Are you taking me on a tour around Southbourne? About time I saw the area. Being stuck at home is giving me serious cabin fever.'

'No tour today.' I look into the hallway. No one's there.

I close the door behind me. Feeling exposed makes me push it to check it's shut. Surely Adam has learned his lesson about eavesdropping on people's phone calls?

'Did you hear a noise?' I ask.

'Sounded like a sneeze,' Emma replies, 'although it was distant. It's probably one of the residents going out.'

'Maybe.'

I don't add how the main door didn't open or close. Nobody went out. Someone was listening outside.

CHAPTER 69

The Watcher

Claustrophobic clouds roll away as if knowing they cannot linger above me. A gust pushes against my body, signalling the impending storm in the sky and inside me. The walk from Harmony House to Hengistbury Head is a prelude to unleashing my demons. I mumble my misgivings along the residential roads. Upon approaching Southbourne beach, my fists continuously clench and unfurl. I stamp along the winding heathland of Hengistbury Head.

Warren Hill places me on high. At the most elevated point of the Head, I loom above the beach, savouring the panoramic view of Christchurch harbour. Lights from the boats swerve rather than their usual gentle bobbing. The water does the storm's will. Belonging washes over me like the sea crashing below. The first time I took the steps towards the hill, I knew I was entering my domain.

The coastguards' lookout building and I are eyes scanning the coast. Our similarities end here. The lookout seeks to alleviate jeopardy. I create it. The usual walkers and tourists are long gone. When the night steals the view of the green landscape and a rolling path, they want no part of this. Fools. Hengistbury Head comes alive at night.

THE WATCHER

The vicious sea ravages the shore. My torch trains upon raven waves, devouring pebbles and drawing them into the sea's gut. The crashing below re-energises me, like a drum leading this soldier into battle. I am ready.

The sky electrifies. Spreading out my arms, I dare the lightning to infuse a spark within me. I am Frankenstein's creation, breaking free of the one who created me. I'm rewriting the rules.

Rumbling thunder greets my rage. I had to leave Harmony House and seek this refuge. When I saw Zara and Sophie's infiltration of Tobias' second bedroom, I imagined hurting them. Their eyes and hands have sullied the perfection of observation.

As the women raided work spent noting others' foibles, I could've wept. I didn't. Emotions complicate business. I can't remember the last time I shed a tear. If I did, it was for effect.

Tobias' notebooks are a masterclass in recording. A brilliant mind deciphered the minutiae and pivotal moments of the tenants' lives. Whenever I regarded the observation library, its brilliance gave me chills. The oddities benefit his role as a man who captures everything. Polite people turn away from him, believing it's rude to focus on a person who's discernibly different. Tobias is adept at using this. Veering from the norm meant he could observe without detection.

Until now.

Tobias will adapt to the infiltration of his works. His dazzling mind will search for another, grander idea. Am I Tobias standing on a hill, fighting murderous impulses? Should I tell you and await the epic fallout? Sophie, if you become The Listener, your trusting heart will break if I'm him. Gullible people need to learn the consequences of their kindness.

No. I'll leave you to work it out, Sophie. You deserve to remain oblivious for a while longer. Know this, though, no matter where Tobias is, he's always watching. Soon he'll move on to the next stage. I have insider knowledge. Watch this space.

CHAPTER 70
Sophie

'And so ends the story of my disastrous night in Bournemouth's "Cheekiest Nightclub".'

Despite his earlier irritation upon picking up my video call, Ben laughs. I gave him the highlights of my evening at Cheeky's, missing out Tobias following me and how he's convinced someone else was, too. While I need to be more honest with my husband, we've just made up. I'd rather keep things settled for now.

He fiddles with his wedding ring. 'I'm really sorry about having a go at you for being in a club. I'd had a shit day at work and then I couldn't get hold of you for a chat. I overreacted.'

'It's okay. You've apologised enough. I was a dick for not calling you back sooner. My stubbornness set in. If it helps, I didn't want to be there. I'm ashamed to say it, but I was feeling lonely and thought going out might help.'

'Sounds like it turned into a bit of a nightmare. Stay away from Rory.' Ben's clenched fists support his chin. 'I don't like the sound of him at all.'

'I'm giving Rory a wide berth. If he tries to touch me again, his arse will be severely kicked.'

Ben's throaty chuckle makes my body ache with longing.

'That's my Soph.'

THE WATCHER

'Am I still yours?'

'Always.' His hands unclench. 'While you want me, I won't let go.'

Talking is hard work when you're trying not to bawl. 'I didn't leave you. I left the situation we were in for a bit. We need to consider what we want regarding a… baby.'

'I can tell you're not there yet.' Ben sometimes knows me better than I know myself. 'Take the time you need. Whatever you decide, I'm here. If you want a child, I want it, too. I tried to spare you the pain of going through each month, not getting pregnant. Seeing your hurt broke me, too.'

'I'm sorry I didn't consider how this affected you. This is only temporary. Soon, I'll be home.' My tears flow and I let it happen.

'I'll be waiting.'

* * *

After talking to Ben, I went to bed early. My pillow is soaked from where I cried myself to sleep, but it's the least of my concerns. Sobs break through the walls. For once, I'm not the one crying.

A sound I once longed for drills into my ear and hammers at my soul. The injustice of it is destroying. This isn't mine to hear. The unmistakable sound of a baby's wails tug at the place in my heart I've tried to close off. None of the residents have children. The contract stipulates they're not allowed. I thought it strange but attributed it to the owners being anti-kids. Pets are allowed, though. I guess cats and dogs don't doodle on walls or answer back.

The infant's intermittent cries taunt me. Whenever it ceases, I've dared to close my eyes. Determined to resurrect my loss, the bawling begins again. I wonder who's looking after a baby. Nobody in Harmony House seems a valid option, but someone's babysitting.

An anguished cry hits me hard. I may never hear something like this in my own home. Can I live without a child?

I place the pillow over my head, trying to smother regrets and flimsy hopes.

CHAPTER 71

The Watcher

Watching Sophie's fitful sleep was enlightening. I've seen her whimsical sketches of the imagined child she was denied. Maybe she believes art can create reality. It stirred something inside me. Not empathy. Never that. Her pictures remind me of how we're all trying to overcome obstacles.

Even in my youth I learned to surmount barriers. When I was eight years old, I took an overdose. My parents dressed it up as a childish error. Painkillers were passed off as a child mistaking them for sweets. My parents made people think I was stupid enough to make such a mistake.

I didn't want to die. What a waste of this life that would've been. The overdose was my parents' punishment. You're probably horrified at a child having such guile. I've always been cleverer than expected. Even at the age of eight, I knew what dosage would alarm others but not be fatal. My parents had failed me, and everyone needed to know. The appropriate services got involved, concerned for my welfare. My parents learned never to underestimate me. Their apathetic looks shifted to wariness. I won. They dared to put me into therapy a few times. It came off worse for them when I made "allegations" about parental abuse.

Art is Sophie's therapy.

Watching is mine.

THE WATCHER

We crave the visual to make sense of this uncertain world. Sophie manipulates her pencil. I control what's on the screen and use it to my advantage. She must learn to be more controlled, too. Her defences are crumbling. Despite shows of bravado, anxiety is winning. A baby's cries are a cruel trick, but she needs the test. How does she react to horrendous situations? Sophie faced Una's corpse and doubts regarding Louise's death. The results aren't always pleasing.

I relish more nights of Sophie wrestling with nightmares of a child that never was echoed by the evil lurking within Harmony House. It creeps through the cracks, climbs through the keyholes, and glides into gaps.

You'll never escape it, Sophie. You'll never escape from me.

CHAPTER 72
Sophie

No more. It's the third night in a row of the baby crying. This has to stop.

I listen at Una's door. Even though she's gone, I still refer to it as her flat. Now, Una's home is alive. The evidence travels through the front door. How did a child get in?

My options are:
• I'm going mad.
• A baby crawled into a locked property and took up residence.
• Someone's abandoned a child.
• A squatter is in there with their infant.

Fatigue demands I sit at the bottom of the stairs, leading to the first-floor flats. In a release of suppressed grief, I join the crying child. Powerful sobs feel like they're bruising my chest. Whenever I believe I have no mourning left, it rises like a bubbling volcano.

Delicate steps come from behind me on the stairs. Iris passes and stands in front of me. The porch light filters through her winceyette nightgown. Beneath, the outline of her body reveals she's in good shape. She isn't as frail as many assume, although the mind can be fragile. I should know. Aware Iris doesn't realise what she's revealing, I look away.

She joins me on the step. 'Why are you crying, dear?'

I weep on her shoulder. The kindness highlights the caring mother I lack and the mother I'm not.

'I can't take it any longer! Someone has to help the baby next door.'

'What baby?'

'Can't you hear it?'

On cue, the child's sobs increase.

'Hear what?'

I go to Una's door. The stinging of my slapping hands against it increases. 'There's a baby inside. It cries every night, and nobody helps. We need to rescue it.'

'There isn't anyone in there, dear.' Iris leads me back to the step.

'There is! There is!'

A key turns. Across the hall, Zara leans out of her doorway. 'Shut the hell up! I've just got to sleep.'

'Can you hear a baby crying?' I ask, aware I'm sounding more crazed by the minute.

'All I can hear is you two having a chat on the stairs at stupid o'clock.'

Zara gives us a hard stare before slamming the door.

Wrapped in a dressing gown, Adam comes out of his home. 'What's going on? Is it an emergency?'

Dragging hands down his face, highlights his bleary eyes.

Iris hugs herself. Perhaps she realises how exposing her nightwear is.

I rush to the warden. 'Please unlock Una's flat. A baby's inside. It might be hurt.'

He sighs. 'No one's in that flat. We haven't got a new tenant sorted out yet.'

'Can't you hear it either?'

'No.' He tightens the cord around his waist. 'For goodness' sake, go back to bed.'

Sod's Law makes the baby silent.

'It was crying.' I need them to believe me. Knowing I must sound unhinged, I try to control my voice. 'A child's been bawling for the last few nights. There might be a squatter in the flat.'

'A baby broke in?' Adam smirks. 'Smart kid.'

'You know what I mean. Maybe the squatter has a child.'

'No one gets into this building without the key code. Did you hear anything?' Adam asks Iris.

'No, I didn't,' she mutters, concentrating on looking at her scarlet toenails.

'You have to check.' My volume's rising.

Adam turns towards his flat. 'You're overtired. Get some sleep.'

'If you won't go in, I will.' I aim my foot at the door.

'Stop!' he shouts. 'You're making a habit of trying to break that door down. Wait while I get my ruddy keys.'

After Adam unlocks the door, he and Iris negotiate the rooms at a leisurely pace. I dart around Una's home, flicking on lights. I try not to visualise her body previously lying on the floor. Saving the child is all that matters. I cast aside a duvet, throws, and cushions, searching for a hidden baby. Nothing. Desperation makes me move furniture and fling open drawers and the wardrobe. Nothing. The last place I look, an empty bath, forces an acceptance. The baby isn't real.

'No sign of anyone squatting in here.' Adam doesn't disguise his annoyance.

Iris places a gentle hand on my arm and leads me outside.

She whispers in my ear, 'Try to sleep, sweetheart.' Watching her leave, I wish she hadn't let go.

Adam faces me. 'I'm not angry. Remember, I understand how difficult anxiety can be. I apologise for being abrupt. Unfortunately, this is me when I'm tired.'

'Sorry to have woken you.' I can hardly speak. My mouth is dry. Must I accept I'm having a relapse?

He places his hands on my shoulders. 'It's a blip. You've made a huge move coming here and you're fighting the past. Don't do it alone. Maybe pay the doctor a visit and see if they can help?'

'Okay,' I reply, weary already at stepping back on the mental illness referral treadmill. 'Thanks.'

I leave Adam, watching me return to my flat. After closing the door, I slide to the floor. I'm not doing as well as I thought.

CHAPTER 73
Sophie

'The GP offered to put me on a list for counselling,' I say to Ben on the phone. 'Apparently, it'll take a while to happen.'

'It boils my piss how mental health services are getting worse, not better.'

His irritation is justified. He's been through the system with me enough times to be frustrated.

'Anyway,' I begin, knowing he'll rant if I don't interrupt, 'the GP said I've got to register here.'

The sound of Ben's sigh hurts my ear through the phone.

'Is this your way of telling me you're not coming back?' he asks.

'No! I've gone on the counselling list in Oxfordshire. All my life I've run away from things. We both know it's true. Coming here was initially me avoiding things, but now I know it's a chance for me to see something through. I can practically hear my parents saying, "I told you so" from Australia if I came home now.'

'Stuff them. They don't matter.'

'Years of never feeling good enough are hard to undo,' I add, 'but I focus on you because you're the only person who matters. Much as I want to be with you, I have to lay the Harmony House issues to rest. This place won't break me. It's supposed to be a refuge. I must let it be that for me. Southbourne still has so much to offer, particularly for my painting. There's a new author who's setting their book by the sea and the publisher has commissioned me for the cover. It feels like fate is telling me to stay here for now. I will come home to you as planned. Life without you in it isn't a life at all.'

'You can't imagine how relieved I am,' he replies. 'We'll pay for counselling if we need to. All I want is for you to be safe and well. Is it wise to stay there on your own? I can join you.'

I smile, although he can't tell. Video-calling wasn't an option. I resemble something a Victorian grave robber would offer as a specimen.

'This new, more stubborn Sophie needs to see things through, alone.'

'Yikes. Could you get more stubborn?' He laughs.

I affect a giggle that sounds pathetic even to my ears. 'Don't worry about me. I'll be all right. The GP's increased my meds. I may be a little foggy for a while, but I have other therapies here: the beach; new locations to explore; my art; and making friends with some of the residents.'

I told Ben about hearing the baby crying. He was concerned, but gentle with it. This far along the mental illness road, I know I shouldn't feel embarrassed, but I do. Supporting others, I try to be a mental health warrior. Sometimes, though, I have to focus on myself and receive help. The prospect of having auditory hallucinations is terrifying. I'm not ready to accept it. The baby sounded so real. My mind has never created noises or visions.

Ben brings me back to the moment. 'Okay. I can be there whenever you need. Work will understand. Promise to call me if you want me to come.'

'I will. Let me get things straight and then I'll be home for good soon.'

CHAPTER 74
The Watcher

Sophie's mental illness is something I can play with. It's a precarious but fascinating territory. Tipping her too far over the edge will end the chance to be my listener. For what I have in store, she must be fairly robust. You're probably questioning why I haven't chosen someone who's unencumbered by mental affliction. Where's the challenge in that? Anyway, "normal" is overrated. Often those who break free of "the norm" are the victors.

After an enforced psychological assessment, I challenged the psychiatrist to define me. She offered a set of labels, diagnoses, and words taken from a textbook: psychopathic tendencies and narcissistic traits. I asserted not everyone fits into the boxes people are desperate to put them in to. It's a cliché to portray those who don't follow the moral line as mentally ill. Often, we're the most resilient. We have to be. Always one step ahead, we're constantly thinking and assessing.

My psychiatrist suggested I take part in a study. The Watcher was to be the watched! I am not a chimp in a cage, waiting to be poked and prodded into action. The psychiatrist had to pay for her audacity.

For a while, I observed her outside the office. Every coffee sipped, shop visited, and drive home came under my radar. For an educated woman, it took far too long for her to detect my scrutiny. When she finally looked over both shoulders as she ate lunch in the park, I was jubilant. The person who dared to confine me deserved to feel afraid. The weight of the disinterested stare while she totted up how much money she was making from our sessions had to be wiped away. It was the pat on my knee that broke me. No one treats me like a dog. Passive observance tipped over into rage. I forgot myself, but none of us are perfect. A person with diplomas on their wall from a second-rate university isn't allowed to define me. She's in no fit state to practice ever again. Job done.

Contacts are useful. I was grateful for the help I received in cleaning up after the psychiatrist's "accident". She can still walk, which is a bonus. I didn't get my hands dirty to exact revenge. There's always someone willing to do it for you, at the right price. I'm rarely susceptible to anger. If you find those hidden switches and press them, though, I explode.

I won't allow emotions to come into my relationship with The Listener. This is merely a transaction. Sophie can't evoke what cannot be there. She won't find a semblance of sensibility. Instead, I will dissect her. My listener must be taken apart to be made whole. Their brain will receive directives to take my recordings to the police.

When I am finished with you, your heart and mind will be mine.

CHAPTER 75
Louise's Diary

The sound will break me. I remember a horror film where a baby's cries were used as torture. Headphones were glued to the victim's ears. She broke down. I fear I will, too. For the past three nights, I've heard a woman crying, as if she's in pain. The sounds are guttural, almost animalistic. They seem to come from outside my window, but whenever I look, the person disappears.

The first time I tried to ignore it. Maybe a couple had a row and a boozed-up person lagged behind. Despite not being in town or directly by the sea, the pub up the road is a popular haunt. We've all had a heavy drinking session and behaved irrationally, me more than most. I attributed the histrionics outside Harmony House to a silly drunken moment and eventually drifted off to sleep.

Yesterday, it started again. Why does she cry outside this building? I understand this place can give someone plenty to weep about. Goodness knows I've shed many tears here, but she can't be a resident. Can't the woman cry in her own home? Why must she unleash her woes on Gull Lane and then vanish whenever I try to help?

Tobias' mother insisted he visit for her birthday. Despite being at the back of the building upstairs, I know Tobias would've heard it if he were here. Nothing gets past him. Tobias

THE WATCHER

often patrols the building and outside. I asked some of the tenants this morning if they'd heard anything. None of them had. The concern for my mental health didn't go unnoticed. I'm aware of what they think of me. Frowns, tilted eyebrows, and pitying expressions are all I receive. Their concerns are mounting. I'm trying not to give anyone a reason to doubt me.

Last night, I tried again to help the distressed female, right after the cries began. I'm surprised Adam wasn't out there, making her move along. He usually does with stray drunks sitting on the front wall. Did Adam mention being away this week? I'm so tired I can't remember. Yes, that's it. He's visiting his sister.

When I went outside, once again, she wasn't there. I looked along the street; empty. Unless the woman lives nearby and can sprint like an athlete, she vanished.

Now she's back. Or so I thought.

After a day of dealing with irate customers, I was desperate for an early night. At the precipice of slumber, the crying began. The wailing woman returned. Determined to find her, I didn't even put on a jacket.

After flinging open the door, I dashed outside, ready to confront or soothe. Once again, there was nobody there. I went back to bed and prayed for it to be over. God and I were done years ago, but I'll take what help I can get.

The moment my head hit the pillow; the crying began. I need to leave here as soon as possible. The madness is consuming me. I'll join the invisible woman in tears. At least I'm capable of that.

CHAPTER 76
Sophie

Another of Louise's diary entries came through my letterbox. It's the scariest yet. Am I repeating Louise's life? I'm in her flat and she heard noises at night, too.

The sender of the copied diary left an ominous note.

Living here will destroy you. Learn from Louise's mistakes. Get out while you can.

The sting of Adam's scorching tea revives me from disturbing thoughts. I made myself face him after the embarrassment of waking him up, trying to find a non-existent baby.

He notices me puffing out the heat. 'Sorry. I keep forgetting. Here.' He pours milk into my mug.

'Thanks for everything,' I say, 'especially about the baby crying thing. I'm so embarrassed.'

I've decided not to tell Adam about Louise's diary. It could be him who's sending the entries to me. He's already confessed to becoming obsessive about Louise. After discovering Tobias' secret room, I'm learning to be more cautious around people in Harmony House. It's hard when you're trying to fit in as well.

'Don't be ashamed,' Adam replies. 'Takes one to know one, right?' He selects a biscuit and raises it to his mouth. Assessing the custard cream, he puts it back on the plate. 'I'm supposed to be cutting down.' He pats his belly. 'Look, not many are privy to this and I'd rather you kept it to yourself. I had hallucinations after my wife died. I thought I saw her sitting in that very chair, in our old house.'

Despite myself, I shift around, trying not to squash Tina's ghost.

'The doctor thinks I'm overwrought,' I begin. 'He might be right. I've had a miscarriage, moved away, left my husband behind, and strange things have been happening here.'

'Like what, apart from Una's death, which was sadly understandable?'

'How Zara behaves, Rory's full-on, and Tobias makes me concerned.'

'It's your mothering instinct.' He winces. 'Sorry, that's crass, given what you've told me.'

'Don't worry. I've realised I should talk about it more. The amount of people who treat miscarriages as taboo doesn't help. I've accepted Ben and I aren't to blame. It happened. Now we need to grieve and recover.'

'Sounds like you're already on your way.'

His smile confirms there's more than the gruff warden persona he exudes. He's also a father and once a husband. People care about him. Still, did Adam send the diary entries and notes? Why would he want me out of Harmony House?

He continues. 'Talking of Tobias, you won't like this. He's gone.'

Unable to hold the mug due to my shaking hand, I place it on the table. 'Why and where?'

Adam scratches his cheek. 'It's all so confusing. Tobias came here to explain he might have to leave. Truth be told, he was nervous, but I put it down to his character. He kept repeating how he needed to protect himself now instead of others.'

'I don't like the sound of that.'

'Neither did I. I asked what he meant, but he wouldn't say. As usual, Tobias didn't look at me, but he seemed more edgy. Next day I went to check on him and the flat door was open. All his stuff was still in there. He'd left a letter on the kitchen side.'

He takes a piece of paper from a folder marked with Tobias' name. The warden has a dossier for each tenant. I remember seeing mine when I arrived. It's probably admin, but it feels somewhat violating. What's in my folder? Adam hands me a typed letter.

Dear Adam,

It is with regret that I must leave these premises and return to Mother. I understand I've not given notice and therefore the landlord will keep my deposit. I'll arrange for my belongings to be collected in due course.

Yours regretfully,

Tobias.

I wave the paper in my hand. 'None of this makes sense. Why didn't Tobias give you the letter rather than leaving it in his flat? He wouldn't return to his mum. Nancy's a nightmare. Tobias wouldn't leave the door unlocked, either. His routines were fastidious. Did you check the bedroom nearest the lounge?'

'Yes. Compared to the rest of the place, it was sparse. There's lots of shelving but nothing on them. Frankly, I'm annoyed Tobias didn't clear the flat out. His deposit will be docked accordingly.'

'Did you see any notebooks or a photo board?' I ask.

'No,' Adam replies. 'Why?'

Concern for Tobias' safety renders me mute.

CHAPTER 77
Sophie

Tobias is still on my mind. I can't figure out why he'd leave. I thought we'd worked things out after he caught Zara and me in his home. Maybe the sense of betrayal became unbearable. The idea of Tobias leaving because of what I did is upsetting. Zara treated him appallingly too, but was it enough to make him go? Perhaps the shame of the secret room being discovered made Tobias run away.

I wish my mind was clearer to decipher what's happened. I'm trying to catch-up on sleepless nights because of an imaginary crying baby. Now I'm being kept awake worrying about Tobias. I miss having an ally and can't help feeling uneasy regarding his disappearance. It's another mysterious event in Harmony House. What is it with this place?

My muddled thoughts are interrupted by a knock on the door. After opening it, a man greets me with a megawatt smile.

'Hello there,' he says.

'Er, hi.'

His sparkling white teeth are dentist approved. To add to the groomed image, his hair's sleek and he boasts a beard so neat a ruler could've set the edges. Despite the manual labour clothes of a stained checked shirt and torn jeans, this is a man who takes care of himself.

Never one to miss an opportunity to be seen, Zara enters the main entrance from outside.

'Hiya, handsome.' She blows a kiss to the man. 'How's it hanging?'

That bloody donkey laugh will make me commit murder.

'Stop it.' He flashes a sparkling grin. 'I'll have you done for sexual harassment.'

'Too late for that.' Zara winks at him. 'All right, Soph?'

I won't bite at Zara emphasising the shortening of my name. 'Great, thanks.'

Zara juts out a hip, always ready to strike a pose. Madonna's "Vogue" video has nothing on Zara's posturing.

'Really?' She exaggerates the word. 'I heard you were having issues after your night-time breakdown.' She loops a finger in a circle by the side of her head.

'I'm absolutely fine and not crazy.'

I won't rise to the bitchy bait by speaking to her any longer. Instead, I turn to my visitor.

'How can I help you?'

Zara slinks away into her flat. The building shudders with the slamming of the door.

The man smirks. 'Quite the prima donna, isn't she? Zara's harmless, though. Anyway, I'm here because Dad says your boiler needs checking. Not a good time of year for it not to work properly.'

'Who's your dad?'

'Adam.' He points to the warden's flat. 'I'm Neil. Dad gets me to do maintenance around here sometimes. This is me.' He holds up an identity card.

After looking at the photo, I open the door wider. 'You'd better come in then.'

CHAPTER 78
The Watcher

With Tobias off the scene, it may seem like the observation has ended. This isn't the case. Watchers never quit. It's in the blood.

Harmony House is full of observers. The residents claim they're minding their own business, but I see them looking at me, looking at them. Watching is a wormhole of which I must be mindful. When The Watcher is being watched, it leads to close calls.

Once again, I observe Sophie. I have to learn everything to assess her worthiness. For now, having her in a foggy state of mind suits my purpose. Only for a while, though. The Listener can't exist in a permanent stupor. My work deserves the best.

Sophie barely glanced at Neil's ID card. Be careful of who you let in, Sophie, you're still trusting people before you know their full story. Check who you're inviting into your home, although sometimes you don't have a choice.

Evil always finds a way in.

CHAPTER 79

Sophie

'Ow!'

I rush into the kitchen. Rubbing his head, Neil leans over the counter.

'Are you all right?' I ask, trying to assess the damage.

'Occupational hazard. I caught my head on the edge of the cupboard door.' He looks up. 'I'm always bumping into things. Dad says I've got a concrete skull.'

Neil whistles in air as he touches the gash on his forehead.

'I should've closed it.'

I wonder if I left the cupboard open, but I haven't been in the kitchen for a while. Was Neil looking for something? Maybe he's thirsty and was searching for a glass.

'Best you sit down,' I instruct. 'You're bleeding a little. Are you feeling dizzy?' I offer a tea towel.

'No, I'm fine.' He checks the blood flow after pressing the towel against it. 'It's only a scratch. Bump on the noggin might knock some sense into me.'

'If you're sure? I can't have you passing out.'

He chuckles. 'I wouldn't be the first to die in here.'

I wince.

'My bad,' he says. 'I've been working on a building site recently. The inappropriate blokey banter sticks. I apologise.'

THE WATCHER

'Would you like a drink?'

'Coffee, please, if you're making one. I've finished with the boiler. It's fine.'

After switching the kettle on, I lead the way into the lounge.

'Take a seat.'

As Neil walks past, I catch a whiff of his aftershave. It's the same one Ben uses. My husband's absence steals my breath along with the wave of a familiar scent.

'Are you okay?' Neil asks as he sits. 'You look upset all of a sudden.'

'Just a bit knackered and missing my husband.'

'Where is he? Dad said you live alone.'

'He's back in Oxfordshire. I'm flat sitting. We'll be together again soon.'

The force of the need to put him off surprises me. I'm rusty in the ways of flirting. The last time someone showed an interest in me was at a youth club; the man I'd eventually marry.

'How are you finding being here?'

Neil leans back and lays a foot on his opposite knee.

Where do I start? Oh, you know, the usual. I'm ecstatic at living with the metaphorical ghost of a deceased woman, Una's dead too, Tobias has disappeared, Rory gives me the creeps, Zara's hard work, and your dad's difficult to figure out. Apart from that, everything's fine.

Instead, I reply, 'Southbourne is a nice area and the flat's great.'

'I sense a *but* coming.'

He offers another dazzling smile. I'm tempted to ask if he's seen the episode of *Friends* where Ross's whitened teeth were fluorescent. Note to self: do not draw the curtains to test if Neil's teeth light up in the dark.

'Everything's fine. I'm happy to be here.'

Stoic Sophie puts on a brave face. I'm getting better at this.

'Are you freaked out about what happened to Louise?'

Despite not knowing him, Neil's concern seems somewhat contrived.

'A little.' Caution loads the sentence. He's Adam's son, but it doesn't mean I should trust him. 'Not every day you move into a place where there's been a death.'

'True. Louise was nice. Dad said he told you how he watched over her.'

I try to keep my face impassive. 'Adam explained why. He's obviously still grieving for your mum.'

Neil blushes. 'Finding out Dad was watching Louise was awful. When he realised it had become too much, Dad confessed. Louise's death hit him hard. He felt like he was losing Mum all over again. Dad and I argued about it.'

'Why?'

'Dad couldn't understand why I wasn't devastated by Louise's death.'

'Why should you be? It's terrible for Adam how she resembled your mum, but why would you be affected?'

'Didn't Dad tell you? Louise and I dated for a while.'

The kettle boiled a while ago but making coffee is forgotten. Processing Neil's relationship with Louise demands all my attention. The connections between people around here are getting complicated.

'You look surprised,' Neil says. 'It's no biggie. Louise and I were a casual thing that didn't last long. When Dad said she resembled Mum in her younger years, it became weird for me. I'd never noticed it until Dad showed me a particular photo of Mum. Dating the double of your mother is far too Freudian for my liking.'

Despite visible discomfort, he attempts a laugh.

'It's a little awkward,' I reply. 'I expect Adam found your relationship odd.'

'He kept trying to put me off her. When Dad finally explained why, it made sense. Not that it mattered. Louise and I weren't going anywhere.'

'Why?' I pull my legs in underneath me on the sofa.

'She was seeing someone else. It appeared to be a love thing, at least on her part.'

'Weren't you jealous or angry? Sorry, that's a personal question.'

'Don't apologise. I'm enjoying chatting with you.'

A dimple forms in his cheek. This one's a charmer but hopefully not of the Rory school of smarm.

Neil continues. 'Sad to say, but I wasn't surprised Louise died. Her life was a mess. Death seemed inevitable. Where's that cuppa? I'm gasping.'

I go to the kitchen, mulling over his words. Why was Louise's death inevitable?

CHAPTER 80
The Watcher

Sophie, you're right to frown at Neil and his observations on Louise. That man knows more than he's telling.

Sure, he's an obedient son who regularly checks on his father. Neil always seems concerned at Adam's convoluted grieving process. Ever the apparently decent man, Neil spends hours with his father, rifling through photo albums, sharing nostalgic moments, and anecdotes. Sunday afternoons are lost in repetitive nostalgia.

The toil of raking up the past shows on Neil's face. Not once has he left Adam's home without shaking his head. He raises his shoulders and then relaxes them before leaving Harmony House. This has become a routine for shedding the burden of Adam's grief. Tina is dead. Life marches on and Neil wants to live it to the fullest.

He's inherited Tina's vigour and extroverted nature; often in the pub, ready to get a round in. The men from the building site are guaranteed a raucous evening in his company. Bar staff look forward to having a chat, particularly the females. The shining smile is a beacon to incite interest.

Many elderly people applaud Neil's kindness. Southbourne's community praises the jobs he does for the needy while never taking a penny. You'll hear in the local shops conversations about his latest act of altruism. The Southbourne Facebook group extols his virtues. He often gets groceries for the infirm and fixes issues within their homes. I swear they'll have a statue of him on the Grove after he dies. He charms with his seeming goodness.

Don't be fooled, Sophie, by the grin and swagger. Chip away and discover the secret Neil hides under the friendliness. No one is ever that virtuous or nice. Often, those who perform public acts of kindness are the most heinous of beings. Don't expect me to show you Neil's involvement in Harmony House's watching. Prove yourself worthy. Find out the truth. Your life depends on it.

CHAPTER 81

Sophie

I haven't spoken to Iris since the night I imagined a baby crying. Shame made me avoid her. No more. I'm not my illness. I'm not Louise. It's a spooky fluke we both heard things. Although, mine was a baby and Louise's was a woman. It's not the same. But why did I get the specific diary entry about what Louise kept hearing? Coincidence, or is someone watching me?

'Are you okay, dear?' Iris asks.

'I'm all right. A little tired, that's all.'

She settles into the chair and pulls a crocheted blanket over her legs. Mismatched squares compete in a riot of gaudy colours.

'Bitter outside.' She gives a shiver. 'My morning walk was a quick one today. The sea breeze felt like it was burning my lungs. I did a workout here instead.'

'I'm glad Neil checked my boiler.'

'Lovely fella. Devoted to Adam. Neil can't do enough for people. He's such a loyal lad.'

I consider my parents and how they value loyalty; receiving not giving. Their devotion to me is non-existent. Growing up, I was told anxiety was a made-up thing in my mind. I wasn't allowed to see a doctor because I'd be labelled "mad" and then the neighbours would know. When my parents moved to Australia, it was the best gift they ever gave me.

THE WATCHER

'Deep in contemplation,' Iris says. 'Not worrying, I hope.'

'I'm ashamed of the fuss I made the other night. You know, about the baby business. I'm so sorry for behaving like that.'

Iris clicks her tongue against the roof of her mouth. 'Forget it, love. We all go through trying times. Good to hear you've been to the GP.'

'How do you know I went?'

'Adam mentioned it when I asked after you. I didn't want to pester you with questions until you were ready to talk.'

I touch her hand. Despite the stifling temperature from the heater, she feels cool. I look at her hand, noting years of toil settled into liver-spotted skin.

'You're so kind to me.' I say. 'Thank you.'

Iris holds up her hands to inspect them. 'Having green fingers is hard graft. I adore tending to the back garden here. It's a vast space, but it gives me so much joy. Adam says he'll employ gardeners, but I'm not having it. The gardens are my territory. Whenever Adam tries to pay me, I refuse. Pleasure is its own reward. You should see my roses in full bloom.'

I'll be back with my husband by then. An image of my garden in Oxford, with wildflowers bursting forth in the summer, makes me smile. Feeling homesick brings me a little closer to Ben.

'How about some more biscuits?' Iris suggests. 'I love these. Shame they go straight to my hips.'

'Nonsense. There's not a scrap of fat on you, not that it's an issue if there was.'

'I try to keep trim.'

'That explains the dumbbells.' I point to the weights on the floor.

'The doctor says I need to do a little strengthening to support my muscles and bones. They're only little weights, though.'

'Make sure you don't overdo it.' I stand. 'A treat every now and again does you good, too. I'll get the biscuits. You look so cosy.'

'Thank you, dear. You're an absolute treasure.'

A knock sounds at the door.

'I'll answer it, seeing as I'm already up,' I say.

A slip of paper lies on the bristled mat. After picking up the note, I check if the messenger's outside. The upstairs landing is empty.

Shutting the door, I hold the paper. The large handwriting is difficult to ignore.

Dearest Iris. Stop snooping around. I've warned you many times. Stay out of my business or you'll get hurt. This is your last chance.

Although I don't want her to see it, I can't lie. After reading the note, Iris blanches.

'Can you get me some water, please?'

In the kitchen, I take a glass from the draining board. Above the sink, a piece of embroidery states, *Beauty is in the eye of the beholder.* Blood-red roses border the quote.

Iris glugs the water from the glass I've brought. The shock is getting to her. She needs my help.

'Who on Earth would send you a poisonous note?' I ask.

'I don't know.' Her voice trembles. She raises the blanket to her chin. 'This is terrible, just terrible.'

'Maybe it's a prank, although a nasty one.'

'No, it isn't.' She throws the blanket aside, goes to the collection of lever arch files, and selects one. 'Look at these.'

I open the folder. It's full of notes telling Iris to stop looking into deaths in Harmony House, cease watching, and threatening to do her harm.

She hides her face in her hands as I sift through the litany of written abuse.

'You must report this,' I say. 'It's an offence and you have a right to feel safe in your home.'

'I didn't want it to come to that. If the police are involved, I might get hurt. It must be a resident or someone who knows the code to the main door.'

'That's why we have to do something. The police will protect you.' I flick through the pages and then drop them. 'Damn, I've put my fingerprints all over these. I expect you have, too.'

'You see?' Her shrillness could crack glass. 'There isn't any evidence. What can I do?'

THE WATCHER

I hold one of the letters with the cuff of my jumper. It may be futile, but I'm trying.

'I'll go with you to the police,' I reply. 'Best we go to the station. Then, if the letter writer lives here, they won't see the police speaking to us.' I check the clock. It's getting late. 'We'll go first thing tomorrow, unless you'd rather do it straight away?'

Iris rubs her eyes. 'All this drama has worn me out. Besides, I'm not a fan of going out at night. Thank you, though. I don't know what I'd do without your support.'

I scan a letter, trying to commit the details to memory.

'Shall I stay here tonight?' I ask. 'I don't mind.'

'Not to worry, dear. I'll be fine. There are several locks on the door.'

Fort Knox has nothing on Iris' security measures. No one is getting into this flat uninvited, apart from vicious notes.

* * *

Outside my flat is an enormous hamper. I look around, wondering if Adam has left it outside the wrong door. The note reads: *To Sophie, Thanks so much for looking after my flat. It's so good to know someone reliable is keeping an eye on my home. You're a star! Best wishes, Bekstar.*

Shame rises at how I've considered leaving. Bekstar is relying on me. Adam might be the warden, but I'm not sure how diligent he is. Would he bother checking on the flat if it's empty?

After placing the basket of goodies on a table, I concentrate on what I came back here for, rather than worrying about letting Bekstar down. I wade through discarded clothing on the bedroom floor, scolding myself for reverting to teenage ways. Where can it be? Think. Please don't have put it in the bin, or even worse, the wash.

I rummage in the pockets of my jeans. There it is; a note in the same handwriting as that of Iris' vicious penfriend. When I looked at the file full of the letters with a fat *o* dotting every *i*, something pinged in my mind.

Here's the note asking me on a date. Rory is Iris' letter writer. He's afraid of being exposed by her for something he's done. How far will Rory go to guard his secrets?

CHAPTER 82
Sophie

It's a new day and one where Rory will be arrested. Iris and I will make sure of it.

Despite the revelation of his hateful letters, I slept better than expected. For the first time since my arrival, I didn't wake once. Maybe the increase in my usual medication is taking effect. Perhaps knowing Rory will be punished brings calmness.

Stanley was my alarm this morning. The cunning bird knows if he taps on the window with his beak, he gets breakfast. Tobias told me not to feed him, as I'll never get a quiet moment. I'm a sucker for any animal. Whenever we share my toast, it feels like we're bonding. The bird was initially hard to please in his choice of toppings. After some trial and error, I've been trained to only ever spread unsalted butter and strawberry jam on Stanley's toast. Tobias warned me once you let him into your life, the gull will take over. Thinking of Tobias hurts. Even Stanley seems more subdued since our friend has gone. Yes, seagulls have feelings too.

Upstairs, I give Iris' door a faint knock. It's early, but going to the police as soon as possible is for the best. Aware Rory lives next door, I make the knocking soft.

'Iris,' I whisper through the letterbox. 'It's Sophie. Please open up.'

As if wishing someone won't appear creates reverse magic, Rory peeks out of his doorway. 'That's what I like to see, a woman on her knees.'

I stand to face him and give my best "don't mess with me" expression.

'Have you seen Iris?'

Despite not wanting to talk to him, Rory's the most likely to know where she is. After all, he's been watching her.

'Why are you asking about her?' Tension dominates his voice.

Don't let him know he's in trouble. Play nice. Rory will be punished soon.

'You're Iris' neighbour. Being nosey goes with the territory, right?'

Rory sticks a leg out. His dressing gown parts to reveal a lack of underwear. As I turn away, he blasts out laughter.

'Seen something you like?'

He pulls the garment further from his crotch.

'I've seen more meat in a veggie burger,' I say, mustering the confidence to walk past him.

Aware of Rory's staring, I take bold strides back to the safety of my flat.

CHAPTER 83
Sophie

Disturbed by Emma's grunts damaging my ears, I put the call on speakerphone.

'What the hell are you doing?' I ask. 'There's a lot of huffing and puffing going on. Wait a minute, you're not—'

'No,' she says. 'Phoning you when I'm having a shag is plain wrong. Besides, I haven't got the energy. I'm trying to put my jeans on after living in nightwear for ages.'

'Shall I phone later?'

'No way. I live for your gossip right now. Denim is overrated and impossible to get into when you're feeling as weak as a kitten. I'm sticking with my trusty PJs.'

'You're not going out, anyway.'

I pop a chocolate into my mouth and savour it before I fill her in on what happened last night.

'I'm concerned about Iris now,' I say. 'We agreed to go to the police station today and now she's not answering her door.'

'Maybe she's backed out.'

'Perhaps, but she could've said so rather than ignoring me.'

'Iris is a sweet old lady who's scared. Perhaps she's embarrassed you're involved. From what you've said, she has quite a stash of those notes. It sounds like she wasn't going to do anything about it until you saw them.'

I cram in more chocolate, chewing fast so I can reply. 'Meanwhile, Rory's getting away with it. I can't go to the police without the notes he sent, but I won't give up on this.'

'Are you eating something nice?' Emma asks.

'Guilty.'

'I've hardly eaten and am existing on liquids. Don't torture me with your chomping.'

Chocolate flakes land on my jeans as I laugh. 'You can't see what I'm eating, unless you want me to video call and show off this massive box of chocolates Bekstar sent in a hamper.'

'Ooh, you tease.' Emma lets out a long groan. 'That was good of her to send you a gift.'

'It made me feel a bit guilty as I was thinking about leaving sooner. I can't go now Bekstar's sent me that and a note showing her gratitude for me being here. Anyway, back to Iris. Do you think something's happened to her?'

'Not all the old ladies in Harmony House snuff it. You live in Southbourne, not the Bronx. Your imagination's more vivid than mine. Although I'm seriously considering using what's happening there in a crime novel. Reality sounds even wilder than my fantasy novels.'

'You'd better credit me in the acknowledgements. I'm actually living this shit.'

'I'll dedicate the book to my nutty, anxiety-ridden, neurotic but perfect friend, Sophie.'

Only Emma and Ben are allowed to take the mickey out of my anxiety. They've earned the right, considering how long they've supported me. Black humour is our coping strategy.

'Right.' I slap a hand on my thigh, pantomime style. 'That's it. Rory will get what's coming to him. If I have to drag Iris to the police station, so be it.'

'Expose the bastard. Oh, and Soph.'

'Yes.'

'Keep away from Rory. He sounds dangerous.'

CHAPTER 84
The Watcher

Rory tunes out as the person on the end of the line speaks. He laces his fingers behind his head and leans back, focusing on the ceiling.

'You forget how accomplished I am in spotting women's fear,' he says. 'I could see it in Sophie's eyes. She knows something about me. The fake bravado didn't fool me.'

Rory won't allow others to underestimate him. He's aware of his lothario image and uses it to his advantage. Then he hams it up some more. Those who despise it look away, the perfect reaction for a man who has much to hide. Women who like a playboy are drawn in.

The leather of the office chair squeaks as it sticks to his thighs. He favours nudity in his home. Even in private, Rory puts on a show. Privacy is a privilege not given to everyone, not when he's involved.

'Keep out of it.' His words snap through the telephone line.

While listening to the caller's irate response, he clicks on a folder on the computer. The corner of his mouth lifts.

'You know what will happen if Sophie goes to the police,' he says.

Rory moves the receiver from his ear. He changes the setting to speakerphone so he can type on the keyboard.

'Don't forget, I can take you down,' the caller yells. 'With everything I have on you, they'll throw away the key when you're banged up.'

'Hear this?' He turns up the volume on his computer. 'It's the sound of your end. Remember, I have my own evidence. Keep quiet, do as you're told, and nobody will get hurt, including Sophie.'

Rory ends the call and shuts down the computer. He's an expert in bringing things to a close.

CHAPTER 85
Sophie

What started as a heated conversation outside my flat has escalated. Dissatisfied mumblings switched to yelling. Once again, I question where Adam is when his intervention is needed.

I'm confronted by Federico and Zara snarling at each other when I open the door. Aurora holds the stair railing, watching and cowering.

'Everything all right?' I ask, cringing at my meekness.

Zara throws her hands on her hips. I resist asking if she wants to add a pelvic thrust and do the "Time Warp".

'No, it bloody isn't all right,' she shouts. 'This perv tried it on with me. I'm not having it.'

Federico laughs with gusto. 'I wouldn't touch you if you were the last woman alive. Why would I want a thing like you when I have her?' He points to Aurora. She lowers her head. A smile creeps from her mouth.

Zara jabs the air with a pointed finger. 'Explain why you followed me all the way from the corner shop. I clocked you checking out my arse.'

'It's the only route back to this building from there. Isn't a man allowed to walk behind a woman?' Federico advances towards Zara.

She shoves him away. He stumbles backwards from the force of the push.

'Don't you dare touch me!' Zara yells. 'I'm not some pathetic bird you can hit. Just because you knock your missus around doesn't mean you can land one on me.'

Aurora darts upstairs and slams their apartment door.

'Nicely done, you two,' I say. 'You've upset Aurora. Let's get this sorted. Federico, were you following Zara?'

Fire travels into his cheeks, burning scarlet. 'No! I was simply coming back from the beach after my run. I never spoke to that woman, let alone tried to seduce her.'

'Yeah, but you wanted to,' Zara adds. 'I could see it in your eyes.'

Federico's nostrils flare. I mustn't let this situation escalate.

I turn to Zara. 'Come in and have a cuppa with me.'

She fans tears away with a fluttering hand.

'Thanks, babes. I could do with something for the trauma of dealing with him.' Zara points an accusing finger at Federico.

He looks at me. An indecipherable hurt replaces the earlier anger. I usher Zara inside and close the door on the confusing man from upstairs.

Inside my flat, Zara makes herself comfortable once again.

'Do you really think Federico hits Aurora?' I ask.

'Obvious, isn't it?'

Zara kicks her legs up and dangles them over the arm of the sofa.

'Haven't you considered intervening?'

'None of my business.'

She extends her fingers to check her fingernails. Silver glitter shimmers in the light.

I resolve to speak to Aurora alone. No one else will help her around here. My disappointment with the residents increases. Every day I'm closer to leaving Harmony House.

'Have you seen Iris recently?' I ask, hoping my guest might prove useful elsewhere.

'That old bird? Why are you bothered about her?'

THE WATCHER

Pouting into a compact mirror, Zara applies a fresh coat of lip gloss.

'She's a nice lady, actually. Don't be so spiteful.'

Zara snaps the mirror shut.

'You're getting mouthier. It makes you more interesting than the weak little woman who left her husband because of feeling defeated.'

'Just answer the question. Have you seen Iris?'

'Yes.' She swings her legs around and holds out a foot towards me. 'Do you like my new shoes? Thought I'd treat myself.'

I rub the heel of my hand against my forehead. The Spanish Inquisition must have been easier than getting a straight answer out of this diva.

'Your shoes are lovely. Focus. When did you see Iris?'

'Crafty old bird did a moonlight flit. She was carrying loads of bags, so I asked if she was going on holiday.'

'What did she say?'

Zara rubs a thumb over the sharp toe point of her shoe. I've never witnessed such love for a material item.

'What did Iris say?'

I'm bordering on shaking her to activate her brain.

'Calm down, babes. I'm trying to remember. When I saw Iris, I was wrecked. It's a bit hazy. Too many voddies does that to a girl.'

'Along with a shit ton of cocaine, I expect.'

'Touché.' She grins. 'This new catty Soph is fab. Keep 'em coming, hun. A bitch fest is always fun.'

I swear there'll be another death in this flat if she doesn't answer my question.

'Banter later,' I say. 'Did Iris mention anything that sounded important?'

'I remember her saying it wasn't as nice as a holiday. She said she had to… What was it?'

Those bloody shoes are flying out the window if she doesn't stop caressing them.

'Got it.' She bounces in the chair. 'Iris said she was going on a retreat.' Zara's mouth rises to the left, forming her thinking face. 'Nope, that's not right. You're doing that.'

I hold my tongue between my teeth to prevent it from lashing out in frustration.

'Now I remember.' Zara nods. 'Iris said she was making a retreat because she needed to hide.'

'What from?'

'Silly cow said someone was trying to kill her.'

CHAPTER 86
The Watcher

Sophie's interrogation skills are improving. Zara didn't make it easy, but Sophie proved a more than equal adversary. Sophie's learning to ask questions and not be satisfied with the initial answers. She's looking behind face values and finally listening. If I was the cheerleading type, I'd applaud her progress. Sending the hamper and note, pretending they were from Bekstar was a good move. I had a feeling Sophie is too polite to leave after receiving such a kind gesture. People are weird. They will stay in an uncomfortable situation just because someone sends a thank you note and a few luxury food items. Still, it's helped my agenda as Zara could have put Sophie off from staying with her talk about Iris leaving.

Zara plays the stereotypical ditzy Essex girl, but she's cleverer than she appears. She could have gone to Oxford or Cambridge, but the University of Life had more to offer. She learned how to make others do her bidding. The girl from Chigwell made good.

Men give Zara the eye and she looks back, assessing her prey. Marilyn Monroe is her hero. She emulates Marilyn, working her body to get what she wants while concealing an astute mind. Zara enjoys hitting those who underestimate her intellect with brilliance.

Few know her IQ equals Tobias'. This makes him a threat. Tobias wasn't fooled by her heavy make-up, miniskirts, and boosted cleavage. He recognised a clever and controlling mind. As the saying goes, it takes one to know one. Zara had to expose him.

Bluffing Sophie by asking her to look at what Tobias had written on Zara in the notebooks was genius. Sophie's moral compass wouldn't win over curiosity. She's a pushover for a sob story. It's something we need to work on. Tobias' dead sister was the perfect distraction from the tome of Zara's secrets. She can at least thank Tobias for having a troubled past.

Burning pages curl before dropping into the sink. Handwriting is obliterated by voracious flames. Zara smirks at the disintegration. Destroying Tobias' books of observations on Zara fuels her fire of self-preservation. They are gone. So is Tobias.

Zara slaps her hands together; job done. Now she has other things - people included - to get rid of.

CHAPTER 87
Louise's Diary

I can't keep having the same arguments. Whenever we do, another decent part of me disappears. Since we met, he always takes. All he's given me is heartache and low self-esteem. Why don't I ever learn? After enduring years of being physically abused, I found the courage to leave Karl. Now I've substituted one cruel man for another. Except this one's a charmer who messes with my head.

To a degree, I knew Karl was prone to anger soon after we met. His mother warned me to stay away. I attributed it to an inability to cut the apron strings. It turns out she was warning me Karl was the same as his father; a violent bully. I thought I could save my husband, believing the love of a good woman had the power to bring change. How does an intelligent woman become such an idiot around men?

Even when my husband bust my lip open on our wedding day, I covered for him. The clumsy bride had tripped over the hem of her dress. I grimaced throughout the speeches as my "drunkenness" became the butt of others' jokes. Watching the wedding video always made my stomach clench. As friends and family roared with laughter, the camera caught me trying to force a smile against a bleeding mouth.

My mother remarked on my carelessness and gave tips on how to remove blood from lace. I'd have preferred advice on how to get an abuser out of my life. She'd never have believed it, though. To everyone who met him, the sun shone out of Karl's proverbial. Such men have a knack. They adopt an act of chivalry to mask their savagery. These are the kind of people we're shocked to discover are monsters. Tabloids are full of cautionary tales, but still no one takes heed, least of all me.

Another snake akin to the one in the Garden of Eden has charmed his way in. He's never hit me. It's no less dangerous than Karl using me as a punchbag. In fact, it's more terrifying. Spiteful words stay in the mind longer than cuts and bruises remain on the body.

Tonight, I made the mistake of asking him once again to be faithful. He laughed. To my shame, I'm the one who fought this time. Slapping hands and unleashing futile anger are far removed from my usual control. He stood there and grinned, relishing the effect he has on me. Trying to wipe the smugness away, I attacked him. It wouldn't do. He needs his face, along with the patter, to get women into bed. My shoulders protested as he locked my arms behind my back. Then he released me, pushed me to the floor, and left. To him I am litter; damaged and useless.

I'm still here, lying on the rug, wondering if I'll ever rise again. Humiliation has brought me low. This must end. I'll take him down, too. I know how to do it.

CHAPTER 88
Sophie

Rory's flat is tidier than I expected. I visualised a den of depravity littered with debauchery. Discarded wine bottles, the stale stench of a man, and takeaway cartons all contributed to my imaginary scene. It seems Rory isn't the cliché I anticipated. To underestimate him is a mistake. It makes sense his flat is in order. The polished wooden floor, straightened cushions on the sofa, and automatic air freshener pumping out scent are probably part of an act. No self-respecting woman wants to be in the home of a slovenly pig.

I'm not sure whether to thank Neil or wish I hadn't seen him. Adam asked Neil to check a problem with Rory's toilet. When I bumped into Neil in the building's entrance, I took the opportunity he offered to join him in Rory's flat to continue our chat. After Iris previously vouched for Neil as a decent man, I figured I'd be fairly safe. Still, I'm continuing to be cautious about the people I meet. Neil being in another room while I figure him out is wise. I have my mobile with me, and Neil has left the front door open, probably to make me feel more at ease.

'It's obvious you're having a nose around here,' Neil says.

'Not at all.' I'm rubbish at affecting nonchalance. My words sound strangled.

'Really?' Neil raises an eyebrow.

I raise my hands. 'Okay, you've rumbled me. I'm bored and fancied snooping around my neighbour's gaff.'

Neil lugs a toolbox towards the bathroom. 'Off you go then, but don't tell Rory I let you in. It'll be our secret.' He gives me a wink before leaving.

I can't figure Neil out. He seems like a pleasant bloke, full of chatter, and with a kind expression suggesting approachability. There's something about him that makes me a little wary, though. Maybe Neil's too nice. Being in a known playboy's home, alone with a man I don't know, is questionable, but I've had two people vouch for Neil so far. Adam can't stop telling me how wonderful his son is. Parents can have rose-tinted perspectives when it comes to their offspring, though.

Neil knows where he stands with me. I'm not leading him on. Mentioning Ben regularly and how much I'm missing him should be enough of a signal. Apart from Emma, I tend to make friends easier with men than women. It's not a conscious choice. I guess I'm still a tomboy at heart who wants to play with the boys, platonically, of course.

Now I'm here, I might as well see what I can discover about Rory and do my best for Louise. After reading the latest diary entry, once again put through my letterbox, I'm convinced she referred to Rory. It could've been the night he lost his cufflink. Louise knew something that would expose him. This is my chance to find it. I'm also here for Iris. Since she's gone and has taken the notes with her, I must gather evidence of Rory's wrongdoings.

The sender of Louise's diary added another message to the latest extract. Their hatred is increasing. I look at the newest note after releasing it from burning a hateful hole in my pocket.

Read this and weep. I've heard you cry along with an imaginary baby. Despite what you think, you're pathetic and weak. Louise thought she was strong, too. She was wrong. Harmony House will break you, like it did with Louise. Go home.

The writer of the note didn't figure on my stubbornness. Never confuse my empathic heart with weakness. I'm even more determined to stay here and prove I'm an equal adversary. Being in Rory's home is a metaphorical up yours to the person who's trying to force me out.

How long does it take to fix a toilet? Neil seems competent, so it will probably be quick. I head for the computer in the corner of the lounge. Most of our private lives are stored on our PCs, from social media to documents. Let's hope Rory's security is non-existent. His PC is an old model, trying to do new things, rather like its owner. A dying fern slopes on the desk towards the keyboard. As I start the computer, my sleeve catches on the plant. Crisp brown fronds sprinkle everywhere while I try to reposition it. The password screen appears. Please be predictable, Rory. I type *Sexy*. I'm in.

From the bathroom, Neil swears. Hopefully, this means the job will take longer. I check if Rory's on social media. He has a Facebook account. I'll get Emma to friend him so we can discuss what's on there. There isn't time to trawl through. I'm confident he will accept a new female friend to add to the existing multitude.

Think. If you were a sex mad bloke, what would you have on your computer? Porn. It's not exactly damning. Many people watch porn but I have an inkling Rory goes beyond the boundaries. Curiosity leads me to his pictures and videos. I could do with a laugh. Ben and I went to a sex shop once. They threw us out for laughing at the enormous dildos and eye-wincing devices.

Women's names are the titles for video folders. I click on one named *Opal*. A scene begins with a sleepy woman sprawled on a bed. Whenever the man on top of her moves away, her face comes into view. Opal's detached, but perhaps that's her thing.

I open the folder for *Gabrielle*. Lying on a black silk sheet, a woman drapes her arms above her head. Her drooping eyelids appear seductive. I feel compromised in witnessing someone's nakedness. I'm ready to click away when a man appears in the shot. He's naked, too. The man turns to the camera and gives the thumbs up signal. Rory.

I'm watching his sex tapes. This changes my perspective in the viewing. Nothing related to Rory is innocent. What I discover here could be the evidence I need to have him arrested.

After zooming in on the woman, I realise she isn't affecting a lazy sexiness. She's semi-conscious. Her head lolls around and she's struggling to prise her eyes open. I've met her. It's Gabrielle, the woman who confronted Rory in the nightclub. She mentioned going to the police. This video must be the reason. Did he drug her? Why hasn't Gabrielle reported it? Perhaps the shame of being on a sex tape is a deterrent. I'd be mortified if my family and friends saw me like that. I turn from the screen, feeling traitorous to another woman for viewing her vulnerability. She must live in torture, wondering if Rory will make this video public. Upon hearing Neil's footsteps, I click the video off and grab my phone.

'Having fun?' Neil asks, appearing behind me.

I type gibberish on my mobile.

'I'm messaging with my husband.'

Neil grabs a tool he'd left on the side. 'I reckon I'll finish this job in about fifteen minutes. Not that you need to know because you're not doing anything you shouldn't. Actually, maybe you should go. Why is the computer on?' His jovial tone becomes more serious.

I give a bright smile to rival Neil's usual, but now absent, pearly white grin.

'I nudged the mouse by accident, and it came on. Don't worry. I'm just sitting here questioning Rory's decor choices. You'll be done soon, anyway. Fancy going for coffee afterwards? There's a café I've discovered that has amazing cakes. Not a date, though, understood?'

Neil rediscovers his smile.

'You're on. Oh, you probably need to get rid of those ferny bits all over you. There's more on you than the plant. You wouldn't want it sprinkling over the keyboard.'

Neil leaves. After brushing off plants determined to stay on my woollen jumper, I turn to the screen. Time isn't on my side. I scan the folders. Louise is there, too.

Bracing myself, I click on one of Louise's videos. There are several. Like the others, Louise is semi-conscious and at Rory's mercy. I can't look any longer. Since I've learned more about her, Louise is a real person to me.

Despite burgeoning sickness, a sense of justice compels me to continue witnessing women's sexual abuse. Near the end of the alphabetical list, I find someone I expected: *Zara*.

It's obvious she's had a fling with Rory in the past, but I won't abide him abusing her. I play the first video.

Zara's wide awake and hard at it with Rory. I fast forward through the others. Zara's fully conscious in all of them. She had a lucky escape, if you can call having sex with a predator lucky.

I'm ready to move on from Zara's videos when a surprise addition appears on the screen. The man's face is hidden. He uses the camera angle to ensure his identity isn't revealed. As he completes the threesome, I notice a tattoo on his forearm. The idiot didn't consider how distinctive the pattern of an eye bordered by roses and thorns is. He was in another video, too, with Gabrielle. Maybe he's an accomplice.

I open a spreadsheet labelled *Payback*. A list of women's names is in one column alongside amounts of money. A cross reference of the names against the videos confirms it's the same women. Gabrielle argued with Rory at Cheeky's about owing him money. She mentioned they weren't consenting adults. He must be blackmailing women with these videos. The sleaze threatens to show them to an audience unless the victims pay up.

'Nearly finished!' Neil calls from the bathroom.

I begin closing the folders. My trembling finger hovers over the mouse upon spotting a specifically named folder. *Sophie*.

CHAPTER 89

The Watcher

Sophie's senses are heightening. Rather than being a disadvantage, anxiety's making her more focused. I will keep an eye on it. She might want to flee. If she stays, my exposure would be detrimental to the project. Sophie can only be a listener if and when I say she's ready. She must earn the position, not take it.

I've mastered the art of observation in high-rise flats, penthouse suites, and everything in between. An amateur won't usurp me. No one will stand in the way, blinkering my view. By whatever means necessary - deceit, violence, even death - I'll see the Harmony House mission through to completion.

Play your part, Sophie, rather than trying to take over. You'll get your chance later to shine. Believe me, it will be glorious. I'm compiling a schedule for us, if you are to be The Listener. More tests of your capability must come first. It's time for you to make or break.

CHAPTER 90
Sophie

The clatter of a tray hitting the table is a welcome distraction from my disturbed thinking. Neil takes the seat opposite me.

'I got you a large slice of chocolate cake. From your expression, I figured you might need it. Are you okay?'

I fiddle with the fork.

'I'm fine, thanks.'

Keeping time with my breathing, I tap the utensil against the plate. Neil scans the café and then steadies my hand.

'Best stop before someone flattens you.'

Across the room, a scowling woman shakes her head. Her deep wrinkles and flat nose resemble a pug. In solidarity, her companion throws a filthy stare at me from over his shoulder. These are the kinds of people desperate to be offended about something. They probably prowl through social media, poised to set everyone straight with their nasty opinions. The clang of my fork as it hits the table irks the judgemental pair.

'Something's up,' Neil says. 'You've been edgy ever since we left Rory's place.'

'What do you know about him?'

'Not much. Bit of a player, acts like he's younger. Walking cliché.'

Neil knocks back an espresso. I take a sip of my latte. The miniature gingerbread man dangling on the rim falls in. There's no danger of him drowning in caffeine. It's more milk than coffee. Ben would've known to ask for a double shot.

'Has Rory ever been in trouble with the police?' I ask.

'What the hell did you see in his flat?'

'Nothing.'

I break off a piece of cake and chew. My mouth needs a distraction. I don't know this man. He seems nice, but can I trust him?

'You weren't on Rory's computer, were you?'

It's Neil's turn to receive disapproving looks. Our judging panel in the corner doesn't approve of raised voices either.

'Of course I didn't go on the computer. What do you reckon I'd find on there if I did?'

'I can't think of anything. It's a huge invasion of privacy, though, looking at someone's PC.' He straightens in his seat. 'Look, Rory's just one of a list of odd people living in that building, including my dad.' The habitual grin reappears. 'You're spoiled for choice in those flats for mysteries and weirdness.'

'So, you also see it? Sometimes I wonder if my imagination's working overtime.'

'You'd have to be blind not to recognise the stuff going on in Harmony House.'

'On that note, do you know Iris?' I ask.

'Yes, although she's so quiet she's easy to forget.'

'Did you hear she's gone away?'

'Dad mentioned it. He wasn't happy, as Iris didn't say when or if she's returning. As long as she keeps paying the rent, Dad says he's not too bothered.'

I consider my next words with caution. 'For a warden, your dad doesn't notice much, does he?'

Neil crosses his arms.

'You'd be surprised at what he sees and hears. Not much gets past him. Dad has misgivings about some tenants, but the landlord only cares about the money. Dad doesn't believe Una's death was just an asthma attack.'

THE WATCHER

'Really?'

Coffee forces its way down my narrowing throat.

'Dad told the police his suspicions, but they didn't take it further. Una would've pulled the security cord if she needed help. She had a fall before and managed to crawl to the cord.'

'I keep wondering why Una didn't pull it.'

'Exactly. Maybe someone stopped her.'

CHAPTER 91
Sophie

'I'm coming home.' Relief wraps me in a soothing hug as I say the words.

'I can't tell you how pleased I am to hear it!' Ben replies. 'I'm stagnating in a stench of self-pity and junk food.'

Sitting in a café with Neil made me realise the scene was all wrong: wrong man and wrong location. Missing my husband has been miserable. I ran away to a false paradise. Harmony House masqueraded as the answer to my problems. Going it alone wasn't the solution, either. Being with my husband is how to work through our problems, not being apart. I was trying to escape from the baby issue between Ben and me. As soon as I saw the details and photos of the building, I fooled myself it was meant to be: an empty flat, near to the beach, with a beguiling name. Who wouldn't believe the fates were smiling on them? The joke was on me.

Stubbornness has kept me here. I wanted to show everyone I could make it alone for once. Running away felt like asserting my independence and leaving my woes behind. I sprinted into trouble, not away from it. All that's happened in this building was a ruse to make me stay longer. Sophie has to fix everything. Sophie can't admit she was wrong and Harmony House isn't paradise. *Ben* is my refuge, not a building or the seaside. I'm better with him because he gives me the freedom to be me.

I don't regret coming to Southbourne. I've enjoyed the scenery and the discoveries, mainly about myself. The time here has shown me how tenacious I can be. Now, I'm starting to like myself. I've faced so much and there's no shame in going home. I won't admit I'm scared, though.

'All I want is you,' I begin. 'If we get pregnant, that's great. If it doesn't happen, we as a couple are enough. From the moment you put your pocket money into the jukebox at youth club and played my favourite songs, I knew you were the one.'

Ben lowers on the screen so only the top of his head is visible.

'You can cry in front of me,' I say.

When he looks up, his eyes are dry.

'I dropped my bacon butty on the floor and didn't want to interrupt this loveliness by picking it up.'

We laugh together as Ben scoops up his sandwich. He inspects it before taking a bite. Bacon is his religion. Nothing will keep him from it.

'I've got some news,' Ben says, while chewing.

'Empty your gob first.'

After swallowing, he opens his mouth. 'All gone. I can come and help you pack. It's why I called. Remember how I told you our Poole branch is in a right state?'

'Yes.'

'Finally, they're going to sort it out. The new finance manager's making a complete balls-up of the job. They've asked me to train him for a few days.'

'That's great!'

'I'm glad you're pleased, as I wasn't sure if I should do it. I didn't want you to think I was stepping on your toes. This is your time away.'

'It's the perfect way to begin the rest of our lives. You can help me move from here back to Oxford.'

'Home,' Ben adds.

'Exactly. I can't wait to be with you.'

'Good, because I'm going to get my stuff together and leave in a bit. I don't want to wait another day.'

'I can't wait to see you.'

Finally, we will be reunited, and I will be free of Harmony House.

CHAPTER 92
The Watcher

Sophie's decision to leave early has forced my observations to their completion. Hours of strategic planning have gone to waste. Do I punish her for this? Maybe I should thank Sophie for pulling me back from the precipice of conceit. Almost being caught before taught me to recognise when a project should end.

Harmony House has served me well. I've watched and interacted when it's required. Secrets, lies, shame, guilt, violence, arguments, and death; this building has offered it all. Now we must part. No regrets or sadness. This building was merely an observational laboratory. Home is wherever the viewing opportunities are.

Watching is my oasis, my shelter. My next post is uncertain, but I have options. I must disappear for a while. No one will miss me. It's a bonus, not a failure. Wherever I go, I'll become part of the landscape. I will belong. No one will question my arrival. I can practically hear the welcomes to the neighbourhood.

Soon, I'll bid you goodbye, Sophie. Keep on the right track. Your leaving confirms you *should* be The Listener. Distance will bring clarity. Back in Oxford, you'll try to leave Harmony House behind. I won't ever let you forget.

CHAPTER 93

Sophie

Knowing my husband will be here soon, my spirits have lifted. It's right to leave. Events in Harmony House forced the move, but it's helped with reassessing my life. This place of great confusion has also given me clarity. I'm ready to be with Ben.

On today's window visit, Stanley wouldn't let me stroke him. I swear that gull knows what's happening. To ease my guilt at leaving, I gave Stanley extra toast. A prime view of bird butt was my reward.

There's someone else I have to say goodbye to. Before I can knock, Aurora opens the door.

'Hello. What brings you here?'

'Wow, you must've been looking out for me,' I say.

She points to the spyhole. 'I often check outside. You can never be too careful.'

What does she need to be wary about? Surely the threat's in her home, not out here. As if summoned by my thoughts, Federico encroaches upon Aurora.

'Hello.' His usual loudness and theatrical movements are replaced by a subdued man.

'I'm leaving soon and going back home,' I begin. 'I've finished the portrait of you. Ideally, I'd frame it, but I won't have time.'

She claps her hands together and then clasps them. 'What a wonderful surprise! Come in and show us.'

As Aurora leads the way, she backs into Federico. He jumps away and follows his wife into the lounge.

The Gallos' flat is a world removed from mine. Their interior decoration screams of wealth. A curtain pole bows in protest at the thick embroidered curtains hanging from it. My fingers long to touch the silky tapestry woven throughout the material.

Original paintings from modern artists cover the walls. My artist's eye knows they're purchased from an art gallery and not reproduction prints. I tot up an estimated figure for how much the paintings are worth, losing count as it reaches triple figures.

Glass dominates the lounge, from tables to the units. For people prone to fighting, being surrounded by glass is a questionable choice. It's in line with their contemporary opulent lifestyle, though; attractive and sparkling. They aren't a typical young married couple, scraping a life together. No car boot finds or family hand-me-downs for them.

'What a gorgeous home you have,' I say while taking the sketch out of my folio case.

'My father insists upon having only the best. He's a man of impeccable taste.'

Aurora leads me to the table. It takes up a sizeable space, more suited to a house.

Federico notes me checking out the table. '*Signore Alunni* won't allow anything to be changed in here.'

Aurora lays a hand on her husband's heart.

'Papa's good to us, remember?'

'Of course.' His shoulders slump. 'I need coffee.'

He dawdles towards the kitchen and takes a last glance at us before leaving. The lack of invitation to join him in refreshments isn't surprising. Federico always looks out for himself.

Now is my moment.

'If Federico's hurting you, there are places you can go,' I whisper to Aurora. 'There are refuges, or I can take you to friends or family.'

She scowls and then resets her face into serenity. Instead of replying, she stares at me.

'Please don't be offended,' I add. 'Domestic violence isn't your fault and it's nothing to be ashamed of. Federico should be the one who's repentant.'

She throws back her head and laughs. 'You think my husband hits me?'

The booming laughter is disconcerting and certain to alert Federico. A diversionary tactic won't work with me.

'I've seen your bruises and how you cower from him.'

She tosses her hair away from her shoulders. 'Please stay out of my business and attend to your own. It's dangerous to get too involved in my life.' Defiance flashes in her eyes before she smooths out the picture on the table. 'Federico, come see the amazing thing Sophie has accomplished.'

He skulks into the room. 'Are you having fun in here?'

Aurora links arms, leading him to her portrait.

'Sophie's such a joker, making me laugh. She tells such stories. Look. I am beautiful, right?'

Barely looking at the picture, he replies, 'Of course you are.'

I can't witness this strange performance any longer. Aurora needs help and I've offered it. Leaving her here makes me feel conflicted, though. When I go to the police, I'll ask them to investigate the Gallos' domestic situation.

'I must go,' I say. 'My husband is on his way here.'

'I'll transfer payment for the portrait to your bank, as agreed,' Aurora adds.

'Thank you.'

'I'll see you out,' Federico says.

Standing outside their front door, tension makes my neck sore. I won't rub it. Federico is watching me.

As Federico edges towards me, I retreat. He pulls the door to, so it's almost shut.

'I wish you well,' he whispers. 'When you're gone, remember, this one thing; don't believe everything you see in Harmony House. Seeing isn't always believing.'

CHAPTER 94

Sophie

Zara wheels around and kicks the door to Rory's flat. 'Bastard!'

She halts upon seeing me standing at the top of the stairs. 'Hi there, Soph.'

I never thought Zara capable of being flustered, and yet, she is. Her cheeks are flushed, and she won't look at me.

'How come you're paying Rory a visit?' I ask.

'I'm feeding the cat.' She takes an audible gulp.

'Got something stuck in your throat?'

She fans her face. 'Is it hot? Are you hot? I'm hot.'

'Not at all.'

The fanning increases.

'Not like Adam to go wild and blast heat in the hallway,' I say. 'It's usually North Pole chilly out here.'

I touch the radiator. Cold. Zara gives me a lopsided smile.

'Rory's gone away for a few days, probably on the pull,' she says. 'He begged me to look after the cat. Can't stand the bloke, but I'm a sucker for a moggy.'

'Why were you calling the cat a *bastard*?'

'What is this, an interrogation? The cat puked and I had to clean it up.'

'Of course it did.' I exaggerate my suspicious tone. Zara deserves nothing from me, least of all buying into more of her lies. 'I'm going back home in a few days, so I guess it's goodbye.'

'Pop round for one last bevvy, babes. I've not been the greatest of friends, but I'd like to part on friendly terms.'

'Let's leave it. I don't want any more drama.'

Zara swipes at her dry eyes. 'I know I come across as brash and confident, but I get so lonely sometimes. Since I came here, I haven't made a single genuine friend. Please let me make it up to you for messing up so much. One last meet up at mine? I'll be on my best behaviour.'

'I'll come to yours tomorrow afternoon.' As I say it, I immediately have regrets. 'No alcohol, just a cuppa, right?'

'It's a date.' She swishes her hands over her tights. 'Got to go. There's fur all over me, never a good look.'

Zara still thinks I'm a pushover. I don't buy the lonely act. She's up to something. Before I leave, I'll find out what. I need as much evidence as I can get for the police. Zara's closer to Rory than she wants me to believe. I follow her down the stairs, watching her brushing off non-existent cat hairs. Rory couldn't possibly have a cat. There aren't any feeding bowls in his home or other feline paraphernalia. When we first met, Rory said he's allergic to them. What was Zara doing in Rory's flat?

CHAPTER 95
The Watcher

Damn! At the final stage, my hand has been forced. After years of watching, I should be more prepared. I must learn from the mistakes that occurred on the last project. Nobody will bail me out this time. If I'm not careful, Sophie will be my undoing. She's discovering more than I can allow.

It's time to hang up my observer's lens in Southbourne. This project has lasted longer than I expected. When I came here, there were no ties. I severed the connection between my alleged rescuer and me. No one has that power over me. I've paid the price by being dutiful, or so they think.

The only actions I can control are my own. People are unpredictable. If I don't react accordingly, their choices could lead to my downfall. Passivity is not in my DNA. I am the product of adept observers, but I took it to a whole new level. While they were content to sit back and watch, like loathsome voyeurs, I reacted. I'm not some seedy couch potato, getting my kicks from the perverted screen. Watching is as much a part of me as the blood in my veins. I won't rest until the world knows what I'm capable of.

It irks sometimes that I can't do this alone. Sending the tapes and recordings to the police is a hollow victory for being noticed.

There must be a person, a conduit to inflict pain upon before I claim my watching fame.

Sophie will be my nemesis or greatest triumph. Never has a human captivated my attention like this woman. I don't understand what this is. It surpasses obsession. I must not forget she's only a messenger. If she becomes collateral, so be it. Don't think I state this lightly. I've invested so much into Sophie. If she has to die, I'll inflict a thousand cuts upon her body as a punishment.

CHAPTER 96
Sophie

I feel sixteen again, waiting for Ben to meet me. Thankfully, this time around I'm not wearing train track braces and we don't have to sit in the rain, eating chips. The neglected excited feelings at seeing my "date" are unexpected, but welcome. Marriage can stagnate, especially when you've been married as long as we have. Now, our relationship has so many possibilities.

A fizzing travels from my stomach to my throat as Ben's car appears around the corner of Gull Lane. Although it hasn't been long since I left, it seems like ages. Will he still like what he sees in me? Will he understand I'm still his Sophie, even though so much has happened? Reminiscent of old times, the Volvo pulls up behind Vera. I had to stop parking behind Ben's car in our drive as my car's chances of starting are slim. Ben was often late for work because of Vera's stubbornness. Like owner, like car.

I regard the azure sky, unsullied by clouds. Is this a sign of clearer, better times to come? Despite the wintry chill, the sun pushes through, offering hope. Seconds after slamming the car door, the other half of me runs towards me. Everything I ever wanted holds me close. Enveloped within my husband's arms, I know where I belong. We'll never be parted again.

* * *

Ben gives a superb imitation of a goldfish, mouth snapping open and shut, as he listens to my account.

'And that's about it.' I end the long story of my adventures in Harmony House.

'You talk as if what's been happening here is nothing. Why didn't you share this with me sooner?'

'Pride, isn't it always with me?' I twist my hands around each other.

'Please tell me you're not coming home based only on wanting to escape here?'

My husband's bottom lip wobbles. I lean over to kiss it.

'I'm returning because I belong with you. Escaping from all the drama is a bonus. I should've stayed at home in the first place and talked things through with you.'

Ben holds my knee. 'I can't believe what's happened here. People dead, Tobias and Iris disappearing, an abused woman upstairs, and a dead woman's diary entries being shared with you. As for that Rory bloke, if I bump into him, I won't be responsible for my actions.'

I cup my hand over his.

'Rory's not worth it. Stay away from him. He will have his comeuppance after I've gone to the police. Soon, I won't have to see him ever again. While you're at work, I'll crack on with packing and finishing my sketches. Rory can't get to me in here.'

'I've missed us. Chatting with you in person is something I'll never take for granted again.'

'I've missed us too, particularly this.' I lead my husband to the bedroom.

* * *

Ben's kiss is the only alarm call I'd ever allow. No wonder every morning I've woken in Southbourne has been a slow starter. Ben wasn't here. I prise open my sleep-crusted eyes and pull him closer.

'Eurgh! Morning breath.'

I swat his arm. 'Rude.'

THE WATCHER

A rapping sounds against the window pane. Ben pulls the curtain aside and then turns to me.

'Is this the famous Stanley?'

I join my two favourite fellas. As Ben opens the window, he's greeted by a series of squawks. Placing a hand on Stanley's head, I beckon him to come closer.

'Hey there, Stan the Man. This is Ben, the husband I mentioned. Stop being jealous and remember your manners. I've told him what a well-behaved bird you are. Don't show me up. Go on,' I say to Ben, leading his quivering fingers to touch Stanley.

Stanley turns his beak towards us. I feel Ben's breath hitching as he leans against me. Stanley nuzzles into Ben's open palm.

Ben's tight smile springs into a grin. 'He likes me!'

I nod.

'Are you crying?' Ben asks.

'Maybe a little. It's hormones.'

'Of course it is.'

He pulls me closer. Stanley lets out an ear-shattering shriek.

I shrug. 'Stanley's such an attention whore.'

'Much as I'm enjoying this, I've got to go,' Ben says. 'Time to sort out the mess that muppet accountant's made. Catch you later, Stanley. Love you, Soph. You're my favourite.'

'Love you muchly.'

I blow him a kiss, relishing how we won't be apart for longer than a few hours.

Prepared to finish packing, I leave my bird friend to his pooping duties. It's mean to be amused by how he always craps on Adam's windowsill. Adam's not the gruff man I thought he was, but he still needs to lighten up. Stanley's sensitive to people telling him to "shoo" and calling him names.

Empty cardboard boxes litter the lounge. Coffee needs to happen first. The letterbox opens and then snaps shut. It looks like another of Louise's diary entries has been delivered. Determined to catch the sender, I rush to open the door. There's no one outside.

CHAPTER 97
Louise's Diary

Today I will be free of Harmony House and the disharmony it's caused.

Adam's selling my furniture. I thought letting go of the pieces I carefully selected would be a wrench, but I don't want any reminders. Adam's been so kind. I admit to feeling uncomfortable when he shared the photos of his wife. The likeness between Tina and me is uncanny. It explains Neil's aloofness, but I expected better from him. My terrible taste in men rears its ugly head again.

For the first time in months, a hidden hope rises. This was a blip, a mistake I made in desperation. I'm ready to make the fresh start I envisaged happening here. To complete my path to freedom, I'm taking this diary to the police and telling them what I know. Then I can leave all the deceit behind. The darkness can't touch me now.

Earlier, I said goodbye to Southbourne by visiting some places. I forgot Frankenfest, the local Halloween celebration, was taking place. Halloween used to be my favourite time of the year until Karl ruined that, too. My ex-husband was all about the tricks, never the treats. I was a fool to believe the gift inside the box was an apology. No matter how hard I try, the image of a bloodied heart nestled in shredded tissue paper won't erase. I can

THE WATCHER

still hear Karl's spiteful whisper as he wished me a happy Halloween, warning me not to give my heart to anyone else. My ex was always the jealous type. Days later, Karl confessed it was a pig's heart. Yes, I believed Karl was capable of killing a person and ripping out their heart. Yes, I stayed with him. No one gets to judge me unless they've lived through gaslighting, narcissism, and mental degradation.

When I saw a Halloween event taking place in the Grove, I considered leaving. There's still some defiance left in me, though. I have a right to stroll along the streets and say farewell. I needed to lay my Halloween fears to rest.

As I admired the carved pumpkins, a sensation of being watched - no, scrutinised - returned. I decided to ignore it. My mind isn't as trustworthy as it once was. In a crowd, I should've been safe. Child zombies performed a peppy cheerleading routine. I allowed myself to relax. A contagious festival atmosphere crept across the crowd. Smiles of the locals made me wonder if I could leave. I recognised familiar faces from visiting the shops and my own customers.

How will I ever forget the zombie girl who approached me? Despite her menacing mask, childhood innocence shone through in her exuberance.

'Happy Halloween!' she cried as she thrust a note into my hand before joining her undead horde.

Goodbye, Louise. Are you leaving Harmony House in a car or a coffin? Happy Halloween. Don't have nightmares.

An adult dressed as a grinning masked devil waved from across the street as I read the note. I scurried back to my flat and have concentrated on finishing my packing since. The sense of purpose reignited my resilience. I will expose my torturer by revealing this diary's contents. This time I'll win. There's no choice. It's not only me who has to survive. The child growing inside me won't ever know its father. I'll nurture away the heinous inherited genes. This is *my* child.

Someone's knocking on the door. I've called to them to wait a moment. Of course, I'll check through the peephole first. No one can hurt me again. I'm seizing this chance to live the life I deserve, as a mother. I guess now's a suitable time to finish this diary.

Goodbye, Harmony House

CHAPTER 98
Sophie

My tears stain the copy of what was probably Louise's final diary entry. It was written the day she was supposed to leave. The visitor might have been her killer. Did they steal the diary after killing her? Not only Louise died. The thought is almost too much to bear. Biology took my child. A murderer killed Louise's.

My messenger didn't add a note this time. The ominous ending, knowing Louise possibly opened the door to a killer, serves as enough of a threatening message. I can't believe her death was an accident any longer. She was likely killed because of her involvement with Rory. He's the obvious suspect. Did he know Louise was carrying his child? The notion of Rory knowingly killing his baby makes me queasy.

Ben didn't want to go to work after I'd told him what's happened around here. To convince him I'm safe, I put on a brave face. Ben made me swear not to leave the flat unless it's a necessity. It's a promise I was happy to make. The first test comes with a knock at the door. I look through the spyhole and contemplate where to hide.

* * *

Another crisis in Harmony House. I didn't expect to be sitting in Adam's home, faced with an irate woman. Tobias' mum epitomises the bulldog licking piss off a nettle analogy. After taking a sip of Adam's volcanic tea, she splutters. I try not to laugh. Poor Tobias, being brought up by this female Hitler. The stories he told me of how militant Nancy was when he was growing up were enlightening.

Nancy summoned me to Adam's flat after he mentioned Tobias and I spent some time together. Believing I was his girlfriend, she laid into me for breaking Tobias' heart. I soon set her straight, although she wouldn't listen when I said I couldn't leave the flat. Nancy insisted the conversation took place in the warden's abode and nowhere else. Concern for Tobias made me obey.

'Maybe Tobias is with a friend?' Adam says.

'I've been into that little shop of his.' Nancy screws up her nose. 'None of the staff or customers have seen him. Tobias left his job. It's not like my son to behave in such a rash manner.'

She's right. Tobias loved working there. Leaving would've been hard. The letter stating he'd gone home was difficult to believe. Living in Harmony House gave him freedom. Returning to a jailer mother was a punishment Tobias tried to avoid.

'Haven't you seen or heard from Tobias at all?' Adam asks Nancy.

She tuts. 'I wouldn't be here if I had.' Her tone is as scratchy as the tweed suit she's wearing. 'We'd made plans to spend a few days together.'

I'd disappear too if it meant looking at her sour chops for days on end.

'We must report him as missing,' I say. 'I don't like the sound of this. Tobias wouldn't go somewhere none of us knew about.'

Nancy places her cup on a coaster.

'For someone who knew Tobias for such a short while, you seem to think you're an expert on him. As his mother, I'm in a better position to decide what happens. I'll check my sources and only go to the police if deemed necessary.'

'No!' I shout. 'Don't delay. He could be in trouble.'

'Will you kindly control yourself?' She hisses. 'I expected you'd be the hysterical type. Anyone who dresses like that is asking to be noticed.'

Nancy's sour face assesses my multiple necklaces, layered over urban camo dungarees. I won't play nice any longer.

'Maybe if you weren't so busy looking down your nose at others, Tobias might be safe.'

'Well, I've never been so insulted.'

She rises from the chair like her arse has been set on fire.

'Ladies,' Adam says, 'arguing won't help. Mrs Peters, I suggest you report Tobias' disappearance immediately. In fact, I'll go with you. Wait while I get my coat.' He leaves the room.

Nancy stares at me. I glare back. Then I realise we have something in common. We've both lost a child. She may have lost two, although it doesn't bear thinking about Tobias meeting a grisly end. Compassion is required.

'I understand as a family you've been through a lot,' I begin. 'Your son's a good person. Tobias might not match what you wanted, but he's brilliant. His mind is astounding and he's so caring. It's sad you've missed out on it. I hope you find him safe and can build a better relationship.'

Leaving Nancy open-mouthed, I return to my flat. Tobias is missing. I can't bear to consider what might have happened to him. He said someone was following me the night I went to Cheeky's. I'm convinced he knew the identity of my stalker. Is Tobias' life at risk because of what he saw? Or worse, is he dead? After all, the dead can't tell the truth.

CHAPTER 99

The Watcher

Tobias had to leave. His surveillance secret was exposed. Action had to be taken. Tobias' monitoring altered. It's devastating when a watcher's stopped in the prime of their power. We never disappear. Even when we die, our eyes stay open.

Exercise caution, Sophie. Discovering where Tobias is increases the threat against you. You're getting too close to the truth and making others mad. Still, this could be another test of how you react to a crisis. Let's have some fun and go out on a high.

Look nearby, Sophie. Feel Tobias' vigilant presence surrounding you. Watchers never truly leave.

CHAPTER 100
Sophie

Ben wobbles as he tries to balance on one knee. He flings out a hand to steady himself on the floor.

'Sophie, will you marry me?' He snaps open a box. The ring inside is a band, dotted with amethysts. 'It's an eternity ring because we're forever.'

'Get up, you numpty. If you haven't noticed, we're already married.' I hold up my left hand and wriggle my ringed finger.

Ben remains kneeling. 'I meant a renewal of our vows. Let's face it, our wedding was rubbish. This time I want to do something that's really us.'

'Instead of pleasing my mum, you mean?'

'Neither of us are church people. I looked such a dick in a penguin suit. The dress your mum made was hideous, too. Whenever we look at our wedding photos, you always cringe. Throughout the day, your parents made it clear they didn't approve. It was all a bit shit.'

'True, although it's still the best day of my life because I married you. I'd love to marry you again and for it not to be shit.'

He places the ring on my finger. It fits perfectly, just like us. He rises to plant a kiss on my mouth.

'I bloody love you, Soph. This is a turning point. Our lives are going to change.'

'For the better, I hope.'

'Of course.' He hugs me. 'Where's the pizza? It's taking ages to be delivered.'

'You ordered a takeaway for the night you propose? So romantic.'

'How long do you reckon until the pizza arrives?'

'Long enough.'

Ben closes the bedroom door behind us.

CHAPTER 101
The Watcher

Enjoy your last night in Harmony House, Sophie. Shiver at your husband's touch upon your skin. Bask in the glow of being back in Ben's arms. Your complacency at a happy ending will make the shock of the final act more powerful.

Will you share my recordings with Ben, or will this be another instance of you keeping secrets from him? A night of passion won't fix your marriage. The shadow of hiding your pregnancy obsession from Ben lingers. One day, you'll wake up and blame him for your lost chances. You foolish people believe marriage makes you whole when it actually divides. Enjoy returning home and living in a fantasy for a while. Press *Play* on my recordings and listen to the bubble burst.

Your self-satisfied smile confirms a belief you're on the way to a better life. Think again, Sophie. Life is about to change forever, for us all. Some won't get to live at all.

CHAPTER 102
Sophie

One of my traits that annoys me is worrying I'll let others down. I'm leaving tonight and still have lots of packing to do. Instead, I'm in Zara's home, having a last drink together. Hopefully, Ben won't be furious when I tell him I've broken my promise and left the flat. I figure Nancy dragged me into Adam's place, so I've already messed up. Besides, Zara's got some explaining to do, and I intend to make her do it.

Zara's lounge didn't disappoint my expectations the first time I was here. It stirs my amusement again. More designer handbags hang from the curtain railings, probably ornaments of parental guilt gifts. I'm still amazed neon pink furniture is a thing. It's a migraine waiting to happen. Zara enters the room, holding two margarita glasses. Liquid sloshes over the rim, landing on her hand. She slurps it off.

'I'm not drinking that,' I say. 'No alcohol, remember?' I don't add I won't allow her to place me in a vulnerable position. Liars can't be trusted.

She puts the glasses on the table and pouts.

'I took ages doing these. It's our last time together, sweetie. Look at the gorgeous parrot straw and all the glittery bits.'

'Only a sip,' I state, needing to get this over with. To her credit, the drink is delicious. 'Wow, you've got skills.'

THE WATCHER

Zara gives the first genuine smile I've seen since we met. I realise she's desperate for acceptance.

'I heard the weirdo, Tobias, has gone,' she says. 'Good riddance.'

'Stop being so nasty. I'm really worried about him. I don't think Tobias left of his own free will.'

The donkey laugh reappears. I definitely won't miss it.

'Always trying to save someone, aren't you, Soph? I was right, wasn't I, saying Tobias would get what's coming to him?'

Panic grips me in its clutches. 'Have you done something to him?'

Zara blasts a hee-haw laugh. I consider strangling her into silence.

'Don't be daft. I'm not a murderer. I meant it's one less evasive fella around here to be bothered about.' Her phone pings. She looks at the screen and scowls. 'Would you give me an art lesson? I'd love to have a go.'

'Really, right now? I've got a lot to do today.'

Her sulky face reappears.

'I need to learn something. Daddy says I'm good for nothing. I need to prove I can apply myself. Maybe I'm more artistic than I thought. My margarita displays are fabulous, right?'

A message pings on my phone.

Going to be back later than planned. This office is in such a state! Sorry. Will bring chocolate and cheese products by way of apology. Love you. Ben xxx

Tired already at the thought of packing alone, I choose procrastination. 'Do you want to sketch, paint or use charcoals?' I ask.

'Bring it all and we'll find out what I'm best at.' She glances at her mobile and places it screen facing down.

'Come to mine,' I offer, aware I've been here too long.

'Sorry, babes. I'm waiting for a parcel to be delivered. I can't miss out on my new dress. Pretty please, for me?'

'Most of my art stuff's packed.' I sigh. 'It might take a while to find it.'

Zara pulls me up from the chair and then pushes me towards the door. 'Better get going then.'

* * *

I'm aware Zara was trying to get rid of me for a while. It's probably linked to the message she received. She's either got a dealer popping round or she's having another crisis. That woman invites trouble.

I've sent a text back to Ben, confessing I was at Zara's. He was surprisingly calm about it, saying I should leave on a positive note, including making peace with Zara. Still, her lies and omissions give me pause. Being around Zara isn't only exhausting because of her extrovert personality. When I'm with her, my hawk's assessing stare is permanently engaged. Watching over her as she creates art will hopefully open up a conversation. Zara needs to provide some answers.

Carrying most of my art equipment isn't easy. Finding it was harder. When Ben began labelling boxes last night, I told him not to bother because I'd remember what's in them. Overnight, I've already forgotten. The easel slips out of my grasp and stubs my big toe. This is how I started at Harmony House, dropping the easel as I unpacked the car. I feel like I've lived here for years. Who knew so much would happen here? The easel scrapes on the floor as I drag it, while balancing bags of paints, charcoals, pastels, paper, and pencils. I should've asked Zara to keep the door open, as I'll have to put everything down to knock.

'You dumb slut! Why are you meddling? Do as you're told!' The man's voice is faint inside Zara's flat, but I can make out the words.

'Why are you so nasty? You said you loved me!'

Zara's high-pitched whine is unmistakable. I've never heard her sound so distressed. Great, I'm walking into another domestic.

'Don't you understand yet? I'll say anything to get what I want.'

It's Rory. I'd recognise that self-satisfied drawl anywhere.

THE WATCHER

'We had a deal.' Zara sounds likes she's crying. 'I did everything you asked.'

'You didn't bring me Sophie, though, did you?'

Rory's words hit hard. Heat rises in my body. My vision blurs. Not now. Have the panic attack away from here.

Ready to retreat, I try to gather my belongings. It's too late. The door opens. Assessing his prey, Rory grins at me.

CHAPTER 103
The Watcher

For a murky day, there were many people strolling along the Overcliff. I swear it's a test. When I've overdosed on watching, I need solace. The nature reserve with its meandering paths usually offers time to process what I've witnessed.

On my earlier morning sojourn, it seemed the world and its dog wanted to steal my serenity. Heading for Boscombe and away from the café and the lift down to the beach, usually guarantees solitude. As I walked, people kept appearing, like vermin on the attack.

You'd probably define me as an introvert or misanthrope. You'd be wrong. The first mistake would be in defining me at all. The second error is in thinking I need to hide. I can shine as bright as anyone else. The set of personas I own for any occasion hangs in a wardrobe of deceit. Every day, I select an appropriate costume for my agenda. For The Watcher, appearances are everything.

The shrieks of a woman carried across the scrub ruined my reflective session. A man held her in a vice grip, teasing at pushing her off the cliff. Her kicking legs betrayed enjoyment at being the centre of attention rather than fear. *Just push her and be done*, I thought. No, today wasn't the day for a walk. Someone could get hurt. I'm toying with inflicting a final blow upon Sophie before she leaves. The happy couple pursuing their perfect ending is making me nauseous.

Maybe a little "accident" for Sophie, Ben, or both before they leave will rain on their pathetic parade. Nothing too serious. A listener needs their ears. They can live without all their limbs functioning, though.

CHAPTER 104

Sophie

As I head for the safety of my flat, Rory seizes my arm.

'Listening at doors?' Fiery breath blows against my ear. 'Careful, you don't jump to the wrong conclusions.'

'You'll get what's coming to you!' I shout and immediately regret it.

'What do you mean?'

He steps back and glares at me.

'Nothing.' I fold my arms, fingers anchoring into my elbows. 'People like you always get their comeuppance.'

Rory sniggers. 'I don't think so.'

He releases my arm and swaggers towards the main entrance. When he gets there, Rory turns around and aims a hand formed like a gun at me. I stand in place, clutching my body. Only when he leaves can I let go.

My art equipment is a modern still life piece, scattered across the floor. I scrabble to gather things together: my mind and the equipment. Clumsy, nervous hands drop more than I'm picking up. Behind me, a door opens.

'Need some help?' Zara asks. 'Let's sort this out and then have a chat. It's time you knew the truth.'

* * *

THE WATCHER

No more living in fear. Since I came to Harmony House, I'm constantly dodging people and their problems. When I arrived, I was avoiding my own issues. The truth is, I brought them with me and then this place added extra. Now I'm preparing to go home, I want answers. I won't allow Zara to intimidate me. She was leading me, like the proverbial lamb to the slaughter, to Rory. Zara's helping him complete the folder he has on me. There would've been a video of me sedated and being raped. She had to get me into Rory's flat. He knows I wouldn't go there willingly. It doesn't matter if the victims agreed to go to Rory's home. If they were there for sex, it doesn't negate the fact Rory drugged them. That's not consent. I shiver at what Rory could've done to me if I hadn't overheard the row with Zara.

I consider the margaritas she prepared. Did she add a sedative? I try to breathe while wondering if a drug's inside me. Was I in her flat so Rory could collect my unconscious body? Buying into Zara's lonely routine was foolish. I believed I was in control, but I'm no match for this level of villainy.

'Oi! I'm talking to you,' Zara shouts.

The front garden is an unimpressive introduction to Harmony House. I've never lingered here for long. It serves more as a frontage to the property than an attraction. Iris tried her best to work with what little creative opportunities she had. Since she left, the front and rear gardens have become barren, devoid of Iris' love. In front of Harmony House is the best place for me to be right now. There's no way I'm going into Zara's flat, and she's certainly not allowed in mine.

Zara inspects the wall, flicks debris off the bricks, and sits.

I pace in front of her. 'You're lucky I'm here and not at the police station.'

She kicks off her shoes and wriggles her toes. 'I'm so tired. It's all gone wrong. Once again, I've cocked everything up.'

'Poor little princess.'

Determined not to be a sitting target, my pacing increases.

'I don't want your pity.'

Zara massages her feet. She suffers for fashion. Good.

'I have zero sympathy for you,' I state. 'After what I heard you saying to Rory, it's clear you've fed me a load of bullshit.'

'To be fair, not telling you what's going on isn't lying.'

'Don't wheedle your way around me!' I yell. 'You and Rory were planning to drug me, let him violate me, video it, and make money from blackmail. You're disgusting. How could you?'

'Daddy's cut me off. I can't pay the rent, let alone afford anything else. I wasn't in on the blackmail, though, and I'd never allow Rory to touch you.'

'Stop lying. I heard Rory say you were supposed to bring me to him.'

She stands in front of me.

'But I didn't, did I? Rory hasn't got his hands on you because of me. He's blackmailing me, too. Because I can't pay him anymore, Rory says I've got to repay him in other ways. So, you've seen the videos. Sneaky.'

I shift to the side of Zara.

'Funny how you're the only one who's conscious.'

'I like sex, so sue me.'

A woman pushing a child in a buggy looks at Zara and says, 'Good for you, love. Can you move out of the way so I can get past?'

Zara steps aside and then continues speaking. 'Rory and I used to hook up and you're right, I am a willing participant in the videos. There's a particular one you can't have seen. The arsehole filmed me having a toot of coke. Rory knows Daddy's anti-drugs. He makes his staff take regular drugs tests. If they fail, they're out. Rory said if I helped him find women to tape, he wouldn't show Daddy the video. When you saw me coming out of Rory's flat the other day, I was trying to find the video on his computer.'

'I know Rory doesn't have a cat. You're not as good at lying as you think.'

'That bastard has put a separate password on that particular video. If Daddy sees me taking drugs, life as I know it is over.'

I turn away. 'You're a despicable excuse for a human being. So what if you're a drug user? At least you weren't raped like the others. You'd rather make sure the designer gear and coke keep on coming than protect other women.'

'I protected you from—'

'What do you want?' I hold my hands out. 'Thanks?'

'It's obvious I won't get it.' She sits on the wall to put her shoes on. 'Don't judge me. You haven't got a clue what I've risked for you.'

'You're talking out of your arse. So, you'll have to return home, boo-bloody-hoo.'

'Who do you think sent you the copies from Louise's diary, along with the notes?' Zara asks.

'You? Why? How did you get hold of her diary?'

'I nicked it from Rory's gaff ages ago. He might be cunning, but he shouldn't leave things lying around when I visit. After Louise died, he stole it. He had a key to her flat. I copied some entries for insurance, looking for stuff I could blackmail Rory with.'

'You two are quite a pair.'

'Whatever. I gave you the diary pages and nasty messages, hoping they'd put you off living here. If you go back to Oxford, Rory can't hurt you. I never figured on you being so ballsy and sticking it out.'

'Did Rory murder Louise?' I ask.

'I honestly don't know, but I'm beginning to think he did.' Tears flow down Zara's cheeks. 'I really cared for Rory. It's complicated. I've watched him change into a beast and I think he's going to kill me.'

CHAPTER 105
The Watcher

If there had been more time, I would've taught Sophie how to spot a fake through body language, tone, and voice. Since her arrival, she's been fed one lie after another. There are moments I think she's cracked it, but decency is her weakness.

Thankfully, it's Sophie's integrity I'm using to make my story heard. She needs to believe we're all inherently good and will eventually do the right thing. I don't doubt if I give her these recordings, Sophie will take them to the police. I'm relying on her ardent sense of justice. The world must know what I've done so I can claim my watching fame. People will learn I was The Watcher, but they won't find me. No one has yet. Hiding in full sight is one of my greatest talents.

Harmony House hoards liars. I've been in a privileged position of seeing through them all. They couldn't keep me out. All along, I've had a window into their lives. I've breathed the same air, keyed in the same entrance code, and passed them by.

Sophie tries to put up the good fight of immunity to deceit. The stamping of her anger on the pavement is pleasing. She doesn't want to engage with dishonesty, particularly Zara's. Yet, here we are; mired in lies from the mouths and minds of accomplished deceivers and murderers.

CHAPTER 106
Sophie

The few pedestrians passing by on Gull Lane give us questioning looks, probably wondering whether to spectate or intervene.

'Stop being so dramatic!' I yell at Zara. 'As usual, you're lying. Rory won't kill you. The drugs video is likely to be another of your lies. You two are in this sex tape blackmail together. I heard you plotting.'

She rushes to my side and places a finger on my lips. I slap it away. Zara looks at Harmony House.

'Did you see the curtain move upstairs?' she asks, craning her neck to get a better view.

'No. Stop changing the subject. Wait a minute, I've figured it out. You had something to do with Tobias' disappearance. I expect Tobias knew what Rory and you were doing, and he put it in his notebooks.'

Zara screws up her face as she continues looking up. 'I swear someone's up there. Keep it down, will you? I haven't got a clue where Tobias is. Remember, I didn't have time to read what he wrote about me because you insisted on listening to a sob story about his sister.'

'It doesn't mean you didn't go back to take another look.'

She reddens.

'You bloody did. Did you steal the books Tobias compiled on you?'

Zara nibbles a precious manicured nail.

'Maybe, but I had a right. He shouldn't have been writing stuff about me. Funny how I'm getting grief, but you soon forgave Tobias for stalking you.'

'Tobias wasn't planning to rape and blackmail me, you sick bitch.'

'So, watching people and noting their every move, along with taking photos, isn't a violation?'

'I've had enough of this.'

Intent on phoning Ben, I aim for the main entrance.

'Before you go, listen to this.'

Zara scrolls through her phone and then taps the screen. She holds her mobile aloft. A recording begins of Rory leaving a message.

'You've messed up, Zara. Cheeky's was your last opportunity to bring Sophie to me and you failed. Daddy will see his little girl on drugs. How upset do you reckon he's going to be? Even more so when he identifies your corpse.'

As she cries, the brokenness of a usually brash woman confuses my instincts. Hugging a person I'm wary of doesn't seem right.

'Why did you let Rory into your flat?' I ask. 'Inviting someone who's threatened to kill you is flaming stupid.'

'He has a key.' A tear drips from Zara's chin, staining her dress with liquid mascara. 'I made the mistake of giving him a spare when we were getting it on. He won't give it back and Adam refuses to change the locks because of the expense. I'd do it myself, but the bloke thinks he owns the place. I can't tell him why I want a new lock, can I? I'd do it myself, but Adam would ask more questions and Rory will know what I've done. He's only upstairs, after all. When he turned up earlier, I thought that was the end of me until he heard you outside.'

'Does anyone around here not have a key to everyone else's flats?' What was intended as a glib statement gives me pause. 'Wait a minute. Do you and Rory have a key to my place?'

THE WATCHER

'Of course I don't. Rory shouldn't either. Adam changed the lock when Bekstar moved in. Lucky, I got into Tobias' flat to get the notebooks on me before Adam changed that lock. Look, Soph, you saved me from Rory just now. If he hadn't heard you skulking outside, I'd be dead.'

'I'd laugh at the fact I rescued you if this wasn't so twisted. That's if it's really what happened.'

I assess Zara, searching for guilt and finding it. Her acting skills are weakening.

'We must save each other. I accept I've done wrong by you. If you want to tell the police my part in this, so be it. I've felt so ashamed, knowing what Rory did to those women.'

'Well, you deserve to,' I reply.

'You need evidence. The police won't act on hearsay. You can't say you were in Rory's home. They'll nick you for trespassing and going through his computer.'

'That's rich coming from you. Besides, Neil let me in.'

'You didn't have permission to look at Rory's computer, though. Anyway, I've got some of the videos on a memory stick —'

'You absolute—'

'Keep it down.' Zara drops her volume to just above a whisper. 'Rory might return soon. Let me finish what I'm saying. I downloaded a few videos when Rory left me in his place alone. He popped out for wine. I'd been waiting for an opportunity and carried a USB with me whenever I was there. Truth be told, I was trying to get a copy of the video he has on me. I copied some of the sex tapes, too. It's insurance against him. The blackmailed was becoming the blackmailer.'

'You and Rory are the perfect couple.'

'Touché, but I don't threaten to murder people. Rory will have me bumped off and I reckon today's the day. I'm no longer any use to him now you're aware of his plan to put you in a tape. I've got an advantage over him, though. He doesn't know I have the videos. We can take the memory stick to the police. I'll make up something about Rory sending sex tapes to me for kicks because we don't need to mention my involvement.' Zara chews her lip.

'Backtracking already,' I reply. 'What happened to being ready to accept responsibility? It's typical of you to weasel out of it. The tears soon dried up, too.'

'You, more than anyone else, should understand about self-preservation. It's why you're here, isn't it, to get your head together and survive? Do you want to live or not?'

'Of course, I don't want to die. Why do you think Rory wants to kill me?'

'You overheard us. Now he can't have you, you're a liability. I'll keep you safe, but it means doing things my way.'

'Why didn't Rory grab me when he saw me outside your flat?' I ask.

She shakes her head. 'Hun, you've so much to learn. Rory never acts impulsively. Don't doubt he's planning your death, Soph.'

'Stop calling me *Soph*. I'm not your friend, but I'll go with you to the police station. I don't trust you and I'll be watching you every step of the way.'

Zara regards her outfit. 'I need to grab the memory stick and change my clobber.'

'Why do you have to get changed?' I ask, rolling my eyes. 'The police don't give a damn what you look like.'

She twirls a curl around her finger.

'Soph, babe, if I'm entering the final showdown, I'm doing it looking fabulous. Don't even think of sneaking off to the police station on your own. I'll deny all knowledge. Without me, you have no evidence. Remember, we're doing this my way.'

CHAPTER 107
Sophie

Back in my flat, whenever someone walks past, I flee from the window. Looking for Rory is exhausting. As shadows from the changing light dance on the walls, my trepidation rises.

I've tried several times to call Ben, with no reply. He must be busy sorting out the issues in the Poole office. I type a message to Ben.

Things are escalating and I'm going to the police with Zara. Rory's worse than we thought. Zara's dodgy, but I'm staying alert and will be safe at the police station. Tell you everything later. Love you xxx

Leaving a voicemail detailing what's happened would take too much time. Worry will make me falter and concern my husband. He has a job to do and it's to my advantage he concentrates on it. The sooner Ben's finished, the sooner we can leave.

I check my watch. Zara said she'd knock on my door when she's ready. How long does it take to put a dress on? The last five minutes have felt like an hour. Please don't return yet, Rory. I consider how this could be a set-up and he's waiting for me. Despite Zara's threat, maybe I should call the police and go it alone. Memories of hearing an imaginary baby still haunt me. Underneath Adam and Iris' kindness, I saw their expressions, considering if I was mad. I can't have the authorities questioning my sanity. I never want to be an in-patient in a mental health hospital again. The betrayal of my parents palming me off on doctors rather than listening to me remains. I understand such places are important, but the fear of being discarded by family who didn't care left an emotional scar.

Going to the police without evidence is futile. Iris isn't here to provide the notes Rory sent. He can wipe the videos from his computer in seconds. Unfortunately, I need Zara, the memory stick, and the threatening message from Rory on her phone. She won't abide being pushed out of the limelight. If the police questioned her after I'd been to them, she'd claim I'm making it up. I may need Zara, but I choose not to feel powerless. Zara and Rory will eventually be exposed, and I can leave.

Dusting furniture will keep me busy. I ought to leave the place clean. No matter how well Adam and I are getting on, I'm certain he'll dock my deposit in a heartbeat if he finds a speck of dust. I get the feather duster out and flick at the ceiling. I sweep over the air vents, placed just below the ceiling. The duster catches and pulls away the front of a vent. After grabbing a chair, I stand on it to check for damage. It isn't a vent at all. There's only the wall behind the removed casing and no gap for ventilation. It's not the strangest part, though. A red light flickers and a camera lens comes into view.

CHAPTER 108
The Watcher

Sophie's face looms large. I'm witnessing my potential doom. She has discovered me. I may have wanted a smart listener, but this is forbidden. Sophie isn't allowed the luxury of knowing before I chose to share the truth.

Everything must change. She is a threat. It's time to reveal myself.

The only question left is whether Sophie will be The Listener or a corpse.

CHAPTER 109
Sophie

Someone is watching me.

I contemplate all the other vent frontages I've pulled away. Some vents are as they should be. Many aren't. Cameras are dotted across the flat. Each one is placed within a larger slat gaping in the middle of the vents. Like most pioneering technology, the cameras are tiny. If I hadn't dusted, I'd probably never have found them.

Every second I've spent in Harmony House has been seen. All the private moments where I've cried, danced like a fool, spoken to Ben and Emma, been naked, performed daily routines, and laughed at the television, I've had an audience. My life is a reality TV show.

In a desperate act to rid myself of the filth of violation, I wash my hands. They've touched the cameras. I'll never feel clean again. Who's watching me? Is it Rory? How did he set this up? Does he have a key? I have so many questions. Considering Rory's involvement with Louise, it makes sense it's him. I've underestimated his resourcefulness and depravity. Zara and I have to leave now.

While grabbing my jacket and keys, the knock on the door makes me startle. Panic overrides the practicality of checking the spyhole first.

THE WATCHER

He stands there, grinning with self-satisfaction.

'Well, hello. Going somewhere?'

I peer behind my visitor to check the hallway. Rory must still be out. I hope I didn't miss him coming back while I was ripping vents off the wall.

'What are you doing here?' I ask.

'Nice way to greet a fella,' Neil says. 'I need to fix the leak under your sink.' He holds up a spanner.

'This isn't a good time. I have to go out.'

He frowns as he touches my arm. 'You're shaking. What's the matter?'

Despite trying to be brave, I begin to cry. 'Please, let me go. I have to be safe.'

He lets go of my arm. 'I promise you're safe with me.'

I hear a door slamming upstairs and turn back towards my flat. If it's Rory, I can't run outside. He'll surely catch me. Inside is safer for now. I turn to close the door behind me. Neil slips inside.

'I didn't say you could come in,' I say as he slinks around me.

I slam the door, caught in making a choice between being hurt by Rory and trusting Neil. Rory may be able to see me via his cameras, but he can't walk through a closed door. Hopefully, having Neil nearby should be a deterrent. Still, the way he walked in isn't cool.

'I didn't say you could come in,' I repeat to Neil, who's lingering by the closed door.

'Sorry, I just thought you needed someone with you. You looked terrified. Maybe playing the white knight wasn't a good move.'

I try to focus on my uninvited guest instead of my fears.

'I don't need you to rescue me. If I want help, I'll ask my husband.'

'Not here though, is he?'

Assessing Neil's face, I fear the worst and find it. The eyes always tell a story. His interest in me goes beyond friendship.

'Ben is actually here. Well, he's at work.'

'How can he be at work here when he lives in Oxfordshire?'

'He's helping out at the Poole office.'

'That right?'

Neil gives me the smirk reserved for those who disbelieve. A sudden thought hits me. I'm not the only liar in this flat.

'Wait a minute,' I begin, 'there isn't a leak under the sink. I haven't reported anything.'

The tips of his ears redden. 'Dad asked me to check. It's a long-term problem he's finally got around to sorting out. You know how lapse Dad is sometimes.'

'Sorry, I'm really busy at the moment. Can you do it another time? I'm going tomorrow.'

I step to the side.

'Where are you going?'

He edges closer.

'Back home with Ben, where I belong. Look, I'm not available. I'm a happily married woman.'

'I want to talk to you before you go to set a few things straight.' His usual buoyant tone is replaced with seriousness.

The tendons in his neck stretch. Neil pulls up his sleeves. A distinctive tattoo of an eye, bordered by roses, appears. It's the same tattoo belonging to the man who completed the threesome in Rory and Zara's video.

I will my breathing to be normal.

'How well do you really know Rory?'

Neil regards the spanner still in his hand.

'I'm here to tell you the truth.'

CHAPTER 110
Sophie

Neil narrows the space between us. The tool in his hand becomes more menacing. Braced for the strike, my eyes follow its movement.

'I hated lying to you,' Neil says. The threat permeating his muscles and stature seems to increase his size. 'There's something about you that captured me from the moment we met. I've never felt this way before. The desire to watch over you is overwhelming.'

My attempt at casual laughter sounds more like hysteria.

'It's really flattering, but I'm happy with Ben. Let's forget this happened. Fix the sink after I've gone. All this stuff won't be in the way then. I'm so messy and—'

As I move backwards, I lose my balance and fall. Neil halts. His arm jolts up and he raises the spanner high. I huddle on the floor, a snail retreating into its shell. Clanging against the wooden floorboards makes me shudder. My mind searches for the sense in him dropping the spanner. He offers an open hand. Pushing with my feet, I scoot away on my backside. The unit by the doorway serves as a prop for standing.

'I wasn't going to hit you!' Neil cries. 'I grabbed the spanner earlier to make it look like I was going to fix a leak. I just got a cramp in my arm. When I hold up my arm, the blood flows into it. It seizes up from an old rugby injury. I'd never hurt you. What kind of man do you think I am?'

'The kind of bloke who invents reasons to be in my flat. A man who features in a "special" film with Zara and Rory.'

Neil holds his head in his hands. He looks up through splayed fingers.

'You watched it then? Rory promised he had deleted it. I saw you looking at the videos in his flat. In the hope you'd do something about them, I peeked at what you were doing. That's why I let you into Rory's home. From watching you, you strike me as someone who wants to help others.'

'It wouldn't have been great for you, though.'

'Why? To my shame, I was a willing participant in one of the recordings, not like those poor women Rory drugged.'

'Did you know about it?'

'Not for certain until you played the videos. When I saw the one featuring Gabrielle, I was stunned. She's an old school friend Rory saw me chatting to in Cheeky's.'

'I don't believe you. There's no way I wouldn't have seen you peering from the bathroom.'

'I *was* watching. I'm telling the truth!'

The bellowing hurts my ears. I mustn't retreat into the safe places within my mind. Alertness will save me.

'You're lying!' I yell back, 'and don't think I missed the reference you made to watching me. I bet you were stalking me before we properly met. Well, I can also watch. I've seen more than your threesome video.' My hand snakes behind me. 'The tattoo exposes you. It was in one of the videos of Gabrielle. You held up her head to the camera while she was semi-conscious. Don't give me that crap about seeing the video for the first time when I played it. You were the main star. I expect you've been blackmailing these women, too. Does Rory offer a cut?'

'No!'

He aims towards me. I seize the palette knife I use for mixing paint. It dangles between my fingers, threatening to slip. I grasp the knife in my palm, sending thanks to Zara that it was on top of

THE WATCHER

the unit. After our showdown, I put it there. Zara's fake request to learn about art might save me.

Neil holds out a hand towards me. I'm not falling for the cramp excuse. With eyes shut, afraid of seeing what I must do, I jab the knife in front of me. A cry forces me to look. Confusion spreads across Neil's face as he assesses the wound in his arm. While he's distracted, I push Neil outside.

CHAPTER 111

Sophie

Surely someone will hear Neil's incessant banging on the door? Where's Adam with his usual disciplining of people's noise when you need him? There's no guarantee of when a rescuer will arrive or if they'll get here in time. I race around the flat, trying to find my phone, and cursing my disorganisation. I had it when I messaged Ben earlier. Where did I put my mobile afterwards?

The thudding stops. I tiptoe towards the door. Thump! It vibrates with the force. Neil's toying with me.

'I found Gabrielle in that state,' he cries. 'I didn't know Rory had hooked up with her. He made me deal with the situation. Please believe me.'

I can't figure out if it's whining or pain is tinging his voice.

He continues. 'Rory phoned in a panic. Gabrielle wasn't coming around. Rory wanted me to take her home. He said I owed him one because he hadn't shown Dad the threesome video. I couldn't bear my old man seeing that.'

I move closer to the door.

'It's the least of your worries after Adam hears about you drugging, raping, and videoing women, along with stalking me.'

'No, I've never done any of that!' he yells. 'I saw you a few times coming out of the building before we first met, that's all. Rory got me on tape, trying to rouse Gabrielle. He left the camera running after having his way with her. I wasn't aware he was filming. The bastard used my appearance as ammunition against me. Rory said if I told anyone what he was doing, he'd show the video and claim I was part of it.'

'A likely story. I'm so pissed off with people around here thinking I'm gullible.'

'I'm in pain here.' He groans. 'My mobile's in the van, so I can't call for help. At least phone for an ambulance.'

Why doesn't he care about the emergency services turning up? Neil isn't aware I can't find my phone. The risk of him getting arrested is obviously minimal against the pain. Did the knife go in that far? I thought the bluntness made it benign. In my desperation to push him out of the flat, I didn't have time to look at the extent of the wound. Through the spyhole, only Neil's legs are visible from where he's collapsed against the door. Am I a killer, too? Clasping the door handle is forcing a life-or-death decision: my life or Neil's possible death.

As I've already rendered him immobile, hopefully he doesn't have any fight left. I grasp the key in the lock, ready to open Pandora's box. Before going outside, I take another peek through the spyhole. An eye appears on the other side. Its menace makes me collide with the shoe stand.

'Sophie, I need help.'

Does he sound weaker, or is my guilt making this seem worse?

'I'm telling the truth,' Neil whines. 'You should fear the residents in this building, not me. Installing cameras is a dick move.'

'Bloody hell, you know about the cameras in my flat?' I scrabble around in my pocket to grab the amethyst. '*You* put them in here.'

'No! I do maintenance, which means I notice lots of things. You're not the only one with cameras. They're everywhere. I was told to keep quiet, or they'd pin it on Dad. After all, being a warden is the perfect opportunity to watch others.'

'Who's behind them, then?'

No reply.

'Tell me!' I shout.

'Help me and I'll tell you.' His whisper is barely discernible through the door.

My wobbly legs demand support. I shuffle to the sofa; a life-raft against fatigue and terrifying thoughts.

'It's not safe out here,' Neil says. 'Please help me. The person watching can see us. Now I've exposed them, I'm in danger. You are, too.'

Can I trust a wounded man who's been so secretive? He's a stranger. When we first met, he turned up unannounced. Is Neil responsible for setting up the cameras or someone else? Maybe he's mentioning them to assert his power.

I continue looking for my phone, pulling up sofa cushions and flinging clothes aside. Perhaps I can use my laptop to email Ben or even the police. I consider the crime dramas I've watched. I've never seen anyone send an email to the police, but I have to try. The volume of packed boxes makes me groan. My laptop's in one of them.

Outside, Neil emits a raw scream, followed by a wail. A heavy bang resounds against the door. Then silence.

I dare to take another peek through the spyhole. Once again, his legs are laid out in front of him. He's stationary, but it might be part of the act. What if it's not, though? What if I've killed him? Is this similar to Zara's trick of leaning against the door to tumble into my flat when I open it?

Thinking about it, Zara and Neil were flirtatious the day I met him. Maybe Rory, Neil, and Zara are all in this together. But Zara played me the message of Rory threatening her. My brain hurts with the conflicting devious possibilities. Were they waiting for a new resident they could mentally torture after finishing with Louise? Bekstar had a lucky escape.

I regard the palette knife on the floor, trying not to focus on the blood staining it. The handle is too thick for the purpose. I take a butter knife from the cutlery drawer. Sliding it into the gap at the bottom of the door, I poke Neil. He doesn't respond. This means nothing when dealing with a deceiver. I need to see his reactions.

THE WATCHER

Ben often marvels at my resourcefulness. When I run low on art supplies, I mix paint with household products so it will last until my order arrives. I've invented systems around my home to make things work. I can do it now. The band, previously securing my ponytail, forms part of the kit. Placing the butter knife on the floor, I stand on it. The handle points out to the left side of my right foot. There's enough of the tip sticking out of the right side of my shoe to have an impact. I tether the knife to my foot with the hair tie. The knife slides under the door. I jab it into Neil. Through the spyhole I can see he doesn't move. I poke a little harder. His legs shake in reflexive response. He doesn't say a word.

A man's slumped outside my door. He might be in trouble. Whatever Neil's done I can't leave him like this. If I do, I'm as bad as him.

I draw the door open a crack. Neil falls backwards. I fling the door open. The body hits the floor.

Neil is dead.

CHAPTER 112
Sophie

The door may be shut, but I can't close off the vision of Neil's body in my head. Dragging him inside isn't an option. If I have to keep looking at his corpse, I'd never survive the mental fallout. As I shoved Neil back outside, I looked over at Adam's flat. Guilt made me turn away. Adam has no one left. Tina's death diminished him. Losing his son will destroy Adam.

The image of blood staining Neil's T-shirt makes me nauseous. His last cry before dying was my signal to help. Instead, I chose self-preservation. Maybe being mercenary is how I'll survive. There's a murderer out there. I'm likely to be their next victim. Using logic is the only way to get out of here. I couldn't have killed Neil. I only poked him in the back with a butter knife. The palette knife struck his arm, not his midriff. He was murdered outside my flat. I left him out there as a sitting target for a killer. No. I am not responsible. I won't accept it.

Frigid air attacks me as I retreat further into the flat. A frame holding a photo of Ben and me falls from the windowsill. Glass shatters on the floor. I didn't open the window. Why would I considering how frosty it is today? Ben says I should get more air to my body; one of his mum's favourite mantras. Even indoors I like to layer up. Still, Ben didn't open the window. I would've noticed after he left. Stanley's a regular visitor, but there's no way

THE WATCHER

a gull could pull a window wide open. My seagull friend might be savvy, but he's not a bird burglar. I shut the window and notice the lock is broken.

I must consider my next move. Can I step over Neil's body? I've watched too many horror films. Imagining him grabbing my ankle doesn't help with being brave. My phone is missing. Nobody knows what's happened. Hopefully, a resident will see Neil, although it might be some time. Zara might come out soon to meet me. I check my watch. Zara will take every second to work on her appearance. She's also proved I can't rely on her.

Amethyst in hand, I make a decision. I won't be a prisoner of fear. I gulp down air, trying to keep my breathing square. Counting the inhalations and exhalations, I reach for the key. Despite being the one to do it, the turn of the lock surprises me. Another version of me is taking charge. No, I must acknowledge my strength. It's all I have left. I am doing this. I am facing it. I can do this. Think. Move. Act.

The handle slips from my grasp. I seize it again and pull the door open. Don't look down. Step over. Keep moving.

I look down.

Neil's body has gone.

CHAPTER 113
Sophie

Where the hell is everyone? Adam isn't answering when I knock on his door. I don't know how to begin telling him I left his son outside, exposed to a murderer.

I banged on the Gallos' door, figuring even Federico would be a welcome ally. No reply. Zara's the last resort. Someone's murdered Neil and taken his body. It has to be Rory. Neil knew about Rory's sex tape operation and the cameras.

The pounding of my fist against the door intensifies.

'Zara, please help. Let me in!'

No response. With each thump I make, I tell my vivid imagination to stop considering what might have happened to her. Has Rory killed her like he threatened? Am I next? I scan the hallway and the stairs. Making so much noise isn't wise when there's a killer around.

Going outside is my final option. I face my fears and go into the back garden where I can see into Zara's flat. Whenever I sit on the bench, I envy the rear flats with their patio doors. The front ones don't have them. Instead, we have windows facing a small garden and the road. It doesn't matter anymore what the flats looks like. All I care about is getting out of here alive.

The exhibitionist Zara has no curtains in her home. It's obvious she doesn't care anyone can see her when they're in the

THE WATCHER

back garden. Once, I caught her walking around nude. Zara paraded in her bedroom by the patio door - no doubt checking for onlookers - performed a twerk and carried on as if nothing happened. I'm relying on her brazenness now.

Sitting on the bed, Zara stares at her phone. She was probably so wrapped up in posting selfies on social media she ignored the knocking on her front door. I don't want a companion who'd rather apply lipstick than help someone in distress, but she's all I've got. The lack of other residents in Harmony House is eerie. The sense of abandonment heightens my loneliness.

My frantic waving arms try to capture Zara's attention. Competing with her hypnotic reflection is a fruitless effort. I approach the patio door to smack against it. As I prepare to knock, a movement inside renders me immobile. A man appears behind Zara. He slinks an arm around her neck. The hold locks into place.

Rory smiles as he strangles Zara.

CHAPTER 114

The Watcher

Trailing Sophie is making me dizzy. I can't miss a single second. Getting closer to her in body and on the screen is imperative. A final decision must be made.

I flick through the camera views on my phone. Aware Sophie can see me at any moment, I linger nearby. Skirting on the cusp of exposure is the ultimate high.

I assess my options:
• Do I watch Sophie as a series of truths dawn upon her?
• Should I deal with the person who's become a chore rather than a help?
• Will I take my prepared escape route now or later?

Whatever I do, I must bring this to completion. The project has changed. Sophie's behaviour determines her fate. If she ruins my work, I have no qualms about the next course of action.

Sophie must die.

CHAPTER 115
Sophie

Think! Move! Act!

Rory's set to kill Zara. His snake arm constricts around her throat. My leaden feet are rooted. Brain fog descends. A rock forms in my chest.

I see something I wish I hadn't. Rory isn't strangling her. It's an embrace. They're kissing. Once again, Zara has tricked me. Why do I keep letting people to do this? Harmony House has blinded me. No more being a pushover. It's true I've been gullible sometimes, but I won't blame myself too much. Expert liars reside here. I won't feel ashamed for trying to see the best in people. Anyone would've been duped.

I'm getting out of here. Zara and Rory will be punished. They must be behind the cameras set up in my flat. Rory's proven he likes to watch women. The thought of him seeing my nakedness and imagining what he planned to do with it is sickening.

I assess the high walls surrounding the communal garden. Iris called this an oasis of privacy and security. Now it's more of a prison. I must go back along the side of the building to the front. Maybe I can get away before the devious duo catches me. I wish I'd taken up running instead of adopting sofa sitting as my main sport. If I hadn't appeared at the patio door, they wouldn't be aware I'd seen them.

Neil's body is probably in Zara's flat. Those bastards are coveting his corpse as a prize. If only I'd given Neil a chance to explain. He might still be alive. But he *was* in the videos. Doesn't that make him part of it? Do I believe Neil was filmed without his knowledge, helping a vulnerable Gabrielle? My head hurts. Nobody can or will protect me. I am alone. I am enough.

Even under the sturdy tread of my boots the alleyway's frosted path is slippery. My flailing hand catches on the brick. The scratching of my fingertips keeps my senses sharp. I focus on the destination. The front gate awaits me. I haven't got a clue where the police station is. It doesn't matter. Escaping is enough. The edge of the building heralds turning a corner from risk to safety. Gull Lane is in sight. I can make it. Hopefully, Zara and Rory didn't see me.

Hope isn't for the likes of me.

CHAPTER 116

Sophie

I try to wriggle out of my captor's grasp as we go down the alleyway. We're heading back towards the garden.

'Stop fighting. Whether you like it or not, you're coming with me.'

'Get off. I'll bloody scream!' I shout.

'There's no one to hear you, sweetheart. Everyone's out.'

'There are people walking past at the front of the building.'

My impending cry is stifled by a hand clamped over my mouth.

'I thought we could do this the easy way, but, as ever, you're determined to make it difficult. Nothing I do is good enough for you. You always have to be in charge.'

I muffle expletives against my captor's palm.

'If I uncover your mouth, are you going to shut up and listen?'

I nod. The hand lowers but remains near my face.

'I'm glad you're playing nice, Soph. This is wrecking my manicure. At least you're shit at running.'

The patio doors for the bottom rear flats are no longer something I envy. It took Zara seconds, even in heels, to see me, exit her flat, dart across the garden, and catch me.

'Whatever you and Rory have done, I won't tell anyone,' I say.

Zara's usual donkey bray is replaced by a jaded laugh.

'You may think I'm an airhead, but I know you won't keep quiet. The second I let go, you'll run straight to the police and spill all about my part in the videos. I can't allow it to happen.'

'What about what we agreed on earlier?'

She ceases dragging me.

'I've had a rethink. Even if I kept what I did from the police, you'd blurt it all out. Do-gooder Sophie can't resist righting wrongs. There's no way I'm doing time. Have you seen what they make you wear in prison?'

'You're unimaginable. After what you've done to Neil, you'll be wearing prison issue clothes for the rest of your life.'

'I hardly think recording a threesome is a reason to be banged up.'

'You killed him!'

The donkey hee-haw returns.

'Get those meds changed. Neil isn't dead. I saw him earlier, going into your flat. For once, I was ready early. It's obvious Neil has a thing for you, so I gave you some time together.'

'Don't lie. His body was slumped outside my door!'

'I think I'd have noticed a body lying in the hallway. Seriously, get to a psychiatrist, pronto. You're seeing things, like the baby you kept hearing.'

'What do you know about it?'

I wriggle away. Zara wrenches my arm behind my back.

'I've got moves. Daddy made me learn Judo when I was younger to toughen me up. I quit when I discovered fashion and boys. As for the baby stuff, Adam told me you were hearing noises. Remember, I was there the night you lost your marbles, imagining a brat crying. Adam was concerned and thought I might be able to help you. As if.'

I squeeze my eyelids shut. She won't have the satisfaction of enjoying my tears.

'My life has nothing to do with you,' I say.

'Oh, but it has. Rory and I were having a chat. We were discussing how to end things with you.'

CHAPTER 117
The Watcher

When the cameras were installed, questions were raised about their necessity in the alleyway. I fought for it. Each project I undertake is done with precision. Nothing's left to chance. No expense is spared.

Setting the cameras up without being noticed was a risky operation. It required assistance. People are easily bought or placated when you're aware of their weaknesses. The building was emptied on the ruse of undergoing renovation. Tiny lenses were installed inside and out of Harmony House. Residents returned delighted with their recent all expenses paid luxury hotel stays.

Every camera is trained on a prime viewing spot. I knew the alleyway had potential. So much happens in dark enclosed places: stolen kisses; one-night stands; deals; secrets; and contrition. The narrow space has widened my view of Harmony House.

My catalogue of blackmail was increasing. It's a shame I can't use any of it. There's no sport in torturing someone if you can't see their reaction.

Once I leave a watching post, I never go back and look. New opportunities are now vying for my undivided attention.

The alleyway plays its part in the final scenes. Sophie's future is looking as bleak as the shadows closing in around her.

CHAPTER 118

Sophie

'So, you and Rory are going to kill me?'

The resignation in my voice is worrying. I should be terrified. Harmony House does strange things to me. This place has a magical hold on its residents; dark magic. I was right in knowing it was time to leave.

The hysteria of her laughing makes Zara loosen her grip on me. Her foot gives way on the icy path. Expertise in wearing stilettos keeps her upright.

'Smart arse Soph reckons she's got everything worked out.' Zara's fingers knead into my arm. 'What kind of person do you think I am?'

'A murderer, blackmailer, and a deceitful bitch.'

Against the power of Botox, her forehead attempts a furrow.

'Quite a list there. Not all of it is true. How can I convince you of who I really am?'

'You don't need to. It's obvious.'

A familiar sound comes from behind Zara. Cawing pitches to a squall. Stanley launches, pecking at her legs.

'Get the hell off me!' she cries, still keeping a grip on me.

Stanley opens his beak wide and bellows at the woman holding me captive. I struggle against Zara's hold. Her vice grip increases as she fights the bird. Zara draws her leg back.

THE WATCHER

'If you kick Stanley, I will end you!' I shout.

She drops back into a standing position.

'You're naming seagulls? It's official. You've finally lost the plot. Shoo! Shoo!' She flutters her free hand at the gull.

Stanley hops to the end of the alleyway and takes flight. Zara's phone pings. Her eyes widen as she looks at the screen.

'We've got to go!' she says.

'Where?' I ask.

'Into the back garden. Rory's waiting for us.'

Zara pushes me in front, leading the way to my certain death.

CHAPTER 119

The Watcher

Sophie is the subject who frustrated and thrilled me the most. How can a being, ridden with anxiety, be so strong? She reminds me of a teenager I once admired. At school, their devious ways almost matched mine. I dared to believe kindred spirits might exist, forgetting I'm one of a kind.

That youth is now an apathetic adult whose life is occasionally disturbed by breakdowns. I receive regular reports from my sources. Such a disappointment. Their faulty mind masqueraded as genius. I had to test it. Anyone allowed into my life must prove their worth. They failed. I pushed that person to the brink of madness. They never returned. The school threatened expulsion for my cruelty. There was no definitive proof. My sparring partner was too afraid to name me. I prospered and learned to be more selective in choosing my subjects.

Since she entered Harmony House, Sophie has been my greatest puzzle. I wondered if someone with a mental illness would be a risk for the listening role. Anxiety makes Sophie stronger. Resilience appears when she's skirting rock bottom. Anxiety brings greater alertness.

Witnessing Sophie's stoicism against Zara's threats made me proud. No. This will not do. There's a job to finish. Emotions have no place here. Sophie is a means to an end. She either ends up as The Listener or she ends full stop.

CHAPTER 120
Sophie

In the back garden, a figure hunches over on the bench by the rose bushes. The heavy winter coat and a scarf wrapped around their face serve as a disguise. It's not Rory's usual cowboy style clothing, but it's freezing out here. The retreating posture isn't his habitual cocksure stance. Hiding within the layers, the person seems more fragile. Zara continues pushing me in front of her. Our guest rises from the bench.

'Let go of her!' the person shouts.

In the confusion at hearing a particular voice, Zara releases me. I move from one person's hold to another's. My rescuer shields me. Their arms envelope me in the care and friendship I've come to know.

'What are you doing here?' I ask them. 'I've been so worried about you, thinking you were missing or even...'

Spiralling puffs of frozen air tumble from their mouth. A deep-rooted frown betrays their heroism.

'My dear,' Iris begins, 'it'll take more than that little madam to bump me off. I received a text instructing me to come here. Zara said if I met with her, we'd go to the police and expose Rory. She sent me one of the videos as evidence of his depravity. Despite my fears, I had to be here. I'm glad I am now.'

Zara grimaces. 'I didn't send you a message. How can I when I don't have your number?'

'A likely story,' I reply.

Iris trembles, probably from fear as well as the brittle, biting chill.

'After I left, I believed I was safe. When I got the message, I dithered over whether it was wise to come. After seeing the disgusting video, I had to be here. Rory must pay for what he's done. I want to return here feeling secure. Harmony House is where I belong. No one will keep me away ever again.'

I can't relate to Iris' sentimentality. For me, this place has been a nightmare.

Zara holds up her mobile, the screen facing towards us. 'I didn't send you a message. Check my phone.'

'Like we're coming anywhere near you,' I say. 'I've seen you fight other people. Besides, you might have a weapon in your back pocket.'

Zara waves the precious mobile in her hand. 'I'd never hurt anyone. Listen to me. When we were in the alleyway, I received a message, too. Rory told me to run after you and bring you here while he sorted out the next stage of his plan.'

Iris claps her hands. 'So, you and Rory are in this together? I knew it.'

'I was bringing you to him, that's true. But I'm looking out for you, Soph, as I always have. I kissed Rory to fool him into thinking I'm playing along. You and I were going to confront him. Now, it appears Rory's playing another watching game with all of us.'

We look around the garden, scanning for the next threat.

CHAPTER 121
The Watcher

Look all you want, ladies. You'll never guess what's coming next. I can see. It's on its way. Scrutinising eyes follow you. Your misty breath in the freezing air trails towards me. Often, the threat is where you least expect it. When looking for monsters, you search out those who appear menacing. Seemingly nice people are the real monsters. They make you believe you're safe so they can swoop in and reveal the true face of evil.

Keep watching, Sophie. Don't let your eyes move away for a second. Fix upon the one spot that reveals it all.

Although this is far more exciting than I expected, this scene must end soon. I have to disappear. Someone will eventually call the police. A new location beckons. When matters are finalised with Sophie, I can leave. Someone else will take the blame for the cameras. I've set them up already. The fallout will be glorious.

Unsure where her safety lies, Sophie's caught between two people. The clues are there. They always have been right under your nose. Wake up from your stupor and smell the roses

CHAPTER 122
Sophie

Zara marches towards us. Heels sinking into the grass make her strides less assured. A quick-thinking Iris kicks Zara's leg. The slipperiness of the sodden lawn works against her, along with Iris' foot holding her in place.

'Thought I was a feeble old bird, didn't you?' Iris says as she leans over Zara. 'Don't underestimate me.'

Zara rolls away. She sits up and checks her soaked dress. With a shrug, she finally puts fashion last. As she tries to stand, Zara teeters on her heels.

'Flaming things.' Zara casts her shoes aside and hops from foot to foot.

'We're leaving.' I edge away. 'Back off and accept it. You've been caught out.'

Without the confidence of her stilettos, Zara is reduced.

'Do what you want. I'm not going to hurt you. Before you go, at least let me explain.'

'Talking time is over,' Iris says with a no-nonsense attitude.

She reminds me of the primary school teacher I equally adored and feared.

Zara reaches for me. I move back. She holds up her hands.

'Okay, I won't touch you, but please believe me. Rory was in my flat so I could trick him. I agreed to set you up as the next video girl. He thought I'd sorted it. I was buying some time for you to leave here.'

Iris slaps a hand to her forehead. The earlier fight extinguishes as she sits on the bench in front of the rose garden.

'Rory wanted to put Sophie in one of those disgraceful videos? This is horrific.'

Zara treads towards us, hands held out in a conciliatory gesture. 'I'm not being dodgy, just checking you're okay, Iris. You're looking a little peaky.'

'The shock is getting to me. Don't come any closer.'

'I'll get help then.'

'No need. Stop fussing and don't try anything.'

Zara dares to move nearer.

'My gran had a stroke a few years ago. She went pale like that, too. Are you sure you're okay? I promise I won't harm you.' She kneels. 'I've never killed anyone and I'm certainly not starting now.'

'Then why are you here?' Iris asks, glancing over her shoulder at the rose garden.

She protects her roses, even when they're not in bloom. She told me she's more of a guardian than a gardener. Right now, Iris is the queen on the throne, presiding over her floral kingdom.

'Rory sent me a message to bring Sophie to the garden,' Zara begins. 'I planned for it to appear as if I'd forced her so he'd think I'm doing what he wants. His plan was to make me look like I'm the bad guy, while he'd save Sophie from me. She'd go with him and... well... you know. Rory wanted to put Sophie in one of his videos.'

I take a moment before speaking to process what she's shared.

'I can't trust a word you say anymore,' I say. 'You've had too many chances.'

Still kneeling near Iris, Zara turns to me. 'I was about to tell you what I'd planned when Iris appeared. You and I, Soph, were going to fake an emergency that meant you had to go back to Oxfordshire. I was going to help you escape.'

THE WATCHER

'Where's Rory?' I ask, looking around the garden.

The dying light darkens between the shrubberies, perfect for a watcher.

'Nearby, I expect, spying on us.' Iris' voice has become paper thin. Maybe she is becoming ill.

Zara puts her shoes back on and sways. She holds onto the rose garden wall to correct her balance. As she threatens to topple, Zara concentrates on the stumps of the rose bushes.

'What the hell?' Zara bends over for a closer look.

'Quick!' I shout. 'Iris is having a heart attack!'

CHAPTER 123

The Watcher

There's so much drama in the Harmony House garden.

Rory's dastardly deeds are forgotten as other unsavoury truths are revealed.

Speak, Zara. Tell us what you see.

Everyone's chances run out, eventually. Seize your last one, Sophie, while you can. The Listener must be alive to listen.

Live for your husband, if that's your motivation. A rosy future isn't always the perfect fantasy it seems, though.

CHAPTER 124
Sophie

Iris slides down the bench. Her scarlet fingernails clutch her upper arm. Puffs of air dart from her mouth.

'Try to breathe slowly. We'll get help.' I keep my voice calm to soothe her.

Zara's pretensions about the old woman's health have disappeared. Next to Iris on the bench, Zara leans over the wall bordering the rose garden.

'Call for an ambulance!' I yell.

Zara faces me, open-mouthed. 'Bloody hell! It's—'

A blow to the head fells Zara. Her body lands in the rose garden.

'You might have killed her!' I cry.

Iris takes a cautious step into her domain. I wonder if she's more concerned about trampling on her precious rose bushes than standing on Zara. Standing back, I hope for altruism.

'She's fine,' Iris says. Red cheeks give her a renewed vigour. 'I've checked her pulse. The first aid training finally came in useful.'

'She's definitely alive?'

Iris concentrates on getting comfortable back on the bench. She opens up her bag and takes out a packet of mints.

'Is Zara all right?'

Iris pops a mint into her mouth.

'She's only unconscious. Sometimes I don't know my own strength.'

'You faked having a heart attack, didn't you?' I ask.

'It's the only thing I could think of to stop her. Seeing as she was initially concerned, I expected she'd try to help me. Strange girl wants us dead but shows concern for someone who looks set to cark it. I expect Zara wanted to be the one to kill me, not a heart attack.'

'Why did you hit her?'

We regard the scattered remnants of the smashed garden gnome.

'It was the first thing to hand.' Iris places her hands in a prayer position and bows her head. 'God help me, I've never hurt anyone before.'

'Don't you believe what she said about pretending to go along with Rory's plan so she could help me?'

'Not for a single second. Remember how I was monitoring things before I left? I suspected Zara and Rory were luring women into his flat. A few times, I saw Zara go in there with them. Mark my words, she's Rory's accomplice. You were next. That little minx was setting you up.'

Thinking of the usually immaculate Zara lying in the mud makes me smirk. Despite this, I am the better person.

'We should phone for an ambulance. Can't leave her pushing up the roses, eh?'

If Iris didn't have a mint in her mouth, you'd swear she was sucking lemons. My attempt at comedy has fallen short. Mocking her beloved blooms, even when they're not out yet, isn't allowed.

'Do you have a mobile?' I ask. 'I've lost mine.'

'Sorry, dear. I try not to carry it around. Granted, it's terribly old-fashioned, but I refuse to be glued to a mobile like most people are nowadays.'

'Let's see if we can find mine then or use someone else's. Hopefully, one of the residents has returned. We need to tell the police about poor Neil, too.'

'Such a sad business.'

Iris looks to the ground. We share a moment of respectful reflection. The silence is interrupted by The Ramones telling their baby they love them. The ringtone for my missing phone demands to be heard. I try to locate it before it stops ringing. I lose.

'Help me find my phone!' I shout.

Zara must have my mobile. As I approach the rose garden wall, Iris pulls me away.

'How silly am I?' She roots through her bag. 'In all the kerfuffle, I forgot. I found this over there.'

Iris holds my phone. She points at the willow tree standing on the other side of the garden. The spindly ashen branches reach for the ground, trying to claim the earth beyond its roots. For some reason, this particular tree gives me the creeps. Maybe it's derived from a childhood fear of the talking trees in The Wizard of Oz throwing apples at Dorothy. I've looked at this tree and imagined its wisps curling around my torso and sucking me into its trunk. Emma's dark fantasy novels have a lot to answer for.

'Are you sure my mobile was over by the willow tree?' I ask.

'Yes. Before you arrived, I took a stroll. I needed to work off my nervousness at facing Zara. Your phone was lying on the grass.'

I inspect it for damage.

'I must've dropped it earlier.'

'Of course, dear.' Iris pats my shoulder. 'Can we go inside to call for the ambulance? The chill's seeping into my bones.'

Mine too, but not only from the weather.

CHAPTER 125
The Watcher

Work it out, Sophie. What do you see? What have you seen? Prove yourself a worthy adversary and accomplice.
Listen. What do you hear?
Stay sharp. Keep alert. Decipher.
Look at what's in your hand and remember.

CHAPTER 126
Sophie

I glance at the phone in my hand and smile. Ben called. Finally, there's hope of the cavalry arriving. After I call for an ambulance and the police, I'll phone Ben. Iris clings to me. I take a few steps with her to Harmony House. A lightning bolt revelation makes me halt.

'I should check on Zara,' I say, breaking free of Iris' hold. 'You go inside and get warm. I'll call the emergency services and wait with her. Leaving an unconscious person unattended isn't wise.'

I race towards Zara, although she's not my target. Now, I remember placing my mobile on the windowsill after messaging Ben. I'd left it there to take a final photo of Stanley when he showed up for one of his visits. When I was in the garden earlier, spying on Zara and Rory, I wasn't anywhere near the willow tree. Anyway, my mobile was missing before. This explains why the window was open when I knew I hadn't opened it. From the front garden, someone approached my flat, forced the flimsy window lock, and stole my phone.

Before Iris struck her, Zara was looking into the rose garden. It seemed peculiar she didn't help Iris with her "heart attack". Zara's earlier concern at Iris possibly having a stroke wasn't fake. Something she saw in the rose garden caught Zara's attention.

I look over the wall and wish I hadn't. The tip of a knife pricks my cheek.

CHAPTER 127
The Watcher

You didn't see it coming, did you, Sophie? That's why I'm The Watcher and you're the watched. I don't know why I'm bothering to address you anymore. You probably won't hear this.

People always revert to type, and you're no exception. I learned all I could about you, absorbing your ways, life, and reactions. I read you like the proverbial book. The final chapter is here. A blade decides your fate.

Your expression confirmed you'd worked out what happened to your phone. Well done. At last, your watching prowess shone through. When you looked over the wall and saw what was lying there, the horror was exquisite. I'll make it a screen saver. It will serve as a fitting memorial for Sophie Walters.

CHAPTER 128
Sophie

My feet drag over earth. Lines from my boots leave a trail next to where Zara's lying. Was that a flutter of her eyelashes? I hope she's gaining consciousness. Nothing else will save me from the knife pricking at my throat.

The strength my captor tried to keep hidden is now confirmed. They haul me back over the wall and position me on the bench like a puppet. How the hell did this seemingly harmless person become this?

'You had to look, didn't you?' Iris spits out each word.

'Why did you kill him?'

Rory's death stare haunts me.

'I had every right to take his life. He was as good as family.' Iris smirks at my reaction. 'When he was a boy, I became Rory's guardian. Your face is an absolute picture. It's always such a joy to behold.'

Her sombre mouth finally breaks into a toothy grin I didn't think her capable of forming. Brown stains leech from her gums, eating into yellowed teeth. No wonder she always fixes her mouth into a grim line. Along with the straggly hair, she resembles a sinister storybook witch, guaranteed to give children nightmares.

'Rory wasn't threatening you then,' I begin, 'but what about the messages you showed me?'

THE WATCHER

Iris cackles, completing the witchy persona. 'It's all part of the plan. I made him write the notes, so you'd think I'm a scared, harmless, little old lady, stagnating with her three cats. I enjoyed having those moggies. Watching Rory wheeze when he visited was fun. He needed a reminder of who's in charge. Glad the cats are gone, though. They got in the way.'

'You haven't…'

'The cats are in a rescue centre. That's the least of your concerns.'

The knife caresses my throat.

'How could you murder someone who was like a son to you?' I ask. 'I understand Rory's a beast, but why kill him?'

'He deviated from the plan. Since we arrived in Harmony House, we agreed no one must learn of our connection. Then Rory told Louise. I forgave that slip, but I knew he would've shared the secret with you, too. He'd lined you up as his next film star. You're *my* plaything. I saw your kindness was something I could manipulate. Rory ruined it by developing a fixation with you. Whenever we talked, it was always, "Sophie this, Sophie that". I noticed the obsessive signs, which is why you must die. No one takes him from me.'

Despite my fear, I can't hold in the laughter. 'Even if I was interested, killing Rory means I can't get my hands on him, anyway. To be clear, I wouldn't have gone near him if you'd paid me.'

'A likely story. Rory always charms women into bed, including Zara. I saw him going into her flat and realised they were in cahoots. He pushed me aside. When you overheard Zara and Rory discussing the videos, I had to bring things to an end. As soon as Zara left to chase after you, I got Rory to let me into her place. Silly boy always trusted me. I gave him one of the sedatives he used on those women and then we walked into the garden. It didn't take long for the drugs to kick in. Rory was most accommodating in passing out as we chatted by the rose garden. I made sure he didn't land on my rose bushes, though. Your delicate disposition won't enjoy hearing the details of his killing, so I'll spare you. Just know I'm a strong woman underneath this fragile façade. When you're older, everyone thinks you're delicate.' Iris regards the bodies lying in the garden. 'I was going to bury Rory after I'd sorted you and that little bitch out.' She points at Zara.

'That's why you seemed out of breath when I first saw you,' I reply. 'Killing a man and burying him must be hard work, even if you are strong. I guess you're lifting heavier weights than just the little dumbbells in your lounge.'

Iris strokes her bicep and laughs. 'The heavier weights I use are hidden in my second bedroom. I can't have people seeing through the frail old woman act. Gardening has honed my digging skills, too. Stereotypes of the elderly as weak have been to my advantage.'

'Did you send Zara the message from Rory's phone?' I ask.

'Well, duh. Who else? Don't think I'm not upset he's gone. I adored him.' Iris' chin wobbles. 'If only he'd remained the sweet boy I once knew. He learned everything from me. After his mum had a breakdown when her pathetic husband left, I cared for Rory. Even at fourteen, he craved the female touch. I gave him all he wanted and more.'

The leering smile reveals more of her decayed teeth. She can't mean what I think she's saying.

Iris continues. 'There's nothing Rory didn't know about how to please a woman. My tuition served him well.'

'He was underage back then and you're much older than him,' I say. 'You're disgusting.'

The knife slashes my jaw. Warm stickiness trickles down my neck.

'Don't you dare sully what Rory and I had! It was a love beyond convention.'

Wild eyes kill off any last hints of the sweet lady. All I can do is keep talking and hope someone sees us.

'Did you know Rory drugged women and filmed himself raping them?' I want to hurt Iris like she's damaged others.

'Know about it? My dear girl, I came up with the idea.'

Breathe. I will get through this. I will see my husband again.

'The whole operation was set up by me,' Iris says. 'It was a lovely little earner. My pension could only pay for so much. It was about time he contributed to the rent and bills. Although I loved him, he was a financial leech.'

'Did you install the cameras in my flat?'

'What are you talking about?'

I let it slide. The police can deal with it. I must believe she will be caught, and I'll live.

'You should never have come to Harmony House.' Iris inspects the knife, running it along her finger. She regards my blood on her skin and smiles. Iris waves the weapon. 'This thing is only a threat. Your death will look like an accident. I'm rather accomplished at it. Louise and Una's deaths had you all fooled.'

CHAPTER 129

Sophie

I take a glimpse at Zara. If I can help it, another person won't die by Iris' hand. Was that a rise in Zara's chest? Damn you, Zara, wake up!

'Why did you kill Louise and Una?' I ask, intent on using talk as a distraction. The longer we're out here, the more chance I have of rescue.

'Louise fell in love with Rory. That's a big no-no.' Iris waggles her finger. 'Nobody takes him from me.'

'Finding out she was carrying his baby obviously tipped you over the edge, you psycho bitch.'

Iris' eyes widen. 'How do you know about it?'

I shrug my shoulders. She isn't getting anything from me, including my life, if I can help it.

'All those years I was denied a child and then Rory gets that slut pregnant. He had the audacity to ask me to take care of the situation, never considering how his actions affected me. After Louise threatened to expose our sex tape operation, I paid her a visit. She was desperate to share her pregnancy news. I had to wipe the smile off her face, so I smacked her head against the unit. Afterwards, I poured gin down her throat so it would appear like she'd been on another of her benders.

THE WATCHER

'Then we have Una, the nosey cow who had to go. She saw Rory and me kissing. I couldn't allow the secret to be exposed. Una thought we were friends. Fellow old biddies, waiting for the curtain call. Una's final performance was quite something. Watching someone die from an asthma attack is a noisy experience. My threats terrified Una so much I didn't need to touch her. She died at my feet.'

Breathe. Think! Move! Act!

'If you loved Rory, why did you kill him?'

Iris regards the place where he lies. Her watering eyes glint in the sun's fading embers.

'He claimed not to love me anymore. Said I'm too old and haggard for him. I've given Rory everything, and he was going to repay me by leaving. After his burial, he'll stay with me forever.' She wipes the tears away and grins.

I have no reply to such evil.

'At least he isn't alone in his final resting place,' Iris adds.

Acidic bile bites in my throat. I don't want to ask, but I must. 'Who else is buried there?'

'Your strange friend, Tobias, and that's your fault.'

Thick sobs catching in my throat make it hard to speak, but I must know the truth.

'Did he know about the sex videos?'

'Indeed, he did. I overheard you telling your friend on the phone about Tobias' secret room. If you'd have shut the front door, he might've been safe.' She nods towards Zara. 'Although that stupid girl told Rory about the notebooks. He didn't share all that happened between him and Zara, but did tell me that. So, I guess you're not fully to blame for Tobias' death. After taking the notebooks, Rory killed him with a few whacks on the head, and then typed a letter on his behalf to Adam. Rory buried Tobias here. My boy wasn't pleased. It was his first kill, but I can't be expected to do everything around here. I do have a life.'

I despise this woman and how she's having a strop about murdering people. The lovely, compassionate Tobias didn't deserve this. All he wanted was to protect people, and no one protected him.

'How did Rory manage to get Tobias' body here without being seen?'

'Good job we've got such an inefficient warden here. Rory's and my night-time shenanigans with the trusty wheelbarrow and tarpaulin cover a multitude of deathly sins.' Iris cracks her knuckles. 'People claim to be good neighbours, but you'd be surprised how many turn a blind eye to what's happening around them. No one wants to get involved. It's too much effort. Don't think I haven't figured out you're trying to delay things by asking questions. Let's clear up the other matters for you as well. Neil's alive, just about. He's tied up and gagged in Una's flat. Bad luck for him that Adam's gone away for a few days to visit family. Neil is a strapping lad and not easy to manoeuvre, but I did it. Thought I was a puny granny, like the rest of them, didn't you?'

I refuse to feed her ego by stating I'd worked out she has a stronger body than it appears. Unfortunately, I thought Iris was using her strength to carry shopping and occasionally light weights, not killing people and lugging bodies.

Iris continues. 'Society writes us off when we reach a certain age. What you see is a shell of who I really am. This.' She grabs her thinning hair and tugs at it. 'These wrinkles.' She swishes a hand across her forehead. 'This seemingly fragile skeleton… It's all a veneer. Inside, I'm strong and beautiful. I used to turn heads. Rory couldn't get enough of me.'

'Spare me your egotistical rants,' I reply. 'Your inner ugliness can't be concealed.'

She swings the knife. My defensive hand catches it on the palm. I wince against the sting.

'I'll do far worse if you don't shut up,' she yells. 'If you had survived, you'd have done well to heed my story. You're getting older. Appreciate any attention you can get.'

'I'm fine with my doting husband, who I've been married to for decades, thanks.'

'A bit on the side keeps things fresh,' Iris says. 'You should've given in to Neil. All he wanted was your body, nothing more. He wasn't someone for you to fear. I hid in the cleaning cupboard under the stairs while Neil shouted his innocence in the hallway.

THE WATCHER

He was innocent. Neil helped Gabrielle out of Rory's flat. He didn't take part in the video. I watched every session through a hole in the wall.'

'You sick bitch.'

Iris gives a hearty laugh. 'Neil knew too much and would've told you. Couldn't you see how besotted he is? Maybe your anxious mind is finally failing you. I'll do you a last kindness by confirming you weren't going mad before. You *did* hear a baby crying. I set up a recording to play from a remote-controlled device in Una's flat. Trusting old soul gave me a key, just in case.

'When we were in there looking for the phantom baby, I removed the machine. You were so busy tearing around, it was easy. Louise was also fun to watch, losing her mind trying to figure out where the crying woman was. I often wondered if she'd find the device. It was a risk worth taking. Louise's mental degradation was wonderful.'

I want to tell her how low she stooped, making someone who miscarried distressed at hearing a wailing baby, and an abused woman feel powerless to help a vulnerable person. But she won't care. She's done far worse. It's not over yet.

'Get a load of me, being the clichéd murderer confessing all before the final kill,' Iris says. 'I love a well-executed detective story. The "accident" can't happen now. You're getting too feisty. Another burial it is. When the roses are in full bloom, I'll remember you all.'

Iris raises the knife.

CHAPTER 130
The Watcher

This will be my most precious recording: the evening Harmony House ended for many of us. Whenever you hear this, The Listener, remember me. I was there, too.

* * *

The knife rose, poised to plunge into Sophie's body. Her smile seemed a strange reaction to facing her demise. I thought she was being a coward, accepting her fate. The passivity ignited my rage. I willed the knife to slice her body to shreds.

I underestimated Sophie. The admission is difficult to share. No one has ever surprised me before. She knew what was coming. My unwitting disciple watched, listened, and waited.

A protector took measured treads across the lawn. Considering his height and bulk, Ben's steps were surprisingly light. When a loved one's life is under threat, I guess people adapt. Sophie spotted Ben creeping behind Iris. Not for a moment did Sophie give him away. The tension at not making eye contact with her husband was perceptible. If you look closely, hope fluttered across his beloved's face at his arrival. He pushed his wife aside. She fell onto the grass. Iris' instincts were always sharp. She plunged the knife in.

THE WATCHER

Ben's chest was a scarlet riot. Love for Sophie poured from his heart. She leaned over him. Ben gave a smile, visibly painful to form, but he did it for her. Everything was for her. To freeze frame Ben's expression is to define true love. The couple shut me out as they shared a last moment. I can't dwell on this now. Someone will get hurt. Ben whispered his last words to the woman who wouldn't leave him. For one last time, they linked together.

A single seagull hovered above. It gave a sound so guttural it hurt my ears to hear it. The bird swept around the pair, shrouding them in shared grief, before flying away. Stanley was gone.

Ben must have called the police before he arrived. Upon seeing them, Iris made a decision. With a last stroke of Rory's cheek, she thrust the knife into her stomach. In a twisted parody of the Walters' love tableau, Iris collapsed over Rory's body. She should've learned to be more watchful. Iris' death is retribution for all the women she allowed Rory to defile. Don't you ever dare compare their watching to mine.

I've narrated Ben's death for you with honesty. Use this as the catalyst to act. I watched him step towards his death and did nothing. Channel your indignation. Expose me. Do what is right. Just for you, I've added one video. Watch Ben die again.

Panning out. Fade to black. Harmony House is a wrap.

CHAPTER 131
Sophie: Eleven Months Later

My pencil takes flight over the paper as I capture beating wings. Emma cradles the child. They swing back and forth, their faces pictures of happiness.

Whenever I see my best friend and my son together, joy forms in my chest. Emma has a fierce unconditional love for Luke, the kind of devotion Ben would've had for his son. When I focus on Luke, I delight in him. He has his father's brown eyes and wide mouth, prone to smiling. Wherever my son is, Ben is with him, too.

While Ben died in my arms, his child grew inside me. My husband was always generous when giving me presents. I wish he was here to share our son's life. The anniversary of Ben's death is coming. I hope the memories will become a comfort rather than the stuff of nightmares. The guilt of knowing Ben would've been safe if I'd never moved away still haunts me.

On the upcoming anniversary, the newspapers will probably be divided again in assessing me. For some, I will still be a tragic widow who didn't deserve this. The more tawdry tabloids will continue to question why I stayed despite what was happening. They don't want to hear how I wanted to help others while trying to get over grief. They don't care that I was broken and have survived. I won't think about it now. Focus on the good things. They're right in front of you.

One great thing Harmony House gave me was a tenacious, damaged seagull that inspired me to write and illustrate a children's book. *Stanley Seagull's Adventures*, along with the boy, Tobias, are my dedication to dear friends lost. Despite being miles away from Southbourne, I still inspect every gull I see for a twisted foot.

Emma returns my wave. I couldn't have got through this without her. Returning to Oxford, enduring Ben's funeral, getting through the pregnancy, and giving birth: Emma has been there every step of the way.

Discontent settles in my stomach as I erase the line I've drawn. A shadow looms over the paper. I look up to see who's formed it. Here's the mystery I could never quite solve.

Harmony House has returned.

CHAPTER 132

The Watcher: Eleven Months Later

The opportunity to watch her once more was almost unbearable. This is the one recording she'll never hear. My narrative has changed to the past tense. Sophie and I are over… for now.

* * *

We endured the pleasantries of checking how each other is, along with my condolences for Ben's death. Of course, I didn't share how many times I've seen it on the screen.

'How did you know I'm here?' Sophie asked.

'The landlord gave me your address. I hope you don't mind. I'm passing through the area. A neighbour said I'd probably find you in the park.' Once again, she entranced me with her command of a pencil. 'Who are you sketching?'

'My friend and my son.'

The devotion I've heard mothers sometimes show poured from Sophie.

'You had a child. How wonderful.' Even to my ears, the excitement sounded forced.

'Would you like to join us for lunch?'

I recognised the overbearing look as one she often gave Zara. Wily Zara wriggled out of her wrongdoings and charmed the

THE WATCHER

police into believing she was a victim. Last I heard, she's back home with Daddy.

'Thanks for your kind offer,' I said. 'I'm only passing through.'

Sophie didn't know I was heading to the airport next. The new observational building is one *I* own, not my father. We have a confused relationship. When a psychiatrist diagnosed my psychopathic tendencies, Papa took me to dinner. Pride at how I'd grown to be like him merited fine dining.

As with all his properties, Papa set up the cameras in Harmony House. Originally, I played watching games with him. He wasn't aware I'd deviated from his rules. Papa is on the run from the police for voyeuristic crimes carried out across the world. Mamma filed for divorce. She knew what was going on, but the public face must remain in place.

I've taken some time out to build up my strength. As with everything I do, seeing Sophie was a calculated move. I gave her space. She must have resilience for the next stage.

'This is unexpected. Thank you,' Sophie said as I handed over the wrapped box. I caught her hand as she pulled at the ribbon.

'Please don't open it now. I get embarrassed when people unwrap my gifts in front of me.'

'Are you alone?'

'Yes. I'm free.'

Sophie will never know how the "freedom" was earned. Not that I was ever trapped. Federico didn't hurt me. He despised me for allowing others to believe he was violent. I mastered Federico until he turned on me, threatening to tell the police about the cameras. Federico was just another project, one that irked my snobby father. I only married as part of the façade of appearing human. Federico genuinely loved me, the fool.

A moonlit night in Father's boat, a face smashed against the mast, and my husband disappeared. The constant questioning and upset at others thinking he was an abuser grew tiring. Federico didn't have the courage to question the bruises I inflicted upon my body. When the neighbours gave him judging looks, I watched my husband disintegrate. I did Federico a favour in killing him. His body lies at the bottom of the sea where he can now rest. Federico's family thinks he's left me and is travelling the world.

Seeing Sophie was the last part of the project. The box she now owns contains date-labelled memory sticks of my Harmony House audio recordings and Ben's death video. The video is the final push for Sophie to go to the police. I have contacts who'll keep me updated on what happens.

The police found the cameras around Harmony House after Sophie mentioned the ones in her flat. I was long gone by then. Papa reported this back. Neil believed Papa was responsible and gave a statement confirming this. Adam and Neil now live in Scotland, near Adam's sister.

When Emma joined us, holding Sophie's child, we made our introductions. Emma commented on the beauty of my name: Aurora.

Despite my revulsion, I touched the baby's cheek. 'Let's have a photo of us with your handsome son. Would you mind?' I handed my mobile to Emma.

* * *

The tannoy announces boarding for my flight. Pleasure seeking leads me to looking at the picture on my phone. I erased the child from the photo. No one gets between me and Sophie.

The Watcher and The Listener are together at last.

THE WATCHER

ACKNOWLEDGEMENTS

Thank you, lovely reader, for reading my novel. Without you, authors are nothing. I hope you enjoyed *The Watcher*. Please leave a rating and/or a review. They're gold dust for authors and help other readers when deciding what book to buy.

My beta readers are stars. Much love to the wonderful Kate, Helen, Belinda, Sian, and Sarah for reading and advising.

Belinda, you deserve a second mention. Thanks for celebrating the good times and helping me through the awful ones.

Dave, you're my rock. No matter what life throws at us, we keep standing together. Without your belief, *The Watcher* would never have been published. We've been on quite the rollercoaster with this one!

Huge thanks to friends, family, fellow authors, and readers who continue to support me. I never take it for granted. Writing is an often solitary venture, boosted by the support of others.

This book is also dedicated to those affected by miscarriage, struggling to conceive, and infertility. May the pain of grief and shattered dreams lessen with time, whatever the outcome. I see you. Your hurt and feelings of emptiness aren't invisible. You matter.

LET'S GET SOCIAL!

Facebook: www.facebook.com/lisasellwriter/

Instagram: www.instagram.com/lisasellauthor/

X: www.twitter.com/LisaSellAuthor

Website: lisasellauthor.co.uk

Printed in Great Britain
by Amazon